an englishwoman
in new york

ANNE-MARIE CASEY

JOHN MURRAY

First published in Great Britain in 2013 by John Murray (Publishers)
An Hachette UK Company

Published in the United States of America as *No One Could Have Guessed the Weather*

1

© Anne-Marie Casey 2013

A CIP catalogue record for this title is available from the British Library

ISBN 978-1-84854-831-2
Ebook ISBN 978-1-84854-832-9

Book design by Meighan Cavanaugh

Printed and bound by Clays Ltd, St Ives plc

John Murray policy is to use papers that are natural, renewable and recyclable products
and made from wood grown in sustainable forests.
The logging and manufacturing processes are expected to conform
to the environmental regulations of the country of origin.

John Murray (Publishers)
338 Euston Road
London NW1 3BH

www.johnmurray.co.uk

For Joe, always

Above all, be the heroine of your life, not the victim.

—NORA EPHRON

contents

an englishwoman in new york

PART I

They arrived in early September. No one could have guessed the weather. It was, as the forecast told them one day, as if a blowtorch had gone through the city. "This is meant to be autumn," she cried, "or, rather, fall, as the Americans call it." "Because the leaves are *falling*," laughed little Max. She looked at him and thought, *No, because of our fall from grace.*

The apartment had no air-conditioning. She sweated and was not happy.

They had visited at Christmas and the streets were quiet. She learned quickly this had been an illusion. He had brought his family to the very epicentre of cool, single, young New

York. Apart from everything else, this made her look uncool, married, and old. Opposite them was a bar so trendy the waifish clientele entered through a telephone box next to a hot-dog stand. It was called PDT. Walking down the street she would think, *PDT—Please Don't Tell anyone I am a middle-aged woman.*

When he told her what had happened, she thought he was joking. Sometimes he had a cruel sense of humour, and had once played a practical joke with a talking mirror in the guest bathroom that made his parents refuse to visit them for a year. It took two weeks of conversation and two cases of red wine for her to accept that this was not his biggest-ever whoopee cushion; they had lost everything—well, nearly everything. And he kept saying there was no point in shouting at him, for it wasn't his fault, it was the economy, stupid. In fact, they were lucky. He had one chance at a low-level management job in the New York office. No bonuses, but a salary, and they could live in the eight-hundred-square-foot East Village apartment he had bought as a hotel room years ago.

"You'll love it," he assured her.

"Really?" she replied, rolling her eyes, imagining what she would do if he uttered the words "new" and "start".

She told him he would have to commute from their white stucco four-bedroom in Ladbroke Grove. That's when he told her they had defaulted on the mortgage six months ago and the house was already on the market. It was beyond infuriating.

The Mothers at the School shrieked divorce. She listened in desperate hope. She knew that the divorcées among their number had ended up with white stucco four-bedrooms, child support, and in one case a lump-sum payment for loss of earnings. She figured this could assuage a lot of emotional pain. But when she looked at the business sections of the newspapers it appeared there had indeed been some kind of global collapse in the financial markets and, although she had indeed abandoned a dreary, ill-paid job that bored her to spend the past nine years supervising the Nanny and the Housekeeper and the Children, she had enough brain cells left to know this might not entitle her to much of what remained when nearly everything had gone.

So she cried and cried. Read articles in glossy magazines about the downturn being an opportunity to stop shopping and rediscover the Real Meaning of Life. They did not help at all. Surely they had spent twenty years being told that *greed is good*? Consumerism helps society. No more boom and bust. And then she cried some more.

Her aunt Eva arrived at ten one morning and found her sobbing over the boys' crested school uniforms. She couldn't bear to remember the scene that ensued; suffice to say that she did not consider it to have been appropriately sympathetic. She had brandished a file of yellowing articles from said glossy magazines saying how it was her right to stay at home when her children were small. And a piece from the Saturday *Guardian* about how children who go to day care from an early age are more likely to turn into delinquents and drug addicts, setting fire to wheelie bins and inhaling the fumes.

Then she was angry. The anger fuelled a burst of activity that got them to New York in the autumn.

Every day she dragged the two boys aimlessly around the neighbourhood, always ending up in the new playground in Tompkins Square Park, ignoring the rats frolicking like rabbits and the homeless alcoholics vomiting into black plastic rubbish sacks. One morning, as they crossed a flower bed to avoid two ambulance men removing another ragged, comatose body from a bench, music erupted from a tiny storefront on Avenue A. An elderly Mexican labourer, one of a group she saw most mornings on the pavement waiting for work, simply stood up and danced. He held his body quite upright, moving to the rhythm with absolute control, and then, to her amazement, he held out an imperious hand to a beautiful young girl, from her stork-like proportions and huge eyes obviously one of the models who descended on the area like designer locusts. The girl gave a slight coy bow of her head and then put her perfect hand in his, just like Beauty when she saw the true nature of the Beast for the first time at the foot of his grand staircase. They waltzed.

Passers-by stopped; touched by joy, they laughed and clapped in time. Max and Robbie giggled and bounced up and down, but she froze, her throat constricted, the sudden emotion so shocking she was able to observe it, exactly as if she had cut herself with a piece of broken glass and there were a few milliseconds before blood spurted out. Tears spurting out of her eyes, she had to hurry away round a corner, where they almost collided with a woman with a live snake around her neck, and the boys giggled and bounced up and down again. Really, sometimes she thought it was impossible to walk down a street without seeing something that aroused such a primal response in her, although, even as she blamed the city, she feared that this sort of overemotionalism might be the start of menopause, a horrific condition, according to Aunt Eva, involving sagging and shrivelling and, believe it or not, *"crispiness"*, though that word had not been said, merely mouthed.

That night she couldn't sleep. It was then she realized she had swallowed her last Ambien on the flight over.

She told the story of the dancing, without the tears or the crispiness fears, at Sunday lunch in a three-bedroom duplex in a doorman building opposite the park, after which his new boss, Jerry, and Jerry's Current Wife told them how much they missed living downtown. With a meaningful glance between them, they agreed on the deficiencies of the Upper East Side; it's so *"sanitized"*, they moaned. Jerry and Jerry's Current Wife remembered a time when poets lived on Saint Marks Place and Jeff Buckley sang "Hallelujah" in Sin-é. She nodded in sympathy, but she had realized on previous trips to the city that the epithet "sanitized" used in conjunction with the location of real estate was code among a certain (invariably wealthy) type of New Yorker to indicate their mixed feelings about "selling out". For her it was simply the effects of regular garbage collection.

Later that day, on the 6 train heading home she looked at him and remarked on this. He burst out laughing. She laughed, too. The boys looked at them strangely. Their parents laughing together was a disconcerting sight. Fortunately, things quickly reverted to normal.

Their American health insurance plan had a more stringent policy towards therapy, the taking of antidepressant medication, or even acupuncture. (It appeared you actually had to have tried to throw yourself out of a window, or chased after your children with a mezzaluna before you could be referred.) Thus, with three of her preferred daytime activities removed at a stroke, she was left to self-diagnose her symptoms on the Internet. Unfortunately, hysterical outbursts, headaches, and lethargy were not just symptoms of the perimenopause, but everything from diabetes to advanced brain tumours as well. She began to wonder if it was all the fault of the noise, the cacophony of noise that followed her wherever she went.

Back home, as she still referred to it, she had banished most real sound, except for chatting, of course, from her daytime life. She prided herself on her meditative colour scheme, her candles and small piles of perfectly shaped stones, her panpipe ambient background music ordered from Santa Fe. She had even bought the Housekeeper a special vacuum with a "silent" option on the controls. Now, as she spent hours lying on the bed, mourning the curtains she had left behind, her ears were assaulted by the three couples sharing upstairs stomping around, running their showers, and nursing their lame greyhound. Below there was the neurotic poodle and the teenager's violin practice. It took about a month for it to occur to her that, in turn, the neighbours were treated to the growls of the boys playing something like Transformers tigers and the ensuing shrieking from her about their homework or their dirty clothes or their general selfishness like a strange hybrid of fishwife and robot.

And all this before you considered what was going on outside. One evening, disco rabbis came down the street. This was not something she had ever seen or heard on Portland Road.

SHE HELD OUT a faint hope that she would find a kindred spirit at the school gates. So much of the texture of her "before" life had been provided by her relationships with the Mothers: the coffees, the exercise classes, the helpful tips ("*I put Post-it notes on places I want Irela to clean*"), the discussion of important educational developments, like the affair between Venetia's mother and the dirty (and dirty) young groundsman who was the son of the headmaster. But it was not to be. For a start, there were several *men* doing their paternal duty. Kidult men with short grey hair, wearing tight T-shirts and cargo pants with flip-flops. And she was intimidated by the most vocal group of women, who were always hugging one another before running off to their yoga or their fund-raising bake sales or their suitably part-time creative jobs with their not-in-the-least-grey hair, miniskirts, and Birkenstocks (their slim, tanned legs marred only by the occasional varicose vein or its less knobbly cousin the spiderweb thread vein).

Her concerns about the dramatic change in the boys' educational environment was not helped by the regular spelling and punctuation mistakes on the PTA board outside the school. Apparently *the season for pumkin's* was approaching. When she mentioned this to a more friendly-looking plump woman, the woman had seemed offended. Clearly, her views were going to be an obstacle to her smooth entry into the community. When she insisted Max and Robbie say "please" and "thank you" to the beleaguered teachers she caught a couple of other parents glancing at her judgmentally. She was *"so English"*, she imagined them saying to one another; concerned about petty politeness and grammar at the expense of her children's self-esteem, creativity, and interest in saving the planet. Of course, there were a few actually poor children whose mothers were running off to cook and clean for her neighbours. They didn't look like they cared at all about recycling, but they wouldn't provide recreational activities for her. She gave up on the school at this point. (Later she would realize that she had projected such an air of unhappiness from behind her sunglasses that people had moved away from her in case it was contagious, like an emotional Ebola virus.) Anyway, it didn't matter, because these days he frequently volunteered to do the morning run.

He had made a Father Friend, in fact, a man called Kristian with a *K*, and sometimes, he told her, they grabbed a quick coffee and chatted. Kristian was separated from his wife, Julia, and their two children lived with him. Julia was a successful screenwriter, a "show runner" on a prime-time TV series (whatever that meant), but had the "chip of ice" all creative people need, a coldness in their nature that allows them to use anything and anyone as material. *It's "splinter" of ice*, she muttered. *Graham Greene called it the "splinter"*, but he was on a roll.

"Have you ever seen her?" he asked. "Kristian says Julia's about six foot tall, always wears a hat, and talks to herself."

Before she could decide whether this was factual or disloyal, she remembered that last Friday she had seen such an apparition marching up and down a corridor, shouting, "How long is it since we butchered a pregnant woman with a meat cleaver?" into her phone, oblivious to a clustered group of mothers swapping vegetarian curry recipes as their children hit one another with macramé snakes.

"That must have been her," he said. "Did you speak?"

"No."

She had watched as the person she now knew was Julia switched the phone off but kept muttering, long, bony arms twitching, endless legs vibrating until inevitably the bulging bag on her shoulder seemed to spin off with a force of its own, spilling a red leather-bound notebook, glasses, pens, scraps of paper with one or two words scribbled on them, and a raggedy paperback onto the tiles at the feet of the women discussing broad beans and kimchi.

The book was called *Why Mothers Kill*.

"Workaholism has driven Julia crazy," he concluded.

"According to Kristian with a *K*," she pointed out, but he ignored her. He was trying to make some meaningful point about how relationships are destroyed, but she was distracted, intrigued by this Julia and her *splinter of ice*, which she knew was an inability to play nice like all the other girls.

This was a quality she recognized in herself.

HE LOVED THE SCHOOL like he loved New York, immoderately, passionately. Not only was it free, it was great for what he kept calling his sons' "life education", and even she had to admit that while the prep school in Notting Hill did do an annual charity auction for different countries in the sub-Saharan continent, its idea of diversity among its pupils was white South Africans and the children of the Japanese ambassador. But she gathered herself with her usual rallying cry.

"How will they get into Cambridge if they never do Latin?"

One night he retaliated. "What's the point of a degree from Cambridge if you don't do anything with it?"

This was hurtful, it hit home, but she was glad. She prepared herself to sulk mightily and searched for the magazine articles about child development again, but he simply walked into the bathroom and locked the door. She stood outside.

"I'm like Bathsheba Everdene in *Far from the Madding Crowd*. 'The stuff of which great men's mothers are made.'"

There was a loud chortle from the toilet that could be interpreted only as a diminution of her maternal skills. Max and Robbie joined in. She was horrified. For if she was not a Good Mother, what on earth had she been doing all this time? She accused him of encouraging a male conspiracy against her. He told her to lighten up. No argument ensued. *What was happening to him?*

He was convinced that their new circumstances were good for them as a family. He expressed pleasure at the smallness of their living quarters, delighted at how she had cleaned the tiles round the shower with an old toothbrush and industrial bleach, and described her previous interior design style as "soulless". They were mucking in together, getting to know each other. When she had stopped trying to decide which of these things was the strangest to say, she wondered whether he was writing articles in glossy magazines about the "Gift of Time" under a pseudonym.

Certainly they were seeing more of him. He invented strange ball games and had learned that a washing machine does the clothes and is different from the one that does dishes. He made funny jokes that didn't upset anyone. And although the Mothers at the School in London had predicted he would miss the "buzz" of his brilliant career, he didn't seem to miss the eighteen-hour workdays at all. Sometimes she felt she was going to bed every night with an inspirational speaker of the kind found on DVDs in the lobbies of health spas. And as she had always found *certainty* enormously erotic (she had had a secret two-week crush on George W. Bush in his leather Air Force jacket), she had to admit that their sex life had been transformed. In a good way. She still hated him, of course, but couldn't wait for the weekends. *What was happening to her?*

Now that she had no help, she immediately jettisoned her previous sanctimonious rules about children, food, and television. She used to dread the hours between five and seven, but now she would pour herself a glass of wine, microwave a Whole Foods ready meal, and let the boys gobble it down in front of a PBS show set in California involving adaptations of classic novels narrated by and starring a dog. Struck by their rapt absorption one day, she came out of the bedroom, removed her earplugs, and sat between her sons, their warm heads leaning against her, and watched. The story was *Pride and Prejudice*, and once she got past the actress playing Elizabeth Bennet flirting with a terrier called Mr Darcy and wondering what could be done with that in the adult section of the cable menu, she was hooked. The lessons of Miss Austen were learned during a beach-party social. She had no idea children's programming could be such fun.

In fact, she had entirely forgotten the pleasure of watching television, and now that she had no friends she could see loads of it: daytime drama, documentaries, dinosaur-versus-shark specials. And then she started reading newspapers, taking books out of the library, spotting posters of obscure bands and listening to their music on YouTube. In the evenings they talked to each other. Everything from US economic policy to why Heart were fantastic and how difficult it is for women to rock.

He told her it was good to remember how much she used to love music. How glad he was that she had let it back into her life again, and before she could say anything, he reminded her of the first time they met, aged twenty-seven, at someone's party in a dark basement near Trafalgar Square, and how she had teased him about his record collection. He loved Queen. And Kool & the Gang. Had the twelve-inch disco version of "Rock the Boat" by Forrest (and had never heard of the Hues Corporation). When he finally admitted he couldn't see the point of The Smiths, she insisted he come back to her flat to listen to "Girlfriend in a Coma". He was excited. He had spotted her several years before, at university, where she wore homemade goth outfits with a Groucho Marx badge pinned to her academic gown, but he had never spoken to her, although he wanted to. It had something to do with the rowing team making fun of her, but they were estate agents now, and he could go out with the pale, clever girl who didn't fit in if he could persuade her to have him.

He laughed and laughed at the memory, started singing and waving two wilted roses from the five-dollar bunch on the table as if they were gladioli. Suddenly, she felt the constriction in her throat again, the tears spurting, and announced that she wanted a Snickers bar desperately and would have to get it. Immediately. Once outside, she fought her way through the throng of pierced young people, and by the Australian Tuck Shop she sat down and wept.

For it was as if she had seen them together that first time. Yes. Really. As if it were that very moment. The two of them on her awful futon in Earls Court, snogging, for that was the only word for it, with her black-and-white collage on the wall. (Actually, wasn't that in her room at college? Maybe it was the poster for the experimental multimedia play she had written?) They had even brought an obligatory traffic cone up with them—her idea, of course. The song had brought it all back to her, but there was more to it than that, it was more than a historical record of an event that a date could tell you, it was a sensation, a feeling that wanted to be felt.

It was *love*.

Love for him, for her children, for this wonderful/terrible/boiling hot/freezing cold city that was going to save her. It had stalked her since her arrival, and now it had her, but she wasn't afraid any more. She realized that New York, the enchanted island, with its tragedies and its comedies, its endings and its beginnings, will make you part of it whether you want it to or not.

Her throat relaxed, her tears stopped, and through her damp fingers she watched as life walked past her: in Uggs, in

Jimmy Choos, barefoot. Then she looked down at her green sneakers and thought, *Maybe I'm not that old? Maybe I will go to the Bowery Ballroom and see Iron & Wine?* And the exhilaration of this idea caused her whole body to tremble. She closed her eyes and felt as if the street were shaking, glasses on tables rattling, and the wings of dirty pigeons flapping as they rose into the sky.

She went back upstairs without chocolate. He was peering at the laptop, amazed.

"Did you feel that?" he said. "There was an earthquake. Just a small one. Magnitude three-point-something, but it went on for twenty seconds."

Oh, she thought, *it wasn't me discovering the Real Meaning of Life.*

"I didn't notice."

He tried to smile, but he looked sad.

"You can say it," she said. "I don't notice anything, do I?"

"Not really, no."

She walked over and put her arms around him.

"Why didn't you leave me, Richard?"

"I was planning to, Lucy. But then we lost everything."

There was a long pause. It was certainly dramatic. Then Lucy grinned.

"Nearly everything, you mean."

surrendered lives

The phone rang as Lucy was in the bathroom with the boys. She was laughing. Robbie had asked for ninety-nine rubber ducks for his sixth birthday, and somehow she had sourced eighty-seven little ones on Amazon and disinfected them before wrapping them up in groups of six, with three left over. The ducklings had arrived a fortnight ago, and every evening they named two more. Tonight they had been discussing which one should be called *"Ugly"*.

As soon as Richard appeared in the doorway, she knew something bad had happened. He had that look on his face, but she smiled at him and was about to say "It's okay", for if he had been fired again they would survive. He told her to come into the bedroom, asked her to sit down, and then said her mother had died.

Lucy's first thought was to ask "Was she on her own?" but of course she was. Her father was happily remarried to the indefatigable Paula, who ran four miles every day in a red tracksuit and drank nothing stronger than an elderflower spritzer, while Mother had lived bitter and alone for years, with only the Sky Arts channel and her drinks cabinet for company.

There was no need to ask what the cause of death was, but Lucy did anyway.

"Eva says she was drinking three or four bottles of wine a day. It was just a case of which one of her internal organs gave out first. I'm sorry, Lucy. That sounds awful, but it's what she said."

Lucy nodded. Yes, it was just what Aunt Eva would say. Eva always prided herself on not sugar-coating.

"I have to go. Don't I?" she whispered, and Richard nodded. Eva had also not sugar-coated the fact that she did not consider anything beyond distributing the news her responsibility when her sister had two adult children, albeit in far-flung areas of the globe.

Now Lucy had another thought.

"Has anyone told George?"

Richard shook his head.

"Eva doesn't know what the time difference is with New

Zealand, and she's too scared to ring him in case she wakes Cordelia up."

Lucy sympathized. She had been on the receiving end of only one of her sister-in-law's expletive-ridden rants before, but once was enough.

"We should e-mail him. He'd prefer that, anyway."

Richard said he would make her a cup of tea and then check out the flights. He would even e-mail George. Lucy looked up and said, "Just don't put *Mum dead* in the heading box", and then she started laughing. Richard went over and held her as she cried. Max and Robbie appeared, dripping wet, in the room. She didn't tell them off for their slippery footprints on the floor, just hugged them.

Richard chivvied the boys out and, sensing something in the air, they changed into their pyjamas without dissent and almost leapt into their beds. They were clearly determined to make it as hard as possible for Lucy to leave them. She lay back on the bed and looked up at the ceiling. The blades of the fan were thick with grey dust. She walked into the kitchen, picked up a damp cloth, then stood on the bed and started wiping them. Richard made no mention of this as he walked in and took a weekend case out of the wardrobe.

The car would be coming in half an hour. She was going back to England, and she had lost her mother. It had been four hundred and eighty seconds since the phone had rung. She looked at Richard.

"Call the car company back," she said. "Tell them I do not want the driver to have the radio on."

He nodded, but she knew he didn't understand. She grabbed his hand.

"I don't want there to be a song that reminds me of what this feels like."

SINCE THE BOYS WERE BORN, Lucy had sometimes wondered what it would be like to go to an airport without them, without feeling like a beast of burden under the mounds of stuff that seemed to be required for their happy transport. One day when they were both tiny she had received a call from a former work colleague of hers, a woman she had liked and admired who appeared to have given birth twice without any obvious derailment to her pre-child self. The woman had rung Lucy *"for a chat"* while waiting for a delayed flight in the business-class lounge at Heathrow.

Lucy, who had one child threatening to head-butt himself on the marble fireplace, the other gnawing on her right breast, somehow managed to grunt vague assents to the chatting while gripped with an overpowering sense of hatred that arose from her naked jealousy. Oblivious, the woman sipped her gin and tonic (Lucy actually heard the ice clinking) and opined on how much she enjoyed travelling these days, as she appreciated being on her own. Lucy had resolved never to speak to this person again and demolished her personality when she met up the next day with the mother's group, but today she knew exactly what the woman had meant.

Despite everything, she felt euphoric as she walked into the terminal building. She got a large cup of flavoured coffee and a sheaf of magazines, including one that promised a "cellulite special" featuring the dimpled thighs of celebrities on their summer vacations.

"Lucy?" a female voice reverberated at her shoulder. "It's me. Julia Kirkland."

Lucy said nothing.

"Our boys are in third grade together," she added, although Lucy knew exactly who she was and suddenly became aware that, under the hat, Julia was beautiful.

Julia glanced at the pictures of orange-peel-like buttocks in Lucy's hand.

"What on earth are you buying that crap for?"

Lucy responded truthfully.

"I can buy whatever I want today. My mother just died."

Julia didn't apologize or commiserate; she just put her arm around Lucy's shoulders. She was going to London herself, she said, a co-producer had come on board for a film she had written and he had some *ideas to share* with her (from her tone, it was clear that this was not a good thing). Maybe they were on the same flight? Lucy did not move, so Julia looked in her bag for her boarding card, grinned when she realized they were indeed travelling together, and deposited Lucy up at the checkout, telling her to buy her magazines and wait by the chewing-gum stand.

Then she disappeared. Lucy was obedient. Something strange was happening to her now. Every sensation around her was magnified. Lights were too bright, noises too loud, people's faces distorted. The strange exultation had vanished, and she felt she was trapped in a Primal Scream video. Into this psychedelic landscape loomed Julia, returning.

"I upgraded you with my air miles. We'll sit together at the front of the bus, but you don't have to talk unless you want to. You need to try and sleep."

Julia took the plastic bag from Lucy. It was heavy. ("I can tell you bought the September issue," she said.) Then she gripped her hand firmly and led her to Security where she knelt down on the floor and took off Lucy's shoes, and her belt and her silver bracelet. Then she organized a neck and shoulder massage for both of them, and when they eventually turned left instead of right to their seats on the aeroplane, she asked for extra pillows and blankets to make Lucy the most comfortable bed she could.

"You're very maternal, Julia," Lucy said, curling onto her side by the window.

"Hush," said Julia. "It's our secret. I don't want to lose my cult status up at that school."

Lucy fell asleep almost immediately. It was a relief to escape from the vividness of her consciousness, and she did not surface until the cabin lights went on and breakfast was being served. Lucy, who had not travelled in business class for a long time, was amazed by the choice: fresh fruit, cereal, bacon. It was all a long way from the boulder-like scone perennially served on long-haul flights. She reminisced humorously about the scone with Julia. ("You don't even get the cream nowadays.") Only then did she talk about her mother, who had died.

"The funny thing is," she said, "I don't remember her drinking when I was little, though Dad says she did. Apparently she once put vodka into a plastic water bottle when she came on the school trip to the zoo, and my brother's friend Louis drank it by accident and got sick and the headmistress told my father she could never come again. No one talked about it, though, and as we grew older, she was like, you know, that Loudon Wainwright song 'White Winos'."

"Drinking *'just to take the edge off'*," said Julia softly.

"Indeed," said Lucy. "Eventually Dad and Paula, who was George's friend Louis's mum and who knew all about everything because of the vodka and vomiting at the zoo, ran off together. Dad sat George and me down and told us he couldn't take it any more and he wanted us to come and live with them in West Sussex, but we knew we couldn't leave Mum. The week before she'd tripped over the front step and broken her wrist. But as George always reminds me, I only had another year of it. I left home when I was eighteen, and I never went back. Mum and George visited me in Cambridge occasionally, and we had a couple of disastrous holidays where I treated

George to my views on how he should deal with her, but he was stuck with the mess and now he is *very angry*. He thinks that Dad and I abandoned him. And there's nothing I can say to that. Because we did."

"You were a young woman, Lucy. If it was anyone's responsibility, it was your father's—"

"You're right, of course. But George was younger. Only fourteen then. And he was such a good son. He went to university nearby so he could live with her, and he stayed for a few years after that. But then he was offered a job in France, which he took, and then one in New Zealand, where he got married. He told me it was my turn. I'd have to visit Mum, check up on her. 'It's only thirty-eight miles from London door to door,' he said; he'd driven it himself to check. I did it at first. Occasionally. Grudgingly. Almost always disastrously. So it became less and less, and over the last year I didn't . . . I rang once a week. Usually early in the morning so I could leave a message. Then we moved to New York, and truthfully, leaving it all behind was the only thing I was glad about. I've never met George's kids."

The few times she had told people this they had all said *"How sad"*. Julia did not, for which Lucy would be eternally grateful.

"I have spent years in therapy and learned to comfort myself with the 'there's no such thing as a perfect family' mantra . . . But . . . God, how I would hate history to repeat itself, you know, for Max and Robbie to despise me or Richard or each other. Yet the truth is, when you throw in all the anxiety disorders on Richard's side, my children come from a shark-infested gene pool."

She paused.

"That just came to me, and it's not a bad image, is it?"

Julia nodded. "You're a born writer, Lucy. I won't steal it, I promise."

The pilot's voice came over the loudspeaker. They were to fasten their seat belts as he was commencing the descent. Julia picked up the safety instructions from the pocket in front of her and quickly reread them.

Lucy stared at her.

"I always do this in case there's an emergency. I want to be the cool, heroic person. The one who knows the exit doors open inwards."

"Do they really?" said Lucy. "I never knew that."

"You should. The survivors of plane crashes are the ones who read the instructions. If a panic started, smoke billowing through the cabin or something like that, most people, apparently, would trample over their children to get to the exit doors, but it wouldn't do them any good if they couldn't open them."

"Good point," said Lucy, thoughtfully. Others might have dismissed Julia's vision as overly pessimistic, but Lucy knew it was true. After all, when disaster struck hadn't her mother and father both trampled over her and George? The only difference was that her father had read the instructions on how to escape.

For a moment, Lucy wished for a small aeroplane accident, nothing too scary, a couple of seagulls plucked and diced by the front engine, say, just enough to force an emergency landing on the sea, a spot of floating around in the life rafts for the afternoon. Anything so she didn't have to go to a mortuary with Aunt Eva or choose an outfit for Mother to be buried in. The sudden thought of wrestling support stockings onto a dead body was so horrific that Lucy resolved to risk Julia's wrath and grab her handbag before they jumped down the inflatable shoot to ensure her passport ended up in the water. Perhaps, post-rescue, Immigration would have to put her in some holding facility for at least forty-eight hours.

Unfortunately, the plane landed without a hitch, and Julia did not get the opportunity to demonstrate her crisis-management skills until it turned out her bags had been left at JFK. She walked Lucy to customs, and they hugged. Then she turned and marched away, Lucy recognizing from the stiffening of Julia's back that all hell was about to break loose at the lost luggage desk. Bits of paper flew out of her bulging handbag like sparks, so Lucy ran forward to pick them up: old tissues, a Starbucks receipt, a subway ticket, and then a credit card slip.

Lucy looked at it. It had yesterday's date and was the payment for her upgrade to business class, one thousand one hundred dollars. She opened her mouth to call Julia back and then closed it. What would she say? She could not afford to pay her back, anyway. So she accepted the love and walked through customs.

AUNT EVA BURST out of the doorway when Lucy pulled up in the hire car as if she had been planning it, lurking in the hallway until she heard the rumble of an unfamiliar engine.

"You haven't brought enough clothes" was the first thing she said, looking at Lucy's carry-on bag. "I've rung round the funeral people and they can't do anything for at least a week. I put a couple of slots on hold, but I didn't put a deposit down until you were here."

Lucy stood in front of her, wondering if they were meant to hug, but Aunt Eva didn't move. It was a relief.

"There's so much to do," Eva continued, as if they were talking about going on holiday or redecorating a bathroom. "Do you need a shower?"

"No. I'll dump my bag upstairs; you put the kettle on and I'll hit the phones."

"Good girl." Eva sighed. "I can give you the morning, but I have to get back to the library this afternoon." Eva had worked since she was seventeen and refused to countenance retirement, believing it a sin not to be meaningfully employed during daylight hours.

"I knew I could rely on you," she continued, and Lucy disappeared up the stairs two steps at a time so she didn't give in to the temptation to say, *Yes, you see, I am available in a family emergency.* Today at least there was no possibility of Eva asking her what *exactly* she did all day.

She walked straight into her old room and threw the bag on the bed. Her beloved duvet cover was on it, the one she had chosen at age seventeen, a bright floral pattern to match the wallpaper that she had once considered the height of sophistication, but over the years the light streaming in through the window had faded and dulled it so now it looked permanently dusty. On the top bookshelves were rows of Pullein-Thompson horse novels with pictures of ponies emblazoned on the front, then enormous paperbacks like *Gone with the Wind* and *The Forsyte Saga*, their spines cracked, the titles illegible, leading down to textbooks, literary theory, and the contents of various reading lists never returned to different libraries, from the local village to Newnham College, Cambridge.

It was the history of her education in four shelves six feet by four. On the wall still hung a poster-sized crayon drawing of her done by an art student as they sat on the grassy bank beside the River Cam. The young woman had come over and asked her if she could draw her, just for practice, and Lucy, who was nineteen, said yes, feeling it was the sort of thing that should happen to a person when they are young and newly up at university.

Afterwards the woman had given her the drawing and Lucy had treasured it because it was the first time anyone had told her she was pretty and she actually believed it. The sunlight had faded this, too; the paper was brownish cream and curled, although Lucy could still make out the green in her eyes, and the blondish tint in her hair she had in those days, thanks to the copious use of lemon juice and Sun-In bleaching spray.

"LUCY!" called Eva, her voice accompanied by a series of loud thumps. Was it possible, thought Lucy, that Eva was hitting the ceiling with a broom handle in order to chivvy her along? Although Aunt Eva and Uncle Malcolm had been married for nearly forty years, they had never had children, and she tended to treat her niece and nephew in ways she had seen in television programmes in the seventies. This little exchange was just like something out of a sitcom, but Lucy respected her aunt for it. You always knew where you were with Eva, which is not something she could ever say about Mother or Father.

"Coming . . ." Lucy called down the stairs as she sent Richard a quick text.

Then she picked up a plastic pen in the shape of an elephant's trunk, which she had been given during her summer job in the safari park in 1990, grabbed an old diary she had resolved to write in the same year (she had found within one month that the entries comprised of what she had eaten for lunch and there were no great insights she wished to record for posterity), and set about organizing her mother's funeral. This took three hours (to her relief, the funeral director told her he could retrieve and dress the corpse) and included a trip to the local sandwich shop to discuss catering options: egg-and-cress sandwiches, sausage rolls, iced buns, and tea and coffee, though as Lucy had no idea how many people would show up, she said she would confirm numbers nearer the end of the week. The only moment of discord between Lucy and Eva came when Eva tried to insist there be a bar, wine and spirits, and Lucy refused.

At this moment, Lucy's telephone rang and a long international number came across the display.

"It's George," she said, and Eva stopped mid-sentence.

"I just think people will expect a gin and ton—"

"Eva thinks we need to give people a drink. An alcoholic drink, George. At the afters."

"I'm doing fine, Lucy. How are you? Tell Eva that if people want a drink they can fucking well come back to the house and start looking for the bottles mother hid round the place and then forgot about. Last time we were over, Cordelia found three vodkas in the kids' toy box."

Lucy put her hand over the phone receiver and mouthed, "George really doesn't think that's a good idea." Eva nodded sulkily, which Lucy ignored.

"What day is it booked for?" barked George, and when Lucy told him a week from tomorrow, he announced he would arrive the day before.

Lucy bristled. "Oh, so you're happy for me to make all the arrangements?"

"No. You can e-mail everything to me and I'll"—he stopped himself from using the word "approve"—"check them."

Lucy rolled her eyes. At least this aspect of the day was predictable.

"Service is at Saint Luke's, new priest, he sounds very nice, met Mum a couple of times at least. There's no room for a full burial in the graveyard there, so how d'you feel about cremation and we'll put a small plaque on the outside of the church wall?"

There was a pause, a crackling on the phone line. Lucy realized that George was talking to Cordelia before he agreed, which he did.

"We can use the church hall afterwards, and I've booked the Tasty Bite to do finger food."

"No flowers," George said; Lucy heard Cordelia saying something now, "It's awful to have to deal with loads of wilting flowers, so tell everyone to make a donation to . . ."

"Alcoholics Anonymous?" suggested Lucy, and Eva winced.

"No, that'll upset Eva," said George correctly. "That centre where Mum played bridge sometimes. They were very kind to her there."

Lucy fell silent. She knew nothing about this centre or the kindness of the strangers there.

"For the coffin, get a bunch of yellow chrysanthemums. They were her favourites. And I'm working on the service. I'll send you through some suggestions for hymns and readings. You can add anything you like. Do the bidding prayers or something."

Lucy felt ashamed. She had not even thought about the funeral service and had no clue about what should be in it.

She had been so self-righteous about her efforts. And she couldn't bear to admit to George she had forgotten what a bidding prayer was.

"Let's try and find a decent organist. I know Mum would love to have 'Jesu, Joy of Man's Desiring', but we can't do it if the organist isn't good."

"What's that?"

"You know. Bach." There was another pause, so he started to sing. *"Dum, dah, dum, dah, dum, de dah, de dum, dum de, dum dah."* Now exasperated. "It's at the beginning of the Beach Boys song 'Lady Lynda'."

"Oh, yes." Lucy began to sing along. "I love that song. Did you know Al Jardine co-wrote that?"

"I did, Lucy. I remember an entire summer when all you listened to was the Beach Boys. When you weren't reading the Brontës, that is. Mind you, now I know that Dennis Wilson was the unrecognized genius of the band."

"Bollocks!"

"Lucy!" said Eva.

"You don't know everything! You should listen to Pacific Ocean Blue*!"* shouted George, his voice cracking. Lucy imagined Cordelia reaching her right hand forward to stroke his cheek.

"I've got to go. Talk later." And he hung up, the choke still in his voice.

Lucy looked at Eva and their eyes welled up.

"George is upset," she said.

Eva looked at her.

"Of course George is upset. It's terrible for him. Your mother and George . . . they really loved each other."

She wiped her eyes. "Where the hell is your father?"

Lucy said she would ring Paula and find out. Eva snorted.

"Paula won't let him out of her sight since the stroke."

"*What?*" said Lucy. "When did he have a stroke?"

Eva calmly told her there had been a small stroke four months ago, but no one had wanted to worry anyone. Lucy looked at her.

"We all thought you'd been through enough." Unusually for Eva, she faltered under Lucy's accusing glare. "We worried you weren't coping. With what happened to Richard and his job. Losing your home, the life you had . . . and everything."

Lucy thought about what she had said to Julia on the plane about her family; she had not been truthful enough about the astonishing dysfunction of it all. The last time she had spoken to her mother they had argued. Her mother had not wanted her grandsons to live in the apartment in New York because of global warming.

"Don't you understand?" she had kept saying (it was after lunch, her time). "Manhattan will be underwater in fifteen years."

IN HER ROOM, *Lucy sits on her dusty bed and looks out of the window at the rows of comfortable, identical houses lining the road.*

Some have toddler furniture in the driveway, others small cars with L-plates, others midlife-crisis motorbikes, then for-sale signs for the move to the retirement home. Whole lives are lived in these front gardens, but Lucy wants no part of it all. She remembers the eighteen years plotting her escape. What had she yearned for when she stared out of that window? Why hadn't she achieved it?

She glances at the books on the shelf, the brown cardboard box full of her old records; she picks up George Benson, "The Greatest Love of All". Thinks how the day her father took his racing-green Jaguar to a happier life near Glyndebourne she tried to cheer up her mother by playing it to her and reading out the words.

She wonders how she became the sort of woman they think she is. She knows they all have an idea of her role in the drama of this family, so should she play it, or will she throw in some new lines? What has she ever done to any of them, apart from be herself? Is that why her mother didn't love her?

Then it dawns on her that she feels exactly the same as she did all those years ago. And this is the worst feeling of all, for surely as your fortieth birthday approaches, looming inexorably over the horizon and darkening your sky, you are meant to have some answers.

There is a perfunctory rap on the door, and Aunt Eva, coat buttoned up, walks in to find Lucy curled up in the duvet, sobbing.

"It must be the jet lag," Aunt Eva says.

THE MOMENT Father arrived he made straight for his old chair, an orangey-brown Parker Knoll positioned in front of the television in the living room. He looked a lot older than Lucy remembered and was definitely a little shaky on his pins, but when he sank into the chair with a little moan of contentment, Lucy's pang of pity quickly turned to resentment. She had often thought that bloody chair was the only thing he really regretted leaving all those years ago. She decided that she was not going to mention the stroke, either.

She had got it together enough to walk to the corner shop to buy some bourbon biscuits, his favourite, and he was disproportionately grateful for her thoughtfulness. There was no evidence of any food in the house at all, apart from a box of crackers and two tins of tomato soup past their sell-by date. Lucy knew that whatever meals her mother had consumed in the past few years had been provided by Aunt Eva. Paula confirmed this as they stared into the empty fridge together, saying, "At the end she looked like a Belsen victim", which annoyed Lucy intensely; *The Belsen victims had no choice*, she wanted to scream, but she knew that Paula always said inappropriate things like this (her lawn was like "the Somme"; sunburn was like "a trip to Bhopal"), so Lucy nodded with a suitably non-committal expression, as she couldn't think of any other, brought her father a cup of tea with a little milk and two sugars, and sat beside him on a low stool to make a few minutes of small talk about his grandsons.

"Of course, they won't get to play much sport, will they?" he said. "They don't have playing fields there, in New York City, do they?"

She and George had been sent to the local Catholic junior school, where three hundred kids ran round a tarmac area that doubled as the car park. It wasn't exactly Eton. Lucy looked away; today was going to be an exercise in self-control. She was glad when Paula emerged from the kitchen in her mother's apron and yellow rubber gloves.

"We're talking about New York, love," said her father.

"Ooh, yes. Such an exciting place."

"Have you been there, Paula?" asked Lucy, surprised. Paula nodded.

"Yes, I went on a girls' weekend for my forty-fifth— remember, Lawrence?"

"She had to buy two new suitcases to bring all the stuff home, I remember that," he muttered grumpily, but she trotted over and kissed the top of his head.

"We went to the outlet malls. It was incredible. I bought a Max Mara coat and suit I still wear."

"She's still the same size, Lucy. Never gained a pound. Gorgeous as ever."

And he patted Paula on her bottom. She giggled flirtatiously, and Lucy remembered that Paula, in her skintight Levi's and red leather blouson jacket, had been an object of much desire among her brothers' classmates.

"How's Louis doing?"

"Much better. He's got over his ups and downs." (Louis had been a full-fledged heroin addict for ten years, but the month in an open prison after he was caught dealing seemed to have sorted him out.) "And he's just had a lovely little boy with that new girlfriend of his. They've become Quakers."

"Oh." Lucy was genuinely interested in this. She often toyed with the idea of becoming a Quaker. "Have you been to a meeting, Paula?"

"Yes, I went last month to look after the baby. Very interesting. I sort of agree with all the pacifist stuff after Iraq and all that. But I couldn't do it myself. You can't have jewellery."

Her father burst out laughing at this. It took a moment before Lucy realized his laughter was indulgent, a sort of "ooh, you are awful" laugh. Paula and her father were soulmates, it was true. No wonder her mother had turned to the bottle.

"D'you want more tea?" Paula said, and her father grunted "yes". He pointed at the row of videotapes of George playing football on a shelf by the telly and asked Lucy to put one on. She walked over. He had recorded them religiously every Saturday of George's thirteenth year.

"Any game in particular?" she asked.

"No."

She selected the under-fourteens' Buckinghamshire five-a-side and stuck it in the antiquated VCR. She handed her father the remote, and he reclined his chair a little, raising the footstool so he could watch in the greatest comfort. He switched up the volume so he could hear the running commentary he had done himself in the style of John Motson while he was filming.

When Lucy went into the kitchen, Paula was sobbing.

"It's so sad. It's so sad," she kept saying, over and over again. "We should have been friends. Once you get older you realize you should just forget everything and be friends, but your mother wouldn't have any of it. Even after twenty-three years she still referred to me as *'that cow Paula Arnold'*. She always made out that I stole him away. But, Lucy, you know he walked out of that door himself."

He bloody ran, thought Lucy.

"Your dad begged her for a few of those wretched tapes. He just wanted to see them. But she refused, said she'd burn them if he asked her again."

Lucy hugged her. She smelled of face powder and Anaïs Anaïs.

"She wasted her life. That's why I say to Lawrence it's good that you had a bit of a career. And it's why I've always helped out at the golf club. You have to have something for yourself, Lucy. Otherwise what happens if they leave you?"

Lucy wanted to say that her father, with his stroke, and his lame left leg and his bottom firmly planted in the Parker Knoll, was not going anywhere. But she knew that to Paula, who loved him, he was still Lawrence Cunningham, aged thirty-five, heartbreakingly handsome in his cream polo neck, the object of much desire among the Mothers at the School, as he climbed out of the racing-green Jaguar and opened the doors to take schoolbags and children out.

Paula pulled herself together. "Now, I've brought something for you; I hope you don't mind." She shuffled over to her bag and pulled out a sheet of stickers.

"You and George have to decide what you're going to do about the house, but before he gets here, have a little mosey round, and anything you want, stick one of these on it."

Lucy burst out laughing. The stickers had smiley faces on them.

Paula looked offended. "I know you might think I'm being"—she paused, searching for what would almost certainly be the wrong word—"indelicate—"

Lucy, relieved, immediately said, "Of course not—"

"But that Cordelia was talking about your mother's royal wedding commemorative plate last Christmas, and I'm just saying you might regret it if George packs everything up and ships it to Auckland and you don't even have a photo."

Lucy took the stickers.

"Thank you, Paula. That is thoughtful of you."

"We're nice people, Lucy; we think people don't do things like that. But you ought to have seen how my brother's kids behaved when my mum died. It was carnage. They went through the house like a *tsunami*."

Paula shook her head at the memory. Then she had an idea.

"While you're over, why don't you see a few friends? You can't sit here on your own for a week. Life goes on. You should call someone."

That's right, thought Lucy. *Life goes on.*

CAMILLA WAS WAITING, as arranged, behind the taxi rank outside Victoria Station, but Lucy didn't see her at first because she was hidden behind the enormous steering wheel of what appeared to be a farm vehicle. Camilla caught her expression.

"Don't say anything," she said. "In the settlement the Bastard was meant to buy me a 4x4, but he kept arguing on and on, said a Fiat Punto would do for the school run, but my lawyer wouldn't let it go and this arrived. I think he shipped it over from Eastern Europe full of refugees. He's so cheap, that's what Americans say, isn't it? He was always cheap."

"Yes," agreed Lucy, safe in the knowledge that the chances of Camilla and the cheap Bastard reuniting were nil. "He never ever bought a drink, did he? The first time Rich and I met him and he should have been trying to impress us, he made us gin-and-tonics from those small plastic bottles he got free on the plane."

"Want to know something worse than that?" said Camilla, *"He reused lemon slices."*

Lucy looked at her in disbelief.

"Oh, yes," she continued. "After anyone left, he would fish the lemon slice out of the bottom of their glass, wipe it with kitchen roll, and leave it sitting in the side of the fridge till the next time."

"Did you ask him why?"

"He said he didn't want people to be interested in him for his money. I said there's no danger of that, love."

Lucy and Camilla had once been best friends but had not seen each other since Camilla's wedding four years previously. Since then, Camilla had had a child and got divorced. It seemed to suit her, though. Her long legs, encased in lacy tights under a tight grey pencil skirt—a look Lucy had never liked, but on Camilla it worked—were slender and muscular, and there was no sign of the creeping roll of midriff fat that Lucy felt gathering above her own low-rise jeans.

"You look good," Lucy said.

"I know," replied Camilla. "I caught this vile bug that was going round the Montessori. Threw up and out of both ends for a week. Fantastic. I'm back in all my old clothes. It's *totally* recession." She giggled momentarily. Then her face became serious again.

"You should have said something to me, Lucy. If you thought he wasn't right, you should have said it. It's not like I was desperate to get married."

If Camilla had been Pinocchio, her nose would have hit the windscreen at this point. Camilla had been thirty-five, tired of drifting from one low-profile job in the art world to another, fed up of renting a studio flat on Portobello Road, and had tried and failed to land the kind of chap her father craved, so when the cheap Bastard appeared from nowhere, with his off-shore companies and his overuse of aftershave, she asked no questions, brought him home to the family pile in Scotland, and the deal was done at Soho House six months later.

It was the only wedding Lucy had ever been to where the marriage felt doomed from the very beginning. She tried to explain it to Richard at home the next day—he had remembered an urgent trip to his dentist at the last minute—but it was impossible to describe the sense of foreboding in the room. It hummed over the canapés and the seating plan like petrol fumes rising from the Hammersmith flyover. It was not until a thank-you note for the two brass candlesticks arrived that Richard understood.

"Talk about the *unhappy* couple," he chortled. Lucy pooh-poohed it, but she knew he was right. She peered at the black-and-white photo inside and knew that Camilla and her new husband didn't love each other. Camilla had gone through with it because she had read too many articles in the *Mail on Sunday* about desperate childless women in their forties, and, although she was genuinely delighted with her son—"At least I got Tristan," she repeated—the marriage was over before she could provide a spare for the heir.

The Bastard's motives turned out to be something to do with tax and residency, although he had some sort of penchant for marriage, as he was now on his third girlfriend since Camilla and they had just got engaged.

"She's a nice girl, actually, but when I congratulated her I said just don't get older, because then he'll be off."

To fill the tense silence that fell, Lucy tried to cheer Camilla up by telling her about the dramatic change in her own circumstances and her new life in New York. She illustrated this by the fact that they had only one bathroom in their apartment. Camilla was appalled.

"You mean there's only one toilet? How could Richard do that to you?" she exclaimed, in the same tones she had used to describe her ex having sex with an air stewardess at a hotel in Disneyland when they brought Tristan to see It's a Small World. Lucy started saying that the collapse of the international banking sector wasn't Richard's fault, but she knew that Camilla would take Lucy's defence of any male member of the species personally, so she shut up. Anyway, Camilla and Richard had a difficult relationship. Camilla was suspicious of Richard because, despite his father being a diplomat, he had chained himself to the railings in front of the South African embassy the summer before Mandela was released. (*"Couldn't he just have bought the song?"* she said.) Their tongues had also once tangled rapturously on the floor of the drinks tent during a College Ball, but Richard had subsequently pretended it had never happened.

Camilla now pondered the doomsday scenario facing Lucy.

"Are you going to have to get a job?" she intoned, in a voice like Vincent Price at the beginning of "Thriller".

"I don't have a proper visa yet," replied Lucy.

"Thank goodness," muttered Camilla.

"And I'm not sure what I would do."

"Oh, Lucy, you could do anything. You had a bit of a career, after all. Not like me. At least when the cheap Bastard tried to make me earn some money the lawyer was able to confirm that I was qualified for nothing. All those years on the front desk at Christie's doesn't really get you anywhere, except a chance to marry some duke who's flogging off a Canaletto."

Lucy couldn't help laughing. She was beginning to remember why she and Camilla had been such close friends, despite the enormous differences of background, politics, and aspiration between them. They had met their very first day at university, as their rooms were side by side. It transpired they were also tutorial partners, and Lucy watched in awe as Camilla, with her confidence born of entitlement and her resilience born of boarding school, ran rings round the various professors. Posh, slightly potty, and very clever, Camilla was what Lucy had always imagined a true bluestocking to be, and she felt it was a shame that Camilla had not been nineteen in the 1930s, when she could have danced to Cole Porter, hiked her skirt up to slide down banisters, or been a pioneering Girl Guide. There was something lost about her; she had been born at the wrong time, into a class that was dying, to parents who had no way of providing the life they themselves had enjoyed for their children.

"You know what my mother said to me the other day? 'Camilla, darling, Cambridge wasn't meant to be finishing school. Daddy and I thought you'd be a lawyer.'" She paused. "Coming from her, can you imagine? A woman who did nothing in her life except read Mills and Boon and occasionally change some curtains in the north wing."

Remembering her only night in the north wing, shuddering in mildewed sheets as she clutched two foul-breathed terriers to her to try and keep herself warm and Camilla's lecherous brother Benedict out, Lucy thought of her dinner of half-thawed shepherd's pie with Lady Fiona, who assured her that all the secrets of a *heppy* marriage could be learned from the animal kingdom, specifically the big cats.

But Lucy had learned a lot from Camilla. She had arrived at Cambridge silent and cowed; Camilla taught her not to be afraid, not to smoke, and that the quickest way to get a buzz on was a cocktail of champagne and cough mixture. In turn, when Camilla went to parties dressed as a spider and drank distilled alcohol from great punch bowls, Lucy kept a wary distance, ready to rescue her when she couldn't put her key in her door, and even stayed at the police station with her the night she was arrested for being drunk and disorderly while riding a bicycle.

"Why did you stop work, anyway?" asked Camilla out of nowhere.

Lucy was a little startled. No one had ever asked her this outright before. No one, that is, except herself. Unfortunately, she and her self had failed to come up with a satisfactory answer.

"I was so sick when I got pregnant with Max that I left straightaway, and I thought I would just take a few months off afterwards, but . . . then I felt so tired. That was it, really. And I can't decide if I was tired because of the baby, or tired because I'd worked so hard for so long with so little to show for it. Then Richard started doing really well and he was travelling all the time and suddenly we had this house and this life and another baby, and soon . . . None of the women I met worked—"

"Outside the home," Camilla chipped in.

"—and . . . I don't know. Now when I think about starting all over again I feel old . . . and afraid. It's like I was running the marathon, and I hit the wall."

"For ten years?" chortled Camilla.

"You're right. I hate myself. I've been asleep for ten years."

"Darling, no praise, no blame from me. I don't mean to be tactless after Mommie Dearest, but . . . we need a big drink. Look at the state of us. Couple of fucking suffragettes, eh? And to think we used to be like George Eliot heroines, you and me. Especially you. I remember you telling old Miss Whatsher-face-tweed-skirt-old-English that you felt you would stick your head in an oven if you couldn't use your mind."

"Did I?" Lucy was startled. She had a terrible memory and was always interested when people told her things about herself she had forgotten.

"Yes, we'd been reading *Middlemarch*. Remember the bit, *'you would die . . . from that roar which lies on the other side of silence'.*"

There was a long pause.

"I do need a drink," said Lucy.

"You need several," giggled Camilla. "And then if you're up to it, we're going to go to Rose and Jasper Hardy's joint surprise birthday party that's not a surprise any more, because I accidentally put it on Facebook. No one told me it was a secret because *you know who* might be there."

Lucy knew instantly that *you know who* referred to nice but unmemorable Peter Aldridge, who used to hang round the edges of discos in his V-neck sweater and, during the years Lucy had had her ten-year nap, had apparently become Home Secretary. From the frisson of excitement in Camilla's voice, Lucy knew this was meant to be a Big Deal, but in her current state she failed to drum up much excitement.

"I don't care where we go," she said. "I'm just glad to be away from the house of death. I'll go with the flow."

"You have changed," said Camilla, pushing the agricultural vehicle into fifth gear.

CAMILLA LEFT LUCY at the cheap hotel Lucy had booked for the night and gave her strict instructions to get some rest while she went home to check that the new German au pair wasn't letting Tristan watch *Sex and the City* on DVD again on the pretext of extending her English vocabulary. (Tristan had asked for a cosmopolitan at a play date the previous week, and it had reinforced people's perceptions of Camilla.) Camilla would return at seven.

Lucy rifled in her bag to see what Richard had packed, and,

in fact, groping for anything black in her wardrobe, she found he had thrown in a pre-austerity ruffled Prada top with a sequin trim that, over her jeans and boots, would do very nicely for a fortieth birthday party for people who did not wish to be forty at all.

It was commonplace for Lucy to declare whenever she met anyone from her college days that they hadn't changed a bit. In fact, they always had. Normally it was the straightforward deterioration of their looks or the sense that some bright light inside them had been switched off by a force greater than themselves; but sometimes, in her own case, certainly, the years had made them look better, grown into themselves somehow.

Rose Hardy, the hostess, unfortunately fitted into the former group, standing in the kitchen looking oppressed and miserable, despite her picture-perfect breadmaker and children. She was devastated because *you know who* had not appeared and was not likely to appear, it seemed, due to another problem with the euro, which required the entire Cabinet to sit in an office with a big red phone. Well, that was what Lucy imagined, anyway. For Rose, this was a disaster; she knew several people had accepted the invitation only to ask *you know who* about whether the government could safeguard their pensions and were disappointed to have a couple of mere junior civil servants in the Department of Arts and Tourism to ingratiate themselves with. In fact, Rose was so upset she barely registered Lucy's presence, and when Lucy pointed out that perhaps the fluctuations of the European currency market might take priority over a party, Rose disappeared off to find a more understanding ear in which to complain about how "certain people forgot their friends, the friends who helped them into their positions of power", clearly alluding to the days she had spent leafleting in Bayswater before the election.

Jasper was altogether more delighted to see Lucy, clasping her in a slightly too vigorous embrace and marvelling at how much time had elapsed since he had seen her. When he asked, sincerely, how she was, she gave him the only line she wanted to talk about tonight: two young boys, living in New York, happy.

"You look happy," he said. "But then you always were different." And he picked up a plate of mini-sausages glazed in honey and ginger and headed into the living room.

Camilla was shaking Martinis and marvelling that Rose and Jasper had two dishwashers.

"Oh, bloody hell!" she said suddenly.

"What?" said Lucy, confused.

"Miranda Bassett just walked in. I'm off to see if anyone's smoking in the kids' bathroom upstairs. I cannot face Madam consoling me tonight." And she seized her shaker and hurried up the back stairs, leaving Lucy alone and defenceless.

Miranda entered radiantly with husband Simon behind her; he was dutifully carrying a small baby instead of her handbag like he used to, but they were both airily dispatched the moment Miranda saw Lucy.

Miranda was the most conspicuously successful of all the women of Lucy's acquaintance from university. As a shy teenager Lucy had been terrified of her, for Miranda, at age nineteen, swanned around, resplendent in her raven-haired beauty, her permanently airbrushed skin and her maxi-dresses, in which she managed to cycle. In their twenties they had kept a wary eye on each other as their professional paths occasionally crossed, although Miranda was still superior, as, having married Simon at age twenty-three, she had had her first child the year after and was therefore "having it all", a subject on which she regularly opined in her column in a Saturday newspaper. Her brief was to depict the joys and travails of working motherhood with humour and insight, and so every week she detailed an amusing incident about herself, saintly Simon, and her child, whom for purposes of anonymity she called the Saviour. She had published the collected columns in a best-selling book and presented a documentary series on Channel 5, so when Miranda sashayed over to Lucy, Lucy knew she was in the presence of someone who had her own website.

"Thank God, Lucy Lovett. Someone here I can talk to. I've been looking for signs of intelligent life in the other room and can't find any." Her signature peal of laughter burst forth. It never got less strange each time Lucy heard it.

"Was Camilla in here?" continued Miranda. "Thought I saw her running towards her nicotine. Poor thing. We all thought it was bad when she was like Bridget Jones, but now she's turned into Patsy from *Ab Fab*."

From Miranda's rapid appraisal of the company, Lucy knew Miranda was one of the number who had attended only because Rose had promised to deliver *you know who* and had worked out that she must stay for at least half an hour before leaving, in order not to be deemed unspeakably rude. Lucy took a deep breath to gather herself before attempting conversation, but fortunately her participation was not necessary. Lucy was left exhausted by the roller coaster that was Miranda's late thirties. She learned how difficult it was to get anything intelligent made on TV these days, how the Saviour had proved an immense disappointment (dropping out of Westminster to go to a Sixth Form College to do woodturning), and as a result Miranda had been gripped by an overwhelming urge to have another, more Miranda-ish, child and, miraculously, after Simon reversed his vasectomy, she did, another boy, *dammit*, but here's hoping . . . She longed to take life a bit easier, but Simon had got so used to being at home he felt he couldn't possibly go back into the workplace, and they lost so much money after his dodgy investments on the stock exchange, which she had allowed only to make him feel that he was "contributing", that she'd had to take a job writing for a *tabloid newspaper*. Honestly she could have divorced him a couple of years ago, but then you realize, don't you, that there's only one George Clooney, and while perhaps one could have had anyone one wanted in one's prime (Lucy realized she must nod in agreement to this), we're all rather stuck now unless we want to end up like Camilla, bitter and twisted, or like Rose and her ilk in there, the valley of the surrendered wives. *What a bloody waste of taxpayers' money it was educating that lot!*

And with that, Miranda sat down and Lucy thought that despite her support underwear, the uniform of skintight top and maxi-skirt was becoming rather ill-advised. She wanted to say that Miranda was a natural tabloid journalist and this would solve all her financial worries, but something stopped her.

"So what are you up to these days?" said Miranda, changing her tone. She tilted her head to one side in the "tell me about the tragedy" mode. "How are you *coping* with things?"

For a moment Lucy panicked that Miranda had somehow heard about her mother, but no, she was referring to the demise of Richard's share options. Lucy remembered Camilla's horror at the prospect of the Consolations of Miranda. So she announced that she had taken the opportunity of the move to New York to reinvent herself and that *these days* she was writing.

As she said it she knew what had come over her.

Miranda was impressed, though she tried to hide it. The hint of faux sympathy disappeared from her voice.

"What sort of writing? It's not like everyone else—*I'm working on a novel about the mothers at the school gates*—is it? The world simply doesn't need another female hack rambling on about retail and reproduction. Tell me you're tackling the big issues." Lucy gulped, disconcerted by Miranda's aggression, which was not passive. She had often considered writing, and, if she were to try, her stories would be about the school gates and the women she met there, the tales they had to tell if you listened, indeed, the roar that lay on the other side of silence.

"I've been working on TV, actually. A crime show. *Rage Undercover*, it's called. You won't have seen it, I expect. It's on Living. Extremely violent, elemental-type vibe."

She could tell from Miranda's expression that although she certainly had not seen it, she would be scanning the cable menu later that night. Lucy sat straight upright like Julia did and adopted Julia's breezy tone.

"I did it under a pseudonym to allow me to explore a whole different side of my personality, a masculine side, really. Richard's so conventionally macho that I felt I was becoming absorbed into a very traditional role. Julia Kirkland's my writing name. Look out for me."

Miranda positively bristled. She had had enough of Lucy. Fortunately, at this moment Simon appeared to warm a bottle.

"Here, give me that," she demanded, and Simon started, unsure as to whether she was referring to the bottle or the baby. "Sounds like everything's going really well for you," she muttered through gritted teeth.

"It's amazing what positive things can happen from a reversal of fortune."

It was the only truthful thing Lucy had said.

She smiled sympathetically at Simon and moved away, knowing that she needed to find Camilla to prevent her from being arrested later for drunk-and-disorderliness while driving an Eastern European 4x4. As she headed for the stairs she glanced into the living room, looked at the women, obediently clustered on armchairs, talking about the common entrance exam, the men standing by the mantelpiece, guffawing. It was positively Stepford. And yet only a few months ago she would have been firmly in the female area, or else sitting on a cushion like a dog at Richard's feet.

Camilla was lying in the bathtub with a bathrobe on and a towel rolled up like a pillow under her neck. Lucy sat down on the toilet.

"Are you okay?" Camilla asked.

"Sort of," replied Lucy. "I'd forgotten what it's like when you haven't seen people for a while. I hate giving the one-line description of my life."

"I know," agreed Camilla.

They both considered this for a moment.

"Mine is, 'One kid, one divorce, life sucks.' I don't want to say it, and no one wants to hear it," Camilla said.

Lucy leaned over and kissed her friend on the cheek.

"You're not bitter and twisted, are you, Milla?"

"*No!* My life didn't turn out how I imagined. But then neither did yours, right, Lucy? You used to be so *Breakfast at Tiffany's*, and now it sounds like *Last Exit to Brooklyn*. Cheers!"

She handed Lucy the shaker, and Lucy drained the last gulp.

THE MORNING OF THE FUNERAL, Lucy awoke to a thin layer of frost on the window and a robin perched on the ledge outside, staring straight in at her.

She shrieked and George rushed in, bleary-eyed, grey-faced, in striped pyjamas.

"What the hell?" he cried.

"That robin is looking at me strangely."

"*What?*" George turned, but the robin had disappeared, and now he looked at Lucy strangely.

"I'm telling you. It was kind of malevolent. Like in *The Birds*."

"Robins are territorial and aggressive. They mark out their living space and will attack trespassers."

Lucy's vision settled, and she peered at her brother. She noticed the flecks of white in his stubble. "You look dreadful."

"My mother died, and I've been on an aeroplane for twenty-six hours."

"*Don't start—*"

"The springs on my old bed are completely useless. Should have known you'd grab the only decent mattress in the house."

He sat on the edge of her bed and swung his legs beneath him. Lucy knew he was controlling an urge to suck his thumb.

"I wish Cordelia and the kids were here," he said.

Lucy, by contrast, did not wish Richard and the boys were there at all. She had always wanted to keep them as far away from all this as she possibly could. George stared out of the window for a moment. Lucy followed his gaze, wondering if he was thinking the same thing as her, remembering the weekends they roamed the park behind the house together while Mother lay in bed.

"There's something I want to run by you. Obviously, Mum has left the house to the two of us."

He paused. Lucy looked at him, curious.

"I'll get it valued before I leave, and then . . ." He hesitated. A brown moth fluttered against the glass, futilely crashing against it. Lucy reached for a magazine, rolled it into a baton, and raised her arm, but George opened the top window and tenderly guided the disorientated insect outside. As it flew away, he continued, carefully, as if he had been practising. "Cordelia and I would like to buy your share. Whatever the estate agent says, we'll give you. In fact, we can get a few valuations and then average them."

"Okay."

"No, I want you to talk it over with Richard—"

"Richard won't have a problem."

"It's just Cordelia knows a brother and sister who did this, and then ten years later when the house had tripled in value one of them came back for more money, and we couldn't have that; it would be a one-off thing."

(Gosh, thought Lucy, *maybe it is true that there's no such thing as the perfect family?*)

"I said it's okay." Lucy suppressed her urge to pat him on

the head and moved the conversation on. "What will you do with the house?"

George looked at her, surprised.

"We're going to come back and live here. We've been thinking about it for a while, and now . . . I love this house. I had happy times here. I can't think of anywhere better to bring up my kids."

Lucy did not know what to say. It seemed unspeakably inappropriate to start listing reasons why they had had a terrible childhood. So instead she replied, "That's cool."

"Cordelia knew you'd be fine with it. She sees auras round people, and she's says yours is yellow."

"Is yellow good?"

George nodded. Lucy decided to peel the smiley-face sticker off the royal wedding commemorative plate. Cordelia could have it if she really wanted it.

"George. It's only seven o'clock. You must be exhausted. Why don't you lie down in here and I'll bring you some breakfast? It's going to be a horrid day."

"Thank you, Lucy."

"And George . . . I'm sorry—"

"For what?"

That I could not sacrifice myself to save you, she thought, but she said, "For everything. Everything that happened. Everything you went through that I didn't."

Lucy pulled an old school sweatshirt she had found in the

bottom of her wardrobe over her nightshirt and headed for the door.

"Did I tell you Cordelia's training to be a therapist?" said George.

Lucy turned, unsure what she felt about this piece of news.

"Anyway, the first thing they said to her in therapy school is that everyone of our age has to give their parents an amnesty. No one had a clue about parenting in those days, so they just muddled through and did what their parents did to them. The challenge for us is not to repeat the mistakes they made. Cordelia thinks Mum and Dad were completely useless. The important thing is that we shouldn't blame each other."

"That's actually very helpful, George."

And she walked down the stairs to the kitchen, thinking about Cordelia and her exemplary perception, until George shrieked and she turned and rushed back upstairs.

"That robin *is* looking at me strangely," he said, amazed.

LUCY IS STANDING *holding a plate of wilting egg-and-cress sandwiches and avoiding her portly second cousin who stuck his hand up her skirt at her eighteenth birthday party. As she looks around the church hall she thinks this, this strange cocktail party bit, with the complimenting on the organization and the sausage rolls, and the peals of laughter from corners of the room, is the very worst bit of the day; worse than having to sit next to a coffin containing the body of* someone in whose body you grew; worse than watching George choke on tears as he read out a letter his eldest daughter had written to her grandmother; worse than watching people struggle to describe this difficult, disliked woman in euphemisms; worse than the hideous Wizard of Oz curtain moment at the crematorium.

She looks over to see George towering over Aunt Eva, deep in conversation, probably about the house and his return to England. She watches her father, his face red and puffy, sitting isolated on an uncomfortable chair at the side of the room, forever the villain, with Paula beside him, holding his hand, occasionally getting up to bring him another cup of tea. She feels his bemusement that his life should have turned out like this and Paula's relief that their remaining years on earth together will be free of the tormenting phone calls, the demands for money, and the guilt, the interminable guilt of it all.

Lucy wishes them well.

She puts down the sandwiches, asks the two sweet teenagers from the Tasty Bite to make more coffee and tea, and heads to the ladies' bathroom, pausing to splash water on her face before going into the disabled stall and sitting down for a few moments.

Outside, the door opens and a familiar clip of heels and a high-pitched whisper indicate the entrance of Camilla, who has driven down with Rose to support Lucy, for which she is grateful. Camilla goes straight to the small window and opens it, and Lucy hears the click of a cigarette lighter, a deep inhale, and there is a bustle as Camilla climbs on the sanitary towel disposal unit so she can stick her head and shoulders out and smoke while Rose pees loudly, ending with a few intermittent splashes to strengthen her pelvic floor.

Lucy remains silent, gripped with curiosity, listening as Rose comes out and washes her hands.

"Do you think we can go now?" Rose says.

"Absolutely," replies Camilla. "We've done our bit for poor dear Lucy. She looks dreadful." She pauses to climb down onto the tiles. "George turned out surprisingly attractive, though, didn't he?"

"That's it, we're leaving."

But Camilla is having a reflective moment.

"You know the worst thing about these sort of funerals, funerals of people who were just awful, is that everyone has to stand up and say how great they were, and how it was all the fault of the 'illness', how they really did love their husband or their kids despite every-thing. But the truth is, I never saw Lucy's mum smile except when a large bottle of Chardonnay was heading towards her. Do you remem-ber her performance at Lucy's twenty-first, when she tried to pick up one of the waiters?"

"Don't remind me. We picked up the pieces of that one for days afterwards—"

"She was a total bitch."

"CAMILLA!"

And they giggle guiltily, Lucy craning her ear against the metal door for further illuminating tidbits as they leave. She thinks for a moment. And then she makes a decision.

She walks out and goes to the cloakroom, where she puts on her coat, throws her bag over her shoulder, and takes the keys to the hired car out. She walks back into the church hall and says good-bye to her father, Paula, and Aunt Eva, and wraps George in a huge hug, telling him she is happy for him to do whatever he wants, and George, seeing her the way she actually is and not through the prism of their mother's resentments, hugs her back and smiles. She tells him she's done everything she can and now she wants to go home.

She walks out and throws her bag playfully onto the back seat of the car. She jumps in and turns on the engine, driving through the roads of her childhood to the motorway, where a sign for the airport soon appears.

She switches on the radio; she starts singing along, loudly, her upper body dancing as much as a person can dance while holding a steering wheel with at least one hand. She is free.

She realizes that she, Lucy, has not yet surrendered.

the attack dog

If Julia had been writing what happened as a script, which was unlikely, as Julia avoided "woman-y" stories and much preferred *Apollo 13* to *Beaches*, she would have started with a voice-over, and sought an arresting opening sentence to catch the audience's attention.

Julia liked voice-over as a dramatic device; it was an economical way of setting a scene and creating a tone. And tone would be critical to the retelling of this episode, as Julia would seek to replicate her very particular sense of regret and disbelief as she looked back in anger.

There were several options. She could have chosen

During her month's vacation at the Wellness Center
in Connecticut, Julia devoted many sessions with the
family therapist to her complicated feelings about
motherhood . . .

but would have rejected it immediately. Too much setup, far
too earnest, and, most important, "complicated" wasn't the
right word to describe her feelings, as, without any qualifica-
tion, it felt too negative. Julia had been surprised how happy
motherhood had made her. It was all the other crap that had
done her in.

She might try

WOMAN'S VOICE (OOV)
So every day they went out walking, the ugly dog
and Julia—

which, in theory, could be good, particularly if juxtaposed with
a series of striking images of downtown, a sort of "woman
with dog on First Avenue" opening, but Julia wouldn't have
liked it. There was no subtext.

No, in the end Julia would have hit upon an introduction
over three mojitos one Tuesday night with Lucy, as she explained the dramatic reversal of her fortunes.

It was

WOMAN'S VOICE (OOV)
Everything changed because Courtney from
upstairs turned thirty-nine and got a dog.

and while others would have dismissed it as too quirky, too self-conscious, or too left-field, Julia liked it, and she had been a writer long enough to know that if you find a sentence you like, you go with it.

You always fear you might not get another.

EVERYTHING CHANGED because Courtney from upstairs turned thirty-nine and got a dog.

Of course, as these two events coincided, Julia assumed it was a cute, fluffy, baby-substitute dog, most likely a bichon frise, the *chien du jour*, apparently, although the growling and scrabbling she heard from upstairs never sounded cute. There was something feral, urgent, and enraged about the canine noise that she recognized instantly. It was how she felt at that time, after all.

Although Courtney and Julia had owned apartments in the building for nearly twelve years, they were neighbours, not friends. Before Julia and her family moved to the loft on Rivington Street, they had all lived there and Courtney had managed not to learn either of the children's names, quite an achievement in a four-unit co-op with communal entrance hall. Julia and Courtney had both made a decision to cultivate a cordial, if distant, relationship, far easier to manage if there were any disputes in the building about floor coverings, noise in the hallway, or unsuitable new tenants. But as the years went by they became united, mainly because their apartments nestled on floors two and three of the 1895 town house, sandwiched between the basement with outside space (owned by two elderly Marxist academics who harangued them at the annual co-op meeting about making property history) and the penthouse with roof garden (owned by Michael and Johannes, the litigious and unpleasant life coaches, who wanted the other freeholders to sell in order to make the property all theirs).

So when Courtney broke her ankle in a freak accident and looked around for help from her neighbours, she realized that there was only one possible candidate. Courtney decided to take a chance that Julia, who had recently reappeared in the building on her own, had a better nature (not something she could have known for certain at that point) and asked if she would walk the dog.

Her gamble paid off. Julia's better nature recalled the sound of step THUD, step THUD, step THUD on the stairs outside her bedroom and agreed.

And then Julia met the dog.

The dog was without doubt the ugliest animal Julia had ever seen.

She was called Marjorie.

The bastard puppy of mastiff and bull terrier, with perhaps a little pug thrown in, Marjorie looked like she had been the unfortunate result of an experiment in a film like *The Fly* where the Mad Scientist combines DNA from excrement on the ground of the dog run in Tompkins Square Park and this was what grew in the test tube. And unfortunately this animal was not compensated for in the personality department. Courtney announced, with a slight tremor in her voice, that Marjorie had had a difficult childhood and certainly there had been failings in her parenting. No one had taught her to cultivate a winning manner, an affectionate demeanour, a perky wagging of a tail. In fact, she emanated the most extraordinary noise, a low, vicious growl, and did amazingly potent farts. But as they sized each other up across the reclaimed floorboards, Julia decided she liked this bitch's style, and if the truism that people choose dogs that mirror their personalities was actually true and not an "ism", she was getting an insight into Courtney that she would never have imagined. Only a very uncompromising sort of woman would walk past all the cuddly puppies in the rescue pound, nose round the half-chewed cages at the back, and choose this thing. *Interesting.*

So every day they went out walking, the ugly dog and Julia. And Julia discovered that, in contrast to the experience of pushing an ugly child through the streets, where people have no idea what to say once they've peered at it (an all-too-frequent occurrence, really, as one of her witty novelist friends once said, as few babies are *objectively* attractive), there was plenty of conversation to be had on the subject of the dog's repellent aspect. A man playing folk guitar dropped his plectrum, a couple of schoolchildren sniggered in horror, and then, as they started walking along the East River, Julia became conscious of admiring glances from a group of tough men loitering under the Manhattan Bridge. One came over to stroke Marjorie, resting a huge hairy hand on her head, and she growled so ferociously, Julia felt compelled to admire the penmanship of the Tough Man's tattoos. He just laughed, nodding at dog and owner approvingly. It was all very curious, and Julia walked away imagining herself in the smog-filled streets of the East End of London in 1838, her mastiff beside her, like Bill Sikes and Bullseye in *Oliver Twist*. (It is a measure of Julia's mental state at the time that she saw herself as Bill Sikes and not Nancy.)

Sometimes Julia bought Courtney a coffee and a double-chocolate cupcake, and, Marjorie dozing at their feet, they would talk about Courtney's troubled relationship and her co-dependency issues—with New York. The city was the only serious relationship Courtney had ever had. She had met it at age twenty-five, full of dreams, a highflier, adored. After ten years in the advertising agency she had gone freelance, designing, copywriting, consulting. She had bought her apartment, she could afford occasional weekends in the Hamptons and frequent microdermabrasion, but Gotham had turned into a cruel and demanding lover, requiring serious money and total commitment. There was no room to consider another way of life when, if you paused to look over your shoulder, you could slip from winner in Manhattan to loser in Hoboken. And Julia had been right about the baby-substitute thing. Courtney had had her ovaries checked, her blood tests were perfect, there was just no man, and, as freezing your eggs is a dodgy business, it was now or never.

Courtney knew she had to do something big, she wanted to *break free*, she said, she thought about moving. There were other fantastic cities in America, after all; what about San Francisco, or Miami, or Chicago? Julia did not dignify this with a response. They both knew that for a true New Yorker, wherever they come from, only New York will do. She herself thrilled to the dirt and the smells and the noise, for as a young woman silence had terrified her and she had run from the gardens and the convenient two-car driveways of the suburbs to the only place she had ever felt truly at home. She explained it simply as a passion, one beyond logic, for of course one could live sensibly in San Francisco, or Miami, or Chicago. As the children had got older, whenever Kristian tentatively suggested that what passed as bad behaviour in their school, or at home (to be discussed at great length or pored over in parenting manuals), might simply be due to the fact that they lived like caged animals, Julia went pale and refused to talk about it. How could she leave the shrimp rolls at Luke's Lobster? The perfect coffee shop? The life she had lusted after for so many years?

Courtney told Julia she was haunted by a trip to a psychic on West Houston she had made with a group of drunken girlfriends in 2002. The first card the bescarfed woman had dealt

Courtney was reversed (Julia knew this meant Courtney was unlucky in love, as she had once written a whole story line about a psychotic transvestite fortune teller), and Courtney was sure this had prophesied her disastrous romantic destiny. Her last boyfriend had moved to Vermont and become an apple farmer and produced cider and children once a year. "Why wasn't it me?" she asked. "Why didn't he do that with me? (They had once had a furious argument about non-organic cleaning products in front of Julia, which she thought was the answer rather than a gypsy curse, but as it was a rhetorical question, she let it go.)

So Courtney had got the dog. Her mother, a devotee of Oprah's magazine, had suggested it. It might help her get in touch with her maternal side, and she would attract a man who wanted to impregnate her.

Julia thought for a moment, then said the two words she knew would calm Courtney down. *Susan Sarandon.* Courtney nodded vigorously. And then they found a copy of *People* and went through the pictures of all the female celebrities with their children and worked out their ages. Courtney was soon feeling much better, particularly when Julia pointed out that most female celebrities, apart from Susan Sarandon, lie about their age so some of them were popping out babies at nearly fifty.

"Oh, Julia," she said. "I knew you would be the perfect person to talk to about these things. It's always struck me from how you deal with Curtis at the management company that you are a very practical person."

In fact, it was not Julia's practicality that was helping her. Julia was a kind person, which she attributed to her Episcopalian upbringing. She assured Courtney that New York wasn't just a place that could make you forget to have children. It was a place that could make you forget them if you did.

DURING HER MONTH'S VACATION at the Wellness Center in Connecticut, Julia devoted several sessions with the family therapist to her complicated feelings about motherhood. Although generally she approved of the "holistic hotel"—it was very A-list, and the food came in on china plates, so it wasn't for real crazies who might smash the crockery and attempt to slit their wrists—the sessions did not go well at first.

Julia was used to her weekly counselling with Dr Jenny on the Upper West Side. Dr Jenny was in her sixties, white-haired and wise; sometimes she held Julia's hand, she always had lotion-filled tissues available, and when Julia told her she had left Kristian and the children, they cried together. Occasionally Julia worried about the intensity of the bond between them; she loved Dr Jenny and she felt Dr Jenny loved her back. She said to her best friend, Christy Armitage, that going to Dr Jenny wasn't like seeing a counsellor, more like visiting the mother you always wished you had. Christy said, "But you have to pay her?" and Julia decided from then on to keep that opinion to herself.

By contrast, the family therapist at the Wellness Center kept at least a five-foot distance from Julia at all times, expected her to bring her own handkerchief, and asked her leading questions, even when she was crying. Finally Julia, sitting crumpled in the leather armchair, a ball of sodden toilet roll in one hand, announced querulously that she thought the sessions were meant to be *non-directive*. The Family Therapist looked at her with exaggerated calm and said that the Wellness Center programme was therapy boot camp, designed to get results for even the most self-indulgent clients who were used to counselling as *reassurance*.

Julia took this personally and felt defiant. She folded her arms and stared at the picture of a waterfall on the door opposite.

Inevitably, the discussions encompassed Julia's childhood and her feelings about her family of origin. Julia had always been her daddy's little girl, and when she brought her kids, Romy and Lee, home to Westchester to see their grandparents, she noticed that her father's teenage boxing trophy had been placed right in front of Kristian's side of her wedding photo. If anyone accidentally mentioned Kristian's name, Julia's father would pound on a sofa cushion, the veins on his muscular forearm throbbing, the grey hairs bristling over the tattoo he had got in Korea, and demand, "What did that man ever do for you?"

Julia's mother was more circumspect and less partisan. She had given birth very young and devoted twenty-four years of her life to wiping arses and countertops, ironing sheets, and arguing about homework. She did all this for no charge. But it turned out no charge is what you pay for the ultimate guilt insurance. For the day Julia's younger brother left for college, her mother walked away from that stage of her life without a backwards glance. Aged forty-five, she qualified as a swimming coach (she had been nicknamed "the dolphin" as a child) and had taken the local junior synchronized-swimming team to the National Championships at least ten times.

Julia described how, these days, she had to make appointments to speak to Coach Kirkland, which irritated her and meant their conversations were often chilly and combative, especially if anything about Romy and Lee's physical milestones was discussed. But then she realized that what really irritated her was, first, the knowledge that she had much preferred her mother when they were younger and the more comfortable relationship of servant and master had existed between them and, second, the fear that her own children might hate her, because she could not be their slave. Julia, who was quick of mind and fearless of temperament, reluctantly acknowledged that therapy boot camp might suit her.

The tension between Julia and her mother had come to a head one Saturday morning when Julia's mother was on the sidelines at a swimming gala. Julia rang her, by arrangement, about Thanksgiving. Kristian had taken the kids out for pancakes, and Julia was lying in bed with coffee and toast and peanut butter, and felt decadent and relaxed and deluded. She had made a joke, her mother laughed, and then Julia said that Kristian wanted to have another baby. Julia's mother kept laughing, but not in an amused way. When Julia fell silent, her mother marched out of the pool area, where the water made the sound echo around her, and asked Julia outright if she was pregnant. When Julia said "no", her mother said "good" far too quickly; Julia could tell she was gripping the phone so tightly her knuckles were red, and there was a heartbreakingly serious note in her mother's voice when she finally spoke again.

"Don't do it, Julia. *Please.* I love you, but I beg you, don't have another baby."

"Mom. I don't think that's any of your business." So much for the coffee and the toast and the peanut butter. Julia's mother knew before she did that Julia wasn't coping.

"You've got to learn you can't be the best at everything—"

Julia slammed down the phone.

Then why was there never a prize in our house for "good enough"? she thought.

KRISTIAN HAD DROPPED in one morning to discuss the arrangements for the following weekend, when, after finally taking his admiring gaze from Julia (even under that day's multicoloured knitted hat with earflaps, which on anyone else would make them look like they were goat herding in Peru,

Julia looked amazing), he looked down at the dog and failed to conceal his disquiet. Julia took offence immediately. She was getting fond of Marjorie and had taken charge of her grooming, nail clipping, and even teeth cleaning, as she worried Courtney was not attentive enough to the possibility of canine plaque. Sometimes, though Julia didn't say this to Kristian, Marjorie stayed for a sleepover.

"You didn't tell me it was a dealer's dog. It's a gangland bitch. They're used to attack people."

"Ridiculous. How do you know that? You teach yoga."

Kristian was having none of her attitude. "Look," he said, "she's got a *tattoo*."

And indeed behind Marjorie's ear there was a tattoo, a small star symbol, a sign of something rather thrilling and nefarious. Julia knew better than to tell him about her experience with the Tough Inked Man; the separation had done nothing to lessen Kristian's protective streak, and he often lectured her, ending with "I care about you; you are the Mother of my Children." At such times, Romy and Lee, the children of whom she was the mother, always reminded him of reckless things Julia had done in the past, always in the course of research for the TV crime show that had dominated their lives for ten seasons. It was fun for the four of them to banter like that. Only a year before, Julia's main interaction with her children was to holler at them and then beg their forgiveness.

Kristian was concerned about whether the dog was safe around the kids, and so Julia agreed not to let her near them.

She was the very model of reasonableness these days, she had learned the art of compromise at the Wellness Center, and it seemed that, now that they were liberated from the stress of pretending that equality in marriage ever means fifty-fifty, Julia and Kristian were both different people. The rules and the roles were clear, and Julia often thought, *Oh, if only he had been a woman, thus conditioned for career kamikaze, if only he could have chosen to be the wind beneath my wings*, and sometimes felt that if they had only managed to work that out before what happened happened, what happened might never have happened.

When Julia met Kristian he was twenty-nine and had something of a following in an overdesigned men's magazine for his witty columns about a patrician, handsome All-American boy whose father had gambled away the family fortune on real estate speculation in Eastern Europe. To his credit, Kristian never pretended this was anything but autobiographical. He lived rent-free in his aunt's apartment in the Dakota, wore his father's suits from the 1960s, and drove down Broadway on a scooter. His very existence could have been dreamed up by an art director to advertise handmade Italian shoes, and Julia was incredibly attracted to his sidecar, his grey sharkskin, and his disdain for the grubby business of real life.

Once they had the children, however, in an attempt to impress her or himself with his newfound determination to provide, Kristian lurched into freelance website design, finally starting a business downtown that involved his being in the office sixteen hours a day. To fit in, he wore T-shirts that showed his abs. That was the upside. On the downside he took a loan against their apartment and defaulted on it. Of course, he was suffering from depression (he was an adored youngest son, brainwashed by the cult of New York, living with a woman who was the embodiment of "making it there"); and of course Julia should never have allowed herself to be doing everything. Literally. But Julia would never have succeeded without denial. She read numerous self-help books about work/life balance for women and ignored everything they had to say.

She pondered all this the following week as she and Marjorie strolled along the streets, the locations of many of the scenes from her marriage. She saw the two of them, herself and Kristian, not herself and the dog, of course, staggering hollow-eyed down the apartment steps carrying babies and buggies and bottles and heading into the café opposite so they could pay someone to feed them. But they were still laughing, still madly in love; they made jokes, *"If you have two kids in two years, it's not just the city that never sleeps"*, and there were many nights the four of them collapsed on the super-king-size bed together, and if you saw that in a film you'd think, *That's a happy family, that's a family that will make it*. It's called *show, don't tell*.

But then the crime drama got a new executive producer. His reputation preceded him. He was called the Asshole. By his friends. Within a month the Asshole called Julia into his corner office and, with a customized poster declaring ALWAYS

BLAME, NEVER APOLOGIZE hanging above his head, announced that he had fired two of Julia's colleagues (one for having a vacation, the other for having cancer) and was promoting her.

"You'll never sleep again," he said happily, but she figured that this wouldn't make any difference, because she and Kristian had not slept for three years anyway. She worked her brain, fingers, and arse off, drinking Red Bull and vodka out of a My Little Pony beaker, writing through the nights in a delusional state, and the show's ratings soared, although Julia still never seemed to earn quite as much as her male counterparts. Her agent told her this was because she had other life "priorities", but that made no sense.

She had never told the Asshole she had a family.

EVERY MORNING Julia saw a Ghost of Julia Past among the taut, teeth-grinding women standing outside the day-care centre at seven fifty-five.

One day she passed a woman begging her child to stop crying, the woman's own eyes filling with tears, her voice rising to an operatic pitch, until they actually harmonized in a duet of misery as people scurried past, studiously avoiding them, not wanting to allow themselves those feelings.

Julia went into a café, bought the child a cookie and the woman a coffee. The child, clearly fed muesli and never allowed sweets, a regime Julia had imposed on her own two, which she liked to think of as the "I'm never there, but I feel less guilty if you don't eat sugar" diet, stopped crying, gobbled down the chocolate eagerly, and the woman sipped some coffee and waited for the inevitable judgmental homily. Julia, who had been on the receiving end of those many times from women she encountered in situations involving children, said nothing except "It'll be okay", even though personal experience had taught her that it might well not be. And she was sure the woman would have hugged her, had it not been for Marjorie, who suddenly took an enormous, foul-smelling, yellow shit on the sidewalk, and she had to borrow a baggie to scoop it up.

Julia's children had been picked up every evening by a succession of resentful, undocumented nannies who watched television with them until she staggered home between seven and eight in the evening, put in a load of washing, defrosted dinner, and bribed them into bed. Her beautiful babies had turned into slow-to-read, anxious, unhappy children, disruptive when they started school and always whining and desperate for attention. Kristian found excuses to stay out later and later every evening, and many nights Julia found herself alone in the kitchen with his uneaten plate of pasta at ten p.m. before steeling herself for three more hours of writing. The alarm would go off at six-thirty the next morning, and the whole ghastly business would start again. It was like *Groundhog Day*, except it wasn't funny and occasionally something unusually unpleasant or downright dangerous would occur; Kristian left little Lee, aged five, playing with the cutlery drawer alone in the apartment for a morning, simply forgetting about him in a haze of exhaustion. Another day, Julia nearly broke her arm on a cab door pulling Romy inside so she wouldn't be late for school. They were stuck in traffic, anyway, as a film crew had blocked the road. Julia, curious, wound down the window and asked what the movie was.

"*I Don't Know How She Does It,*" boomed the boom operator.

THERE WAS ONE PLACE in her neighbourhood that Julia avoided, a playground on East Thirteenth between Avenues B and C, a relatively pleasant, clean spot, with a metal climbing frame, a few actual trees, and two pergolas on each side that were covered in jasmine in May. She took the ugly dog on circuitous routes around it, for it was somewhere she had no desire to see again. It was a key location, the scene of the "inciting incident", the snapping point, the straw that broke the camel's back (and Julia was the camel).

It happened on a Wednesday and, that evening, Julia waited until Kristian came home after another futile day *drumming up business*, which seemed mainly to be playing backgammon on his laptop and drinking too many beers, and walked out of the loft on Rivington Street. She took a cab to the small apartment on East Tenth (the unpleasant and litigious life coaches had terrorized her most recent tenant out of the building), pulled the sofa bed out, and crashed for eighteen hours. She did not come back.

Julia and Kristian lived separately, Kristian in the loft with the kids, Julia in the small apartment with her laptop. They took turns taking Romy and Lee to school. Kristian stopped working "outside the home" (Christy told Julia he kept saying this). Julia paid all the bills. Apart from the month Julia spent at the Wellness Center, they swapped over most weekends. Julia became reacquainted with sleep and, although the dull ache of separation never left her (the umbilical cords had been physically cut, but Julia felt them dangling from her heart, invisible to all but her, like amputated limbs), she discovered she could hang out with her children, and enjoy them and even get them to do what she asked, something which had seemed almost impossible before. When she rang her mother to tell her this, there was no weird laughter or heartbreaking begging. Julia's mother was matter-of-fact.

"It may work better for you all," she said. "I was talking to some parents last week, and the mother said that the only good thing about their separation was that they both got time off from their kids."

This reminded Julia of a college friend of hers who had rediscovered religion in order to escape her three sons for two hours every Sunday.

One Saturday the second month, one of Kristian's former partners suggested they go to a yoga course together (they had both discovered yoga as a displacement activity from the website design business), and Kristian found his calling. He decided to train as an instructor, travelling upstate most Friday nights.

He didn't ask for much money for himself (he was far cheaper than an undocumented, resentful nanny), and, although it was expensive to run the two apartments, Julia could never have guessed the dramatic effect the new arrangement would have on her career.

She won an Emmy. She got a new agent. The new agent, Clarice, shouted, *"There's a new sheriff in town!"* at the Asshole and got Julia off the Crime Show. She then negotiated a deal with a studio and instructed Julia to write romantic comedy. Clarice told Julia that Julia had been brutalized by her work environment, and it was time for her to get back in touch with her woman-y side. Although Julia thought that was rich coming from someone who had turned an anger-management problem into a negotiation technique, she appreciated Clarice's point. While ALWAYS BLAME, NEVER APOLOGIZE might be the way to terrorize the Writers Room, it is not the basis for successful interpersonal relationships.

"Everything you write is so depressing," Clarice barked at her. "We all want to see a happy ending."

So Julia stopped worrying about things like the future, or the children, or Kristian, for, particularly with his new body, it was only a matter of time until he was snapped up by some single yoga person with limbs like overcooked spaghetti, and the children would have a lovely young stepmother who might well do a far better job of the whole happy-family thing than she had ever managed. Sometimes, though, Lee would tell her that Kristian had said he had more spiritual insight now and he loved Julia more than ever, that he was so sorry for what had happened and how he wished they could all live together again. And Julia realized that despite everything, that was what Romy and Lee wanted, too. But although she hugged her son tight and told him she loved him, and she knew he loved her, she didn't do anything about it. She was still feeling too feral and urgent and enraged.

"JULIA KIRKLAND, JULIA . . . DARLING!" The mellifluous Britmerican tones reverberated outside the Strand bookshop. Julia looked up from the one-dollar remainders to see Benedict Hart-Barrett in front of her. She was happy. It had been many years; in fact, the last time she'd seen him in the flesh, she was twenty-seven and Benedict had escorted her to a Halloween party in Park Slope, where they had dressed up as red devils. She'd watched him on TV, of course; he had become a bit of a regular on cable, always playing the smooth-slash-dastardly European in roles that had at one time been intended for Hugh Grant, and she had heard he was living in a gated community in Calabasas, occasionally playing in the English expats' cricket team in Santa Monica.

They embraced; he started telling her that he was in New York for a few months, had landed an ongoing role playing a cardiac surgeon in a new series for HBO written by a mutual acquaintance of theirs; "it's *dramedy*, I'm going to be HUGE," he said. Julia squashed her immediate feeling of jealousy and opened her mouth to say something positive when Benedict caught sight of the dog.

"Good lord, love," he said, like Kristian, immediately recognizing the dog's provenance. "Have times got hard? What are you selling? Ooh. *Hark at her.* I'm trying to be a good girl these days."

Julia explained about Marjorie and Courtney and the freak accident, and Benedict fell in step beside her so they could talk. Benedict was marvellous company, unfailingly indiscreet and camp. He started telling her about his co-stars on the dramedy, including a once extremely famous film actress. They had reached Tompkins Square Park by this stage, and he looked around, wrinkled his nose, and said, "Darling, what she's done to herself with the booze and the blow and the Botox. It's vile. If she walked through here without make-up, the rats would *throw* themselves on the poison."

After this chance reunion, Benedict and Julia met most days. Benedict was on call, but the unfortunate-looking ex-film actress was so demanding that shooting was frequently delayed and he found himself at a loose end. One day, to Julia's amazement, he told her he had a daughter, the product of a brief liaison with a make-up artist, which goes to show that you can never tell with upper-class Brits.

(Lucy had said that to Julia, and then, Julia's world being smaller than a village, it turned out that Lucy had been best friends at university with Benedict's younger sister, Camilla.

Benedict cheerfully recalled shinnying up a drainpipe and breaking into Lucy's room as proof of his overwhelming desire for her. Lucy gleefully reminded him that she had pushed him back out of the window onto the bicycle rack below, and he had broken his arm in two places. They roared with laughter at these memories. Julia did not. Why did they find attempted assault or grievous bodily harm, even in self-defence, funny? And then she remembered she had had the same bemused feeling the first time she had watched *Monty Python's Flying Circus*. One morning, she came upon Lucy and Benedict sitting side by side on a bench, earnestly calling the names of London Underground stations out to each other: *"Paddington!" "Theydon Bois!" "Bethnal Green!"* culminating in one of them shouting *"Mornington Crescent!"* Lucy said it was a game made famous on BBC Radio 4 and there was no point in trying to explain, as it would make no sense at all. From that moment Julia would say "It's like Mornington Crescent" whenever she and Lucy experienced culture clash.)

Soon Benedict started coming up to Courtney's, enjoying a larger audience. Courtney was appreciative and amused, and getting more attractive by the day as she limped off to facials and bought shorter skirts that exposed her one good leg. Sometimes Julia left them alone, and her writing would be disturbed by peals of giddy hahhahhahs from upstairs, punctuated by the occasional growl and a door slamming as the dog was locked in the bathroom.

A fortnight or so later, Courtney told Julia that she was worried about Marjorie. Had Julia noticed her behaving oddly? Julia shook her head. She had got so used to the dog's demeanour that it seemed perfectly normal. But Benedict pointed out that Julia was often so matter-of-fact about things, so LITERAL, so *New World*, really, that, lacking the sophistication of a non-American, she mightn't have a clue what was happening under the surface of anyone's world.

"That's true, Benedict, I always thought you were gay," Julia responded, and once again he roared with laughter like he was in an acting class, and Courtney exhaled with such relief that even Julia the Literal American got what was going on.

Benedict took over the counselling role with Courtney, but his recommendations on the subject of Marjorie were not consoling. He wasn't a "one man and his dog"-style Englishman, the kind who have portraits of their faithful Labrador Arthur above the mantelpiece on a larger scale than their children. He was ruthlessly unsentimental about the animal kingdom, a trait he had learned from his mother, Lady Fiona, whose way of dealing with troublesome pets was to load them in the Range Rover, drive down the nearest motorway, and abandon them. Benedict, who had been sent to boarding school at the age of seven, thought this was eminently sensible. He detailed various ways of restraining, muzzling, and whipping animals into obedience, with or without leather implements.

"There's only one way to deal with a difficult mutt," Benedict would conclude. "Let it know who's boss."

It was a good job Courtney was draped on the sofa, because by now she was weak with excitement. Julia made her excuses and left, not that they noticed, and then had to go out walking without Marjorie, as it felt extremely strange to listen to the groans, growls, slamming, and shrieking that then emanated through the reclaimed floorboards from the humans upstairs.

Oh, yes, Courtney looked a little embarrassed in the doorway the next morning when Julia bumped into Benedict bouncing down the stairs, the dog grizzling and snapping at his heels. He asked her if she was coming on the walk, and although Julia felt usurped, she thought Marjorie looked pleadingly at her, so she agreed.

It was a beautiful morning, the sun shone on the queue outside Abraço, the coffee tasted better than any cup of coffee ever, and Benedict was in sparkling post-coital form. It was marvellous to be ten years younger for a couple of hours. Julia laughed and laughed as Benedict reminisced, and then Benedict laughed and laughed as Julia regaled him with stories from her time on *Rage Undercover*, the horrors of it fading by the moment as they became funny stories. She had just got to a bit about the day she had volunteered to lie underneath a mound of fake dead bodies on set in order to propel one into the air during a supernatural sequence, when she looked up and realized they were right outside the children's playground on East Thirteenth Street.

Julia *froze*.

Marjorie, sensing something, clamped her muscly body next to Julia's leg, growled viciously, and farted aggressively in Benedict's direction. He yelped and held his nose and ran over to a bench in the park. With hindsight, Julia would realize that Marjorie's behaviour was odd indeed, but at that moment she gently patted the elephant dog's bulbous head. Her head was full of her own dark thoughts, and when Benedict asked her what was wrong, she told him.

Almost exactly a year earlier, Julia had hidden from the Asshole and absconded from the production office to bring Romy and Lee to the park after school, in a poignant attempt to convince herself that she was in control of her life. She released them into the playground, where they happily charged and screamed, and then ran over to the huge overhanging tree where other children were climbing and playing pirates and swinging on the branches.

Julia was preoccupied, as always. Her phone kept ringing, and the Asshole had handed her a voluminous set of notes, which she was trying to read while preventing Lee from breaking a limb, or Romy from breaking another child's limb. They didn't break any human limbs, but just as Julia had resolved how to connect an A story with a B story in the third act by an extraordinary event that bridged the distinct plotlines in an unexpected but thematically satisfying way, her children hurled themselves onto a large branch so wildly that it broke and they thudded butt first on the ground, laughing hysterically.

Suddenly Julia heard a female voice screaming, *"Stop! Stop!"*

and spun round, assuming someone had been mugged, but no, a woman was charging full tilt towards Romy and Lee, pushing her double buggy in front of her. She skidded to an impressive halt involving a deft sideways tipping motion of her front right wheel and, at the top of her voice, berated them for damaging the tree, *nature's gift to us all.*

Now, at another time, Julia would have been cross with her children and herself. She knew they were acting up, and she loved trees and hated the violent crunch of sap and wood. But Lee began crying and the woman didn't stop. She turned to Julia, her hemp jacket quivering with indignation, and accused her of being a bad mother with out-of-control children. (She didn't use those words exactly, but that's what Julia *heard*, a crucial distinction, as the family therapist at the Wellness Center pointed out.)

And that was it. Julia erupted. She picked up the broken branch in both hands, ran full tilt towards the tree, and attacked it. She thumped the trunk, she whacked the roots, she screamed up into the leaves, "I can't take this any more! I can't take this any more!" and, as the exhilaration of anger coursed through her, she thought of Lee running round the apartment in his inflatable green Incredible Hulk costume shouting, *"The madder Hulk gets, the stronger Hulk gets!"* and, transformed herself, she kept thumping and whacking and screaming *"The madder Julia gets, the stronger Julia gets!"* (For Julia, even while having a nervous breakdown, could not help referencing movies.) Bits of bark flew everywhere.

After only a few seconds, but to the playground visitors standing in horrified silence it must have felt like ages, Julia spun round to Buggy Mother, brandishing the branch aloft. The woman ducked behind the pergola, her baby started to wail, and Julia glimpsed Romy and Lee and the fear in their eyes. A kindly-looking elderly man stepped towards her as if considering an intervention, but Julia stopped herself.

"Sorry," she said to the woman, and she hurled the branch onto the ground. "You see I can't take this any more." Now her tone was matter-of-fact.

Character is action, Julia, she thought.

Benedict put his sympathetic expression on. "We all have to face our demons," he emoted, and Julia was reminded how much she hated it when actors ad-libbed their lines. He took her hand and waited, presumably for her to sob uncontrollably onto his cravat and declare herself healed, forgiven for savaging the East Village mother, or rather Mother Nature herself in the form of the injured tree. They both wanted the big finish, the bit where Julia had an epiphany that would change her life, but it didn't come.

And then Marjorie leapt up and bit Benedict on the ankle.

Julia has tried to reconstruct exactly what happened, but she was shocked and does not know now if it's memory or imagination that has kicked in. She is convinced she heard a CRUNCH! as the dog's teeth met Benedict's bone, but it could be that she was remembering the previous CRUNCH! of sap and wood in some weird parallel experience. Unfortunately for

Marjorie, Benedict had once done six weeks' training with the Special Forces for a thriller that had never gone into production, and, in fury, he grabbed the metal section of her lead, flipped it round her neck, and choked her until she was dead.

"What have you done?" screeched Julia, and she fell to her knees, crying and clutching the dog's corpse as Benedict hopped up and down in agony and asked a passer-by to ring his manager in LA to get the name of New York's best plastic surgeon.

THERE IS SOMETHING so terrible about death, something so finite, so irrevocable, that, whether it be a pet fish floating on the top of a bowl, or a parent in a hospital bed, or an ugly dog inert on tarmac, the realization that there is nothing you can do to bring them back and that life will end whether any of us like it or not cannot be ignored. Julia was so traumatized by what had happened that she took to her bed for forty-eight hours. She was aware this was an overreaction. At eleven o'clock at night on the second day the phone rang. It was her mother calling, and not by appointment, but Julia was happy to hear from her and she described her feelings about the terribleness of death, omitting the bit about the parent in a hospital bed. Julia's mother understood. She said that life certainly did go past in a flash, far quicker than she could ever have imagined, but that teenage Julia had helped her accept that.

"You remember what you used to say, sweetheart: 'Life

moves pretty fast. If you don't stop and look around once in a while, you could miss it.'"

"That wasn't me, Mom," said Julia. "That's from *Ferris Bueller's Day Off.*"

"I don't care," said Julia's mother. "That's why I became a synchronized swimming coach."

And then she started to sing *"Who knows where the time goes?"* in her reedy, slightly out-of-tune mezzo. Julia joined in. It was a most unexpected mother-daughter moment.

When they had finished they both giggled. Her mother said good-bye and sent her lots of love, told Julia her father sent her lots of love, waited for his footsteps to leave the room, and then added in a whisper, "Kristian's a good man, Julia, and you have two wonderful children. I know there were very important reasons for what happened between you, but now that you're aware of the inevitability of death, I want you to ask yourself if on your own is where you want to be."

And she hung up.

Julia got out of bed and ran all the way along First Avenue to the loft on Rivington Street, where Kristian, who had been waiting a long time, ran down to meet her and kissed her and she told him the story and what her mother had said and he listened and said everything would be all right. Although he couldn't resist a small smile as he said, "So you're sure the Attack Dog is gone for good?"

"She was called Marjorie," cried Julia, and he didn't laugh.

JULIA HAD CONTACTS DOWN at the local police station, and they took the dog away and even brought some ashes back for Courtney in due course, although by that stage Courtney was preoccupied with her morning sickness (Benedict had left more than the memory of his personality when he returned to Calabasas), and the beginning of a new romance with her gynaecologist, who had always been attracted to her but, knowing her desire to be pregnant, had ruled himself out, as he was infertile due to a teenage attack of mumps. Julia lost touch with Courtney after that.

Julia told the Life Coaches she wanted to sell (she and Kristian decided to buy a little place upstate with land and lots of trees for the children to clamber over at the weekends), and, eventually, Courtney did, too, when she and the gynaecologist and the baby moved to Brooklyn.

So Michael and Johannes finally got most of the town house, Julia heard from an actress who's been seeing them about her kleptomania that it's stunning, and everyone lived happily ever after.

Apart from the ugly dog called Marjorie, of course.

the doorman

Every morning, when she woke up, Christy Armitage looked out of the window and thought about death. She blamed this on two things. First, last month she had volunteered to go on the school field trip to the Met, where she and the twins had got stuck with a group of Italians in the Temple of Dendur. Her nose was practically jammed up against a piece of hieroglyphic graffiti as the enthusiastic docent described in slow, laboured English the slow, laboured death of the wife, servants, and animals of the pharaoh, immured with his corpse in the pyramid. Christy had felt physically sick, and the funny feeling had never left her.

Second, there was the undeniable fact of Vaughn's advancing age. Awake, upright, with his hair dyed some unrecognizable shade of browny chestnut with artful streaks of grey, his tanned, squash-playing body marching purposefully into the elevator, it was easy to forget that he would be seventy-one on his next birthday. But as she turned from the window and her thoughts of immolation in the penthouse in NoLIta, she watched him sleeping, his face in saggy repose, snorting snores fluttering his white nose hairs. He looked like an *old man*. She shuddered. Dear God, or Buddha or whoever, what had possessed her? Or what had possessed him? The twins were only six years old. They had just been to their half-sister's fortieth birthday party, where Lianne had sobbed on her shoulder, bemoaning her childlessness, and begged her, *Christy, what will I do?*

Christy, ever practical, had discreetly given her the number of the agency where she and Vaughn had got the egg donor, and told her they were affiliated with a reputable sperm bank, Ivy League students, that sort of thing, but insisted that, in the event of pregnancy, she tell her father it was a drink-fuelled one-night stand with a fellow tourist in Cabo San Lucas. She didn't want to deal with Vaughn's rage at the idea that his grandchild might be related to his children in ways he could not even imagine the genetic permutations of. It was positively Egyptian, she reflected, and, *whoosh*, there she was, trapped in that temple again.

Somewhere in the distance a phone was ringing. It stopped. There was a pause, and then a fast padding of indoor shoes along the carpeted hallway to their suite.

"It's the agency," said Loretta the Housekeeper (for that was exactly how she was called). "The Nanny quit." Vaughn sat straight up; he could go from dreaming to despotism in less than sixty seconds.

Loretta the Housekeeper intercepted with only the slightest tremble. "It's all right. They've got someone else. She's called Maria, and she's from Colombia."

Now Vaughn's eyes narrowed horizontally, but the effect on his physiognomy was vertical, as if his forehead was about to meet his chin. It was scary, but Christy was not surprised. They had once had a cleaner from Colombia who had been a disaster. She'd told Christy that the metallic Versace evening dress had been destroyed by hot solvents at the dry cleaner, but Vaughn had discovered her selling it on eBay and become racially prejudiced. What Christy was surprised about was what happened next.

"Tell them no, thanks. They must find us three choices to interview. In the meantime, my wife will look after our children."

It was a measure of Loretta the Housekeeper's years of service that she managed to leave the room without dropping the telephone in astonishment.

Vaughn looked at Christy in the window. Her face had not changed expression, but inner Christy, the one trapped in the

Temple of Dendur, was screaming. She shook herself off and decided to be positive. At least it had taken her mind off death.

Her mother used to say she had married a father. Christy knew that this was pejorative to her father rather than herself, part of an ongoing battle as to which of her parents would write the story of their own marriage, but, in truth, her relationship with both of them was strained. They had never got over the incredible beauty of the child they had accidentally produced (when Christy was a baby, people stopped her mother in the street; one woman took photos inside the pram), and they treated her like a changeling, with a combination of fear and awe, as if the faeries had stolen their natural lumpy child and given them this magical one instead.

It was a relief to all three of them when cross-eyed brother Jake finally came along. He belched and blew up frogs with a straw and took their attention so they could leave Christy in her room, staring out of her window, imagining a quite different life in a galaxy far, far away.

When that life failed to materialize, Mr Vaughn Armitage II did. But their relationship was not at all what her mother diagnosed. For Christy would have quite liked a father, or what she imagined to be a father, a soothing paternal presence, a rock. But Vaughn was neither of these things. He had boasted of the length of his member, as he quaintly put it, the first time she had met him and, apart from his brief and bitter first marriage, he had romanced, also quaintly put, scores of desirable women. In fact, after Christy and Vaughn returned from

Turks and Caicos, the question on everyone's lips was *Why did he marry HER?* She was thirty-five, a bit-part actress and former catalogue model, with no real aspirations to society life or charity work or even luxurious idleness. She was doing a degree in art therapy at the New School, her nails were often chipped, and she bought clothes at Banana Republic. And so it was universally acknowledged that she should have refused him and allowed a better groomed and more deserving woman to spend his money. On good days as well as bad days, Christy acknowledged that, too. But there was no accounting for what Vaughn might do once he had made his mind up about something.

The nine years since their marriage had passed in a blur. After six months of infertility, Vaughn took them straight to a gynaecologist in Sutton Place. The doctor had been calm, he had reassured them that Christy's age was not a problem, the irony of which was not lost on anyone in the room, and he ordered them to relax. Christy, obedient as ever to a strongly expressed view, rounded her lower back and exhaled, but then the doctor made a fundamental mistake. He relaxed, too, and with Vaughn that was always dangerous. He said that in his experience the number-one cause of infertility among professional New Yorkers was not having enough sex. Vaughn was so outraged at the slur on the virility of his member that, from the following week, Christy was booked for a seemingly endless series of invasive fertility tests that traumatized her so much that eventually she agreed to the IVF with donor eggs to make it all stop. Three pregnancies later, the twins were efficiently removed by Caesarean section and Christy never went back to the New School. But she could not quite pinpoint what she had been doing since then. In fact, her life was just like her faulty Toyota Prius. At about age twenty-one she had put her foot on the accelerator, it jammed, and when it stopped, she was a forty-four-year-old woman wondering where it had gone.

The previous week, Vaughn had been sent an e-mail invitation to a dinner where every confirmed guest had a small descriptive sentence after their name in parentheses, a label, presumably to make the event more attractive to prospective attendees. So someone called Misha was not just from Montenegro, but had also founded his own Reconciliation Advisory Agency, and his wife, Elaine, was a mother and Environmental Campaigner. It went on like this for twelve people. Vaughn, Innovative Global Financier, deleted it, but it had struck fear in Christy's heart. How would people describe her other than "the woman to whom Vaughn Armitage was married"? Even the *verb* wasn't active. She was lacking something— it was obvious. She simply did not know how to be a person, let alone a wife or a parent.

But today was apparently going to be the First Day of the Rest of Her Life, so she walked purposefully into the enormous playroom where Sorcha and Sinead were sitting side by side, staring at the wallpaper.

"Don't you want to watch TV, girls?" she asked hopefully. They shook their heads in unison and informed her they were looking for pictures to materialize in their heads that they could tell each other about. Assuming this was some telepathic twin thing, Christy told them she would just sit with them, then. They didn't seem to mind very much. That was as good is it ever got between mother and daughters.

She had once tried to suggest to her best friend Julia Kirkland that perhaps her difficulties with the girls were to do with her unresolved feelings about the egg donation. Julia had snorted unsympathetically. "If you grew them, they're yours." But that was Julia all over. She was a writer. She had opinions. They had met ten years before, when Christy was doing walk-on parts and Julia had just started as a story editor on a new TV show about a private detective with multiple personalities, one of which was a serial killer. The story lines were violent and misogynistic beyond belief, and Julia, who had already decided to have a brilliant career, was responsible for the most violent and misogynistic of them. But to go back to the first point, maybe she shouldn't listen to Julia too much on the mothering issue, for, as Julia said herself, her label was "the woman who walked out on her children", although, and this was said with a rueful chuckle, she thought it should be "misunderstood".

Within half an hour Julia was round with the lattes from Café Gitane, and she and Christy were smoking menthols on the balcony as the girls played solitaire with each other. Julia had brought round an old game of Twister and informed Christy that this would be today's activity.

"That's the secret, Christy—make a plan for every day. That's how you'll get through it."

"My plan for tomorrow," Christy informed her, "is for the agency to ring with a new nanny."

But they didn't. So Christy pulled her padded fleece on over her Juicy tracksuit and took the girls to the playground. It was very interesting to see how children did resort to imaginative play when there was nothing else to do. Also, that you could get three slices of pizza for three bucks if you walked five minutes toward Chinatown. The next day they went to a children's film, a shameless holiday concoction involving elves, a three-legged reindeer, and snow. They giggled and ate green candy and popcorn and ice cream, although afterwards, Christy was perturbed when Sorcha told her that the last time they were at the cinema, the nanny had taken them into the toilets and asked them to take photos of her in her underwear, which she then texted to someone called Rik on the iPhone Christy had bought for her. Christy made two mental notes: first, not to mention this to Vaughn, and second, never to employ another nanny who boasted about familiarity with modern technology.

They ice-skated at Rockefeller Center, where she avoided the attentions of a priapic Santa. They saw the Three Bears at the Marionette Theater in Central Park. They marvelled at the Rockettes, high-kicking their way through a London bus on-stage at Radio City Music Hall. She took them shopping and, instead of buying them coordinating outfits, allowed them to choose their own clothes. They skipped home in purple and blue leggings, demanding Vaughn's approval, and he deemed them "funky", which made them dissolve into laughter.

Christy was the very opposite of the helicopter parents she saw whirring from school gate to enrichment class; her detachment gave the girls space. They were both like Vaughn, independent, type-A personalities (his alpha sperm had beaten the eggs into submission) and, although she wondered how she would cope with a couple of puppy-like, emotionally demanding boys, within days she could see that she was exactly the kind of mother her twins needed.

She was getting a bit cocky by the time she saw Julia after her Wednesday-night meditation class. That night's theme had been *Life provides you with exactly what you need*, and Christy felt enlightened.

"I had no idea there were so many things to do with children in New York. And because I'm so busy during the day, Vaughn's decided we don't have to go out every night or away every weekend. Bliss. And he's taking us to a hotel upstate for the holiday so I don't have to deal with my stepdaughter's list of dietary requirements. Life provides you with exactly what you need."

Julia was approving. She took out her red leather-bound notebook.

"This is happening a lot," she said. "I'm making notes for an original screenplay. Because of the recession, more and more women are having to look after their children again. And a

certain proportion of them appears to be finding fulfillment."
Julia said this in the calculated manner of a scientist explaining an anthropological phenomenon, but her interest was commercial.

"My new agent says there's a *huge* gap in the market for an aspirational movie for women like us who don't know how to be mothers."

Christy thought for a second. "Speak for yourself. I don't know about fulfillment, but I do intend to buy their presents myself this year. I have some ideas about what they might like. And I haven't thought about death any morning since the nanny left."

"*Interesting,*" Julia said, and scribbled something down. Christy peered over her shoulder and glimpsed the words *Temple of Dendur* with two exclamation marks scrawled after it and *had too much time on her hands,* which ended with a question mark.

VAUGHN HAD NEWS FOR Christy when he came into the spare room the following morning. She slept there after meditation, as it often awakened subconscious thoughts in her that made her thrash around or talk in her sleep all night. The previous night after the co-op board meeting he had had to sack the doorman, whom he liked. Raoul had been renting second-floor apartments by the hour to an upmarket escort agency while their owners were out. Vaughn secretly thought it showed great entrepreneurial flair and felt it was the fault of the board members, who were snobby but cheap, for not paying him properly. Raoul's great asset was that he could do pretty much anything—electrics, plumbing, painting—which actually suited the parsimonious owners, and Vaughn often slid him fifty dollars on the side to keep the lobby presentable. However, even he had to draw the line publicly at prostitution, and so Raoul was gone and the management company had sent them a temporary.

"He's Irish apparently," Vaughn said meaningfully. "Let's hope he's legal."

The mention of Ireland always caused a little froideur between them, but today it lasted only a couple of seconds before the next headline.

"Oh, and there's a new nanny who can start January first." Christy looked up. Suddenly she saw a vision of herself, sitting on their cream leather sofa, trapped inside a pyramid, the stones being hauled shut, sand rushing through the cracks. She was screaming, pounding her fists on the walls, as the girls sang and played Twister outside.

"I want to look after them myself from now on," she said.

The words had come out by themselves. She appeared to be channeling a very in-control woman. She was startled but excited, she liked the sound of herself, and, as it was only the second time in their entire marriage she had expressed a specific desire to do something, Vaughn was momentarily discombobulated.

"When will you go to the gym?" he asked. He had clearly not noticed that the girls had started school the previous September.

THE GIRLS HAD a crush on the new doorman. Christy knew this because on Valentine's Day they had made him a card at school and asked her to hide it behind the front desk. She insisted on looking at it first. It had a very peculiar-shaped shamrock inside a star-dusted heart. She pointed out that it was not customary to sign a Valentine's card, but their response was, "How will he know it's from us then?" and she didn't have sufficient mastery of dialectic to combat their logic. She tried to make them give the card to their father, but it really was a lost cause. She had to make a pinkie promise it would be placed in an obvious, but not too obvious, place where he would discover it and feel the warmth of their devotion. Of course, as she staggered in from the school run, an enormous backpack swinging off each shoulder, although he was not present, the lobby was filled with a flirtation of females, as it tended to be these days, and it was not possible to deliver the secret missive.

Christy herself had not seen John Paul O'Sullivan (the girls met him every Saturday morning when Vaughn took them for breakfast and quality time), although she had once glimpsed a muscular bejeaned leg sticking out from the store cupboard and heard *Oh Holy Mother of God* in manly Celtic tones emanating from the laundry area. She figured that she would have to wait until teatime, when the two fantastically *french* French teenage girls living on the fourth floor had to eat some steak, and Miss Sorenson, the octogenarian former ballet dancer from the ground-floor garden apartment, usually had him rescuing Mikhail, her corpulent tabby, who often got stuck on the window ledge outside the French family's kitchen, looking for gristle.

And so it was that at five o'clock the reception area was empty. Vaughn would consider that a sacking offence, but Christy was delighted. She hurried straight over to the desk, pulled open the top drawer, and put the card in, but she was distracted momentarily by a gaudy leprechaun key ring. She picked it up and held it to the light. That was the moment he returned.

"Are you rifling through my drawers, Mrs Armitage?" he said, and stopped, embarrassed when she didn't laugh.

She decided to get the whole exchange over with quickly— Valentine's card, little girls, pinkie promise—and even managed to hand him the pink envelope without looking into his face, a habit she had practised because she had never been able to get comfortable with the idea of staff.

She was almost at the elevator when she heard his soft chuckle. *Sorcha and Sinead, Sorcha and Sinead.* She paused. The words did sound different in his musical brogue, and so she looked at him. His eyes were blue, his hair was dark, he was handsome, but it was his voice that was beautiful.

"It's nice to hear you say their names," she said.

"Are you or your husband Irish? Why are they called that?"

Of course she should have remembered to say that her father was second-generation Irish, his grandfather had come over on the boat and her maiden name, another quaint expression, was Mahon, but she didn't. She made the mistake of telling the truth.

"Our egg donor was an Irish student, and we decided it would be good for the twins to honour their culture."

(In fact, "we" hadn't decided at all. Christy had insisted in the middle of another burst of morning, noon, and night sickness and had prevailed, the first instance of this, which was the reason for Vaughn's froideur around all things Irish.)

The conversation ended there and then. That had shut up his blarney. But as she rode back up to the penthouse, Christy thought, not for the first time, how far she had come from her upbringing in rural Southern California and how out of touch she now was with anything that could remotely be described as normal. It was nearly as excruciating as when she had tried to commiserate with one of the Mothers at the School, whose husband had just been made redundant, by saying that she had decided to stop using a driver for errands. But, as Julia always said to her, at least you know this, at least you attempt an "examined life".

She thought this could be the only reason Julia was her friend.

· · ·

VAUGHN HAD TAKEN a two-week break from work in early March (he had been planning a discreet ribbon lift on his neck, but now that Christy was baking cookies and having play dates and had even joined the reading group at the independent bookstore on Prince Street, she had reverted to her former self with no interest in grooming, and he didn't feel the need to keep up), so he decided to spend the time rereading *The Diary of Samuel Pepys*, letting his daughters crawl all over him, and patrolling the apartment block to see what sort of a job the new doorman was doing.

He was impressed. Although Mr O'Sullivan appeared pretty useless at anything beyond keeping the lobby tiles clean, he was brilliant at exuding a professional air, always had an umbrella ready for the female residents, and seemed to have a vast network of Irish plumbers, builders, and electricians who materialized in a minute and were reasonably priced.

Julia, who had actually had a proper conversation with him, had learned he was an actor, or rather had spent ten years in LA trying to be an actor. Her theory was that he was "playing" being a doorman. Christy found this very interesting. It had sometimes occurred to her that she was "playing" being a mother.

"Action is character, Christy," said Julia.

Julia was absolutely thrilled by Christy's transformation.

And it wasn't just because of her friend's increased happiness. Julia's original screenplay was taking shape.

"It starts with the scene in the Temple of Dendur. Very New York. Very Nora Ephron. You're my heroine. You've been obsessing about death, or rather the death of your personality to your alpha-male husband—that's the interpretation, right?—but you've broken out of the pyramid."

Christy told her it was more literal than that. It was a condition of her pre-nup that in the event of Vaughn's death, she could live in their properties only if she remained single.

"Is that legal?" said Julia, scribbling in her notebook again, as she knew well that you could not make this stuff up. Christy shrugged.

"I just signed it. I knew everything would be fine. And it is."

"That's good," Julia replied. "I'm only writing happy endings these days."

Christy was indeed chuffed by her story so far. She was even beginning to consider the vague but tantalizing possibility that she might get a proper job one day, although Vaughn would probably draw the line at that. But despite Julia's protests, these developments didn't seem very dramatic or "Hollywood" enough. She asked Julia whether a movie could really end with a woman talking about Edith Wharton at a reading group.

"Of course not," replied Julia. "This is only the first ten pages. It'll be a romantic comedy; you'll meet a guy somewhere in act one and fall in *lurve*."

Christy was horrified. "I couldn't do that to Vaughn. You can't have the heroine of a romantic comedy abandon her husband and children."

There was a terrible pause as she realized what she had just said, but Julia didn't take it personally.

"You're right. What a monster you are! Vaughn will have to croak first—"

Some time later, Christy was still tittering in a disturbed way about this conversation when the handle of the fridge came off in her hand. She turned around a little helplessly, looking for Loretta the Housekeeper, but she had gone to collect dry cleaning (the only staff member allowed to do it these days) and Vaughn was having his constitutional nap, so Christy, after ineffectually hitting the handle with a hammer a couple of times, knew that she would have to summon the doorman. She felt a bit weird about it—it was the Irish egg conversation—but she had no choice. Vaughn did not tolerate anything broken around him, particularly kitchen appliances.

In fact, it all went very smoothly. After three minutes' chat about the size of the fridge, John Paul was able to fix the handle, although he decided to call his second cousin Patrick, who was really the man for the big fridges, to check it over later. And then she made him a cup of tea and decided to prove to him that she was not the person he imagined her to be. She asked him about being an actor, and he told her he had spent several years in LA with moderate to poor success. He had stood behind Colin Farrell a few times, had a few one-liners in episodes of daytime drama, done a washing powder commercial once. He grinned slightly manically and riffed on about the power of a white wash, but she did not laugh, and he was glad. She mentioned that she herself had been a pair of legs in a pantyhose commercial, and he didn't laugh, either. In that moment, they understood each other perfectly. They had both walked along the boulevard of broken dreams and ended up in the same apartment block, although one of them was at the top, and the other at the bottom.

Vaughn came in looking for coffee, bleary-eyed and uncharacteristically crumpled after sleep. He eyeballed the doorman, and then, without a word, formed a question mark on his face to her.

"The fridge handle came off," she said. "John Paul fixed it, though his second cousin Patrick, who's the man for the big fridges, is coming back tomorrow to check it."

John Paul seemed to shrink in the laser beam of Vaughn's silence. So this was Vaughn's choice of weapon today, she thought; he would be the dominant lion of the pride by whatever means necessary. John Paul, by contrast, was a beta male, a sort of handsome adjunct, who might be stroked occasionally by a sickly lioness, but he would never father the Lion King. Christy sighed to herself and wondered what it would be like to be married to a beta male. She imagined she wouldn't really mind, though it had proved very difficult for Julia. In the middle

of a vision of herself walking down the aisle with the doorman, Vaughn said something. Both John Paul and Christy were
surprised.

"I said, Will you be here to supervise this Patrick, your
second cousin?"

John Paul shook his head. He told them he had a day off;
it was Saint Patrick's Day, and as he'd never been in New York
on March 17 before, he was going to the parade.

"Christy," said Vaughn, about to surprise her again (it was
happening a lot these days), "you and the girls should go to the
parade, too. You can take them, can't you, Mr O'Sullivan? The
girls have Irish DNA in them."

John Paul shuddered involuntarily. Christy knew he did not
want any more information about their reproductive adventures, but Vaughn kept to the party line.

"Christy's grandfather was from County Limerick. He came
over on the boat, died three years later."

Vaughn could not understand why the doorman had
laughed. *Strange people*, he thought, and hoped the guy was not
a drinker.

THE GIRLS WORE green, white, and orange hats, tried to
copy a troop of flame-haired children reeling, and sang along
at the top of their voices to "Beautiful Day". After a couple of
hours they were all frozen, so they went to a pub he knew
in Greenwich Village where the owner turned a blind eye to

children and they sat in the back by a fire, as Gaelic football played on a small television above the bar, and John Paul told Sorcha and Sinead stories about Ireland, about the faeries and the hill of Tara.

"That's why the recession came to Ireland, you know. Because they tried to put a motorway through Tara."

He made the story of the Celtic tiger sound like an Irish myth.

"After the gold came to Ireland, the people became greedy," he said. "They learned to love their home improvements, and their clothes, and their handbags, and they forgot about the things in their past that were good. And that's why they tried to build the motorway through Tara and the ancient land punished them."

For that was the truth about Ireland, he said. "You don't own the land, the land owns you." Then he bought Christy a half of green Guinness. To the girls' amazement, as she was a Pinot Noir woman exclusively, she sipped it.

"It doesn't taste too bad." She smiled. There was froth on her upper lip. Without thinking, he wiped it away with his thumb. She had often wondered what the word "frisson" meant. Now she knew.

After that, John Paul always seemed to be around when she was coming in and out of the lobby. He hand-delivered packages to the penthouse and, once Vaughn was back in the office, swept outside their door several times a day. She thought it must be exhausting for him, because he had to do the same for everyone, in case anyone noticed. For her part, she usually managed to do her morning errands at precisely the time he took a coffee break, and he would often fall into step beside her as she bought flowers, had a coffee, or, if she was desperate to see him, collected the dry cleaning instead of Loretta the Housekeeper. They found they were able to continue conversations across days or even a whole week when they talked about their childhoods. She supposed this was what it must be like when you met someone you really wanted to be with. She finally understood what all the fuss was about.

After she collected Sorcha and Sinead from school, if it was nice outside, they would sit in the small patio garden and he would throw tennis balls to the girls, who ran about and caught them. Miss Sorenson would sit next to her, and they talked about Elizabeth Street in the 1960s and how she had known Rudolf Nureyev. Everyone was happy, apart from the French teenage girls, who were incredibly sulky, and raised an eyebrow only when John Paul took off his sweater and exposed a thin line of black hair running down his torso.

And the amazing thing for Christy was that she never once lied to Vaughn about anything. She would say she had bumped into the doorman in the street, or he helped carry up the groceries, and soon Vaughn had decided to recommend they make him permanent at the next co-op board meeting. She was delighted. She had convinced herself that she had made a new friend, and she needed a new friend, as Julia was going through a difficult time again, and had become hypomanic, staying up all night writing and occasionally ringing her, sobbing, saying she hated herself, she missed Kristian and the children, *what sort of a woman was she*? Christy did what she always did and took her to the doctor, who immediately signed the insurance forms and sent her to a residential therapy hotel in Connecticut, where he hoped she might find the answer to this question. It crossed Christy's mind that perhaps she should go, too. And then it was spring break, and she told Vaughn she didn't want to go to Turks and Caicos; she would take the girls for day trips instead. And Sinead invited the doorman to come to Coney Island.

JOHN PAUL LOVED CHILDREN. He had a niece he doted on, a champion Irish dancer, and he had a relaxed, easy manner with the girls, chased them, teased them, but always with a lightness of spirit. Christy could see people staring at the four of them as they played on the beach. *What a perfect family*, she knew they were thinking. She watched the sand running through her fingers, and allowed herself six hours to think it, too.

Of course, the loss of Vaughn would be devastating. How would she react? She realized her only knowledge of how to deal with death had come from films. She imagined herself being told the tragic news. Would she fall to her knees? Howl at the sky like Sally Field in *Steel Magnolias*? Or would she be impassive, think only of the children, people murmuring "She's been a tower of strength" as she, the tragic young widow in designer black, led the children, a tableau of perfectly realized grief, behind the coffin out of Saint John the Divine. Where did you find caterers for wakes? Did you pay a funeral organizer like you did for a wedding? She was reassured by the idea that although there was no one in her family she could turn to, Julia either would know how to do this sort of thing or would certainly know someone who did. And then things got more difficult. She realized she had no idea what music Vaughn would want, what his favourite religious readings were, or where he wished to be buried.

She refused to admit to herself that she had little or no sense of what her husband was like at all, whereas she knew already that John Paul wanted to be laid to rest in the family plot in County Galway, his favourite song was "A Stór Mo Chroí", the Bonnie Raitt version, and, though people made fun of it, he loved *The Prophet*. She started to panic. She would have to fast-forward through this sequence.

After an appropriate period of time, John Paul could move into the penthouse with her (if he was still the doorman, no one need ever know, which would circumvent the pre-nup) and they would raise the girls together. If it happened soon enough, maybe she could have another baby, naturally this time, a black-haired son with his blue eyes and her tanned skin. She saw herself giving birth, at home maybe, moving between the bath and her bedroom, screaming with pain maybe, no, breathing deeply, radiating empowerment, discovering that her peasant stock stood her in good stead. She could have had ten children in a field, should life have thrown that at her. John Paul handed her their son, blue and red, wide mouth gaping, crying, and she felt herself start to cry, too.

"The girls want to go on the rides." He was standing in front of her, his hand outstretched. She took it and stood up, still shocked by her inability to control her own thoughts. There were tears on her cheeks. He looked at her tenderly and didn't say a word. Was it possible he knew what she was thinking?

The girls, who had been skiing in Aspen, had gone on a VIP trip to Euro Disney, and had their birthday parties in a private room at the Plaza Hotel, were shrieking with unadulterated joy at playing the slot machines and eating the dirty-water hot dogs, and they took turns recording snatches of video on Christy's phone. Christy and John Paul took them on the bumper cars, where they put a girl each in the seat beside them and vented their sexual frustration by crashing into each other as Sorcha shouted *"Harder! Harder!"* And then, as the afternoon light faded and they knew the day would soon be over, the girls insisted on going on the Ghost Train and jumped into the first carriage together. Without a word, Christy and John Paul got into the next one, and the moment they crashed through the blood-red doors he put his hand on her thigh and kissed her, neither moving until they burst through the cobwebs back into the dusk light.

The girls demanded to go round again, and John Paul quickly paid for five goes each for the four of them. On the third time it occurred to Christy that although she had never been a good swimmer, it was amazing for how long you could actually breathe through your nose if you tried.

Her stepdaughter Lianne was in the lobby with Loretta the Housekeeper when they returned. John Paul was carrying sleeping Sinead, Sorcha was saying over and over again that it was *"the best day EVER"* as she invited him up to have dinner with them, and John Paul had just whispered in Christy's ear that he would sell his very soul to the devil to spend one evening with her. Christy was laughing loudly. Any other time, Lianne might have raised a perfectly threaded eyebrow at such an extraordinary spectacle, but today, very pale, her lower lip trembling, her fingers clutching Loretta the Housekeeper's, she was oblivious. There could be no doubt she was about to deliver a momentous piece of dialogue. Loretta the Housekeeper was not so absorbed in the plot. She seized Sorcha's hand and bustled a very anxious John Paul and Sinead into the elevator, just as Lianne was quivering. "I'm so sorry, Christy."

So this was it. Christy *had* had a premonition that day at the Met, but it was not her own death she had foreseen. And at that moment she knew that her ridiculous fantasies meant nothing, and the appalling reality of this was worse than she could ever have imagined. Bizarrely, her first thought was how awful Julia would feel about the "croaking" joke. Then she was all alone with the blackness and the shock and the truth. Her knees buckled beneath her. She collapsed onto the floor. Lianne looked at her in horror.

"Dad's not dead, Christy. He's had a heart attack."

Lianne made a mental note to herself. She had overdone the preamble. She would have to do better next time, when it counted.

THE FIRST THING Vaughn said when she arrived at the hospital was *"I love you."* Christy burst into tears. Lying in the bed, various plastic leads looping around his arms and chest, it was no longer only in his sleep that Vaughn looked like an old man. He would have to stay there for three weeks, charming the nurses and half-heartedly torturing the doctors by insisting on second and third opinions on Skype from cardiac experts around the globe. His white roots appeared; his muscles weakened. He didn't want the girls to see him, but he insisted on Christy's presence and had a bed made up for her in his room, laughing and calling it their "heart attack honeymoon", but they both knew that really was a joke. When a decision had to be made, even what he should eat, he looked at Christy and said, *"You're the boss."*

And then she had a call from his lawyer, Myron Schulberg. Myron wanted her to know that Vaughn had changed his will. He had voided the pre-nup; she would get what she would get, and the absurd clause about her losing her home if she remarried was gone.

"We were only winging that one, anyway," Myron intoned. "Vaughn wants you to know that whatever happens to him, and that includes being put in sheltered accommodation in the event of another more debilitating attack, diabetes, or Alzheimer's, he wants *your life to go on*."

She put the phone down quickly, as she half expected him to burst into song, and she smiled. How like Vaughn to deliver such a piece of news like that. She was no longer trapped in the Temple. She could have a different life if she wanted.

Christy had rung her mother to tell her what had happened, as it seemed like that was what she should do, and her mother had caught her off guard by announcing that she and Ron, Christy's father, would fly to the city immediately to take care of their granddaughters, leaving Christy free to minister to her recuperating husband. And so Felicia and Ronald Mahon travelled economy on American Airlines to take up residence in the guest room of their daughter's multimillion-dollar penthouse. It was unusually warm for April, so they poured their ample frames into matching shorts and print shirts and huffed and puffed the girls to school and back, after which Ron sat and watched sports in the den, and Felicia chatted to Loretta the Housekeeper.

Fortunately, Christy was so consumed with the new helpless Vaughn that she had no time to worry about dealing with her parents. After the first few testy exchanges with her mother (Christy knew Felicia would not be able to resist a couple of comments about Vaughn's age, she *hadn't wanted to say anything, of course,* and how *all the money in the world can't buy you your health*), Christy decided that she would get through all this by repeating the mantra of that meditation class. *Life gives you exactly what you need.* And certainly the girls adored their grandparents, and they did not seem to care about their irritating corpulence, their devotion to the tabloids, and their refusal to ever validate Christy for her choices, her struggles, and her achievements.

And then one evening, Christy dropped back home unexpectedly. To her relief, the lobby was unattended (too much had happened for her to even know what she would say to John Paul when she saw him again), but Mrs Sorenson was complaining loudly and, just as if she was an observer to the situation, Christy hoped for his own sake that John Paul's lovesickness wasn't affecting his duties as doorman. Because, although she was as sure as she could be that they did love each other, it would feel too weird appealing to Vaughn to save his job, should he lose it through negligence.

The apartment was quiet, and the peace made her feel quiet, too. She found herself creeping along the corridor, where she bumped into Loretta the Housekeeper, who pointed her towards the den. She walked slowly up to the door and was greeted by the extraordinary sight of herself, aged about ten, on the enormous flat screen. It was an old video recording made by her father at a ballet competition, which he had had transferred onto DVD. Little Christy, skinny and blonde, pointed and frappéed and pirouetted for the judges as her girls clapped admiringly and her parents bickered about what prize she had won but agreed that she had been robbed and that no one had shown promise like Christy.

"If she hadn't grown so tall, she could have been a professional," they said.

There it was, proof that her memories of her childhood were unreliable and the story of little Christy, the changeling, who had been swapped at birth and was never truly loved, was not her parents' truth, but the narrative she had constructed to allow her to leave them. She had been a happy, confident, beautiful girl, a girl who could also have been a high school teacher, or the manager of the local bank in Thousand Oaks. She felt her parents' pride and her daughters' admiration, and that moment changed her view of herself forever.

No longer would she be a person to whom life happened. It could happen *because of her*. She made a mental note, as she so often did, that she must tell Julia about this.

Suddenly she felt very grown up. And that was good, because as she jetéed into the room she heard her father ask John Paul to switch off the TV.

From their body language (the shoulder clasp, the rugged bonhomie) she knew that Ron and John Paul had become mates. She suspected Ron would treat John Paul like a son he never had, instantly bonding over the Irish connection. (Her brother, Jake, had not amounted to much. They had poured all their parental aspiration into the wrong avatar.) It made perfect sense, of course. Once Ron tired of watching sports all day, he would have gone looking to do odd jobs round the building and come across John Paul in the lobby. John Paul, desperate to know what was going on with Christy, would have cultivated this assiduously, and so here she was, standing with her daughters, her parents, and the man she had sucked face illicitly with on the Ghost Train at Coney Island. When her parents saw her they emphasized how helpful John Paul had been to them, that nothing was too much trouble for him, and, without looking at Christy, Felicia remarked that "the girls say you all go on little outings together".

Now Loretta the Housekeeper announced there was some dinner ready. Fish pie. John Paul looked up greedily; he was *starving*, he said.

Felicia beamed approvingly. She liked a man who ate and had never trusted Vaughn's calorie-controlled attitude to life.

"What about the lobby?" said Christy. "You can't leave the lobby unattended." Everyone looked at her in horror; she half expected booing and hissing as if she were a pantomime villain. She tried again, modulating her voice, adding a gentler inflection. "It's just I heard Mrs Sorenson going on. You could get in trouble. Lose your job."

Her parents closed ranks with John Paul.

"What would you know about a job, Christy?" said her father.

"Nothing," she replied, and patted his arm kindly, for at that moment she shared his disappointment in her.

So John Paul got what he wanted. They had their evening

and he did not have to sell his soul. He had his dinner in his magnificent apartment with his beautiful "wife", his stepchildren, and his in-laws. He handled it with grace, the perfect host, grateful but not patronizing to Loretta the Housekeeper. Christy was struck by the fact that he was a very good actor. Julia was right. It was a dreadful profession, all about luck and nothing about talent. But she played her part well, too.

When they had carried the girls to bed, and her parents disappeared discreetly to their room, they walked onto the balcony. There was a mist over the city, and the tops of the buildings poked through it, as if the skyline were floating. They allowed themselves one chaste kiss. If there had been a soundtrack it would not have been Céline Dion singing her heart out, but rather discreet, poignant strings. She told him that nothing else was going to happen between them, there was no future, she was going to do the right thing, for, after all, she had chosen her life for better or worse. What would they do, anyway, the two of them? They were too similar, two drifters, but they were too old to go off to see the world. He wiped the tear away from her left eye with his thumb. He held her hand, very still and sad. Then he decided to make things easy.

"I suppose it's a relief," he said. "I'd never be able to say no to you, but what would I tell my girlfriend?"

She would never know whether it was a joke or not. Three days later, John Paul quit. She heard from the French teenagers that he had gone back to LA, but from him she never heard anything again. For the next few years she would go to any movie with Colin Farrell in it to see if he was in the background.

Vaughn was discharged from the hospital with orders to retire, and they started dividing their time between the city and Bridgehampton.

Although she asked the girls to delete the clips of them all in Coney Island, they didn't know how to, so sometimes, if she pressed the wrong combination of buttons, her phone would spontaneously burst to life and replay five seconds of her and John Paul fighting over some cotton candy.

It always gave her a strange feeling. Sometimes she remembered this was happiness.

JULIA CAME back from the month in Connecticut a new woman and, as so often happened with Julia, a catastrophic event in her personal life had vastly improved her professional one. In group therapy she had met a producer she had been pursuing on a networking site for ages and, to cut a long story short, she had pitched him her rom-com idea starring the Christy character. He had negotiated a deal with her agent secretly (phones were, strictly speaking, not permitted, but they made exceptions for Academy Award nominees) and, as Julia told Christy over lunch, "I just have to write it. So, tell me more I can use."

"Well, actually," said Christy, "I had an idea for the story. I thought I could fall in love with the doorman."

Julia looked at her admiringly. "That's genius! What would happen?"

So Christy told her the story, embellishing it in key areas. She was particularly keen on her ending, involving the lovers standing by the ocean, staring out at a moon river, as one of them remarked that it was as if they could walk across it except they would surely drown. It was bittersweet, poetic; she would cry if she saw it in a movie. The only bit she left out was the kissing in the Ghost Train, which was just too personal.

Julia wrote quickly in shorthand until Christy stopped.

"It's brilliant," she said, not taking her eyes off the page. "Two things I'd have to change. I don't believe you wouldn't have sex. There'll have to be skirts up in act two. And the ending. The ending is dreadful. It simply couldn't end like that."

Oh, yes, thought Christy, *it could.*

equine-assisted
learning

I t was Lianne's idea to do the horse course in New Jersey, and she decided that Christy would do it with her. She engineered this by ringing her father, Vaughn, on his private line and suggesting he give a place to Christy for her birthday. It would be nice for her to spend some time with her stepmother, she said, for, unlike Cinderella, it was her own mother who was wicked, and that Christy must be exhausted from the demands of looking after him and the girls. Vaughn had some vague memory of Christy wanting a pony when she was a child, and, as he was tired of buying her expensive jewellery that she never wore (it infuriated him that she had let her ear piercings grow over when there were three sets of diamond studs in the safe), he told Lianne to book the course, what-ever it cost, and he would add the money to her monthly allowance.

Christy found out a week later when Loretta the House-keeper announced that she was looking after the girls for the weekend of May 25 and 26 while Christy was away. Christy was confused and immediately went to the kitchen to check the year planner on the wall. Armed with the knowledge that the days were empty, she found Vaughn in his study, where he put on his calculatedly distracted face and told her that it was a surprise for her and it was all Lianne's idea.

Uh-oh, thought Christy.

Lianne had Vaughn in a headlock of guilt and recrimin-ation; "she imbibed it with her mother's milk," he would joke, although Lianne had been exclusively bottle-fed by Nanny Marta while her mother chain-smoked and got her thighs back into her Pucci slacks.

It was an old, old story. The savage emotional deprivations of his own youth had made Vaughn incapable of two things: denying his daughter anything material and being even a half-way decent father to her. These, added to the fact that the first Mrs Vaughn Armitage II was mentally unstable, ensured that Lianne had the kind of spoiled but unhappy childhood that in-evitably creates a spoiled and unhappy adult. So while Vaughn might say after the fraught family gatherings that happened every five years, *"My money may not have bought her happiness, but she has a better quality of misery"*, it seemed too late now to buy her either a personality or a man, as even the most abject gold digger had been put off eventually by Myron Schulberg's pre-nuptial demands and . . . well . . . Lianne herself.

"She wants to spend some time with you," he responded limply. "You're a role model for her."

"I'm only four years older," she said, but she knew she shouldn't have, because Vaughn never wished to be reminded of the age difference between them, particularly since the heart attack had slowed his pace from hare to tortoise, and sometimes Christy heard him saying to people that *she* was more tired these days, or her ankles were hurting her, or "Christy doesn't like travelling as much as she used to," to explain why his racing-around days were over.

Vaughn fiddled with his wedding ring, a sure sign the conversation was over. Resistance was useless. Christy knew she was going on the horse course, but, to her surprise, she noticed a glimmer of uncertainty in his expression.

"What is it?" she asked.

"The minimum number for a group is five, so Lianne wants to bring a couple of friends with her. I said you'd be fine with that."

Uh-oh again, thought Christy.

The last time Lianne had brought her friends to the apartment, one had found a magnum of vintage champagne that Vaughn was saving for his seventy-fifth birthday and drunk it out of the bottle. Another had pissed upward onto the intaglio etchings of lilacs in the guest bathroom.

Christy remembered that she was no longer living her life in the passive form.

"I'll find three others," she said.

"EQUINE-ASSISTED LEARNING. I'VE heard about it," said Julia as they power-walked the High Line. "It's incredible for children with special needs. And adults with back problems. There's pretty much nothing a horse can't help you with. As Catherine the Great used to say. *Baboom CRASH.*"

"Oh, please. The point is I can't do it on my own with Lianne, and even if I could, I would need you there to stop me from strangling her. When I rang to ask her if I needed to bring jodhpurs, she said 'No, all you need is an emotional dilemma the horse can help you solve.' Hers is 'Should I break up with this new guy I've just met because he's got genital warts from visiting prostitutes in the Far East?' She needs help. I mean, what's Black Beauty going to say about that?"

Julia wanted to interject the obvious here, but—

"You have to come, and you owe me. Remember when I had to play Woman with Bruises at two hours' notice for you on the show and the Asshole hit me with the plastic coffee cup?"

"I don't remember that."

"Maybe we'll all find it healing. Lianne's convinced it will be therapeutic, you know, for her abandonment issues. And you *always* have emotional dilemmas."

Julia ignored this.

"You told me Lianne was trying to have a baby."

"Don't talk to me about that. Vaughn paid for her to have her eggs harvested, and I set her up at the clinic. But when I asked her when she was going to be implanted, she looked at me with this petulant expression on her face and said, 'Do you really think I need to be pregnant right now?' And I said yes, *if you want a child*."

Christy was acting out the exchange, imitating the high-pitched monotone of Lianne's voice. Julia knew that this was a bad sign in anyone and realized that she must be compassionate.

"Stop, stop there. I'm coming. This is going to be good. I'm always open to a new experience. I wanted to do EAL in Connecticut, but they suggested Jungian sand play instead. And I like to see you and Lianne snarling at each other. It reassures me that you're not perfect. She drives you crazy."

Christy stopped and regarded her friend haughtily. "She doesn't drive me crazy, apart from when she calls me *'Mom!'*"

Julia checked the new diary app her kids had loaded on her phone. This took some time, for she had only just got her head around texting. Christy's agitation was fermented by impatience and then bubbled into annoyance when she discovered that Julia had arranged to spend the Saturday, May 25, with her new friend Lucy Lovett. She tried to conceal it, but Julia knew her well enough to know what she was thinking, which was *I thought I was your best friend*, so Julia volunteered to invite Lucy to come, too. They were all Mothers at the School, after all, and, more important, Julia was integrity filled and didn't stiff people when she had a better offer. Usually Christy admired this trait. Not today.

"Lucy Lovett is sarcastic."

"She's *English*. Haven't you ever watched *The Office* on BBC America?"

"I heard her say to Robyn Skinner that if parents can't spell, how can they expect their children to?"

"Who's Robyn Skinner?"

"Robyn Skinner's that woman who's always late for pickup, so someone always has to wait with her kids, and then she's always cross. Like it's any of our faults she's so disorganized. Honestly, it happened last week and she looked at me really strangely. Like she hated me."

"Lots of women hate you. Don't you ever look in a mirror?"

"No." (This was true. Christy avoided looking at herself, as she had acute body dysmorphia, a legacy of her modelling days, and often referred to her "wobbly bits", oblivious to the stab of loathing this induced in every other woman around her.)

"I'm telling you she hates us all."

"Ridiculous. Anyway, back to Mrs Lovett and her crusade against the incorrect use of the apostrophe, which, by the way, I agree with."

"People see her graffitiing on the PTA notices."

"Give her a chance. Maybe in the end *you'll love Lucy*?"

Julia winked, but Christy was in no mood to be humoured.

"You, me, lunatic Lianne, and sarcastic—oh, sorry, *English*—Lucy Lovett. Okay, that's four. Apparently the minimum on the course is five, but I can't take the stress, so I'll just pay for the extra place. Vaughn mustn't know, though. Don't mention it to him."

"Why?"

"You know Vaughn can't bear waste. It's because of his childhood. He eats yoghurts after their sell-by date."

Julia shifted a little, unwilling to join Christy in a domestic lie.

"It's only a few hundred bucks," Christy pleaded.

Now Julia looked at her strangely.

"Hey, Marie Antoinette. Don't say that in front of anyone else except me."

"Oh, I'm sorry, I'm sorry. I'm being awful. It's Lianne and this stupid weekend. At least it can't get any worse!"

Christy's nostrils flared, and she flicked her mane.

LUCY, JULIA, AND CHRISTY sat side by side on wonky plastic chairs at the back of the school hall as the raffle was being drawn. Julia was hunched up in the middle, as, although usually she insisted on the end of a row so she could stick her legs out to the side, she understood that Christy, who had Irish roots, was having some strange post-colonial reaction to Lucy and was scared of her.

Dolores Madden, head of the PTA, a woman who could have run a small country as a dictator but instead had four children and managed the local CVS, was holding aloft a large scented candle wrapped in orange plastic.

"Number seventy-nine. Seventy-nine."

"That's you!" said Christy, nudging Julia, and before Julia could pretend to have lost her ticket the two women behind them started clapping. Julia hurried up to Dolores, made a futile attempt to give the candle back, but Dolores just hissed, "Nobody wants this. Just take it." Julia returned to her seat, blew the dust off the wrapping, and wondered who she might regift it to.

"The next prize is . . . unusual," said Dolores, making no effort to raise her expression above pained. "A place on a weekend course in E . . . A . . . L . . ." She picked up an envelope and read, her tone tightening with every word. "That's Equine-Assisted Learning, which incorporates horses experientially for emotional growth in participants. Kindly donated by Mr and Mrs Vaughn Armitage II."

She looked accusingly at Christy. Last year Vaughn had paid for five new computers, obviating the need for spring semester fund-raising.

"What?" said Christy, turning to Julia, bemused.

Lucy explained.

"I got Vaughn on the phone last week when I was ringing round for donations. He said he'd just had an e-mail from the horse people. There was a place you hadn't filled . . ."

She stopped. Lucy sensed she was tightrope-walking above a treacherous marital crevasse, and anyway, she was confused herself.

"I thought it was a riding weekend."

"Did you?" said Julia innocently.

"Number three hundred and two. Three hundred and two."

"That's me!" came a voice from the front of the hall. Lucy, Christy, and Julia all leaned forward to look.

"It's Robyn Skinner," said Christy.

"Who?" said Julia.

Christy looked at her meaningfully.

"Is that good or bad?" wondered Lucy, until she saw the expression on Robyn's face as Christy detailed the prize.

"So the three of you are going . . ." Robyn was looking up at them, her hands fiddling with the waistband of her baggy skirt. Her hair, scraped back into an unforgiving pony-tail, was ash blonde. Her face, open and freckled, was un-lined, apart from a triangular furrow between her eyebrows. The three sides of the triangle were anxiety, hostility, and bemusement.

"And my stepdaughter, Lianne. It was her idea," said Christy.

"How old is she?"

"Forty."

Lucy filled the ensuing silence. "Have you ridden before, Robyn?"

"No," said Robyn bitterly, "I didn't grow up in that sort of home."

Ouch, thought Lucy. She wanted to say "Neither did I," but she didn't.

"Neither did I," said Julia.

"It doesn't matter whether you can ride or not," said Christy firmly. "The course is psychological. Lianne says you spend time with the horses and you learn life lessons. Then, when you find yourself in a crisis situation, you think, *What would a horse do?*"

"How does that help a crisis situation?" said Robyn. "It's a horse."

None of the others could think of a response to that.

"Is it in a hotel, Christy?" What Robyn meant was might there be room service and an opportunity for two nights of uninterrupted sleep?

"No. It's an equestrian centre. We sleep in yurts."

"What are they?" Robyn was clutching at straws now.

"A yurt is a timber-and-sheep's-wool structure first built by Turkic nomads on the steppes of South Asia," said Lucy helpfully.

Robyn was disappointed, that was obvious, but in her life she had been disappointed by many things far more important than the PTA raffle. As a teenager, Janis Ian's "At Seventeen" was her favourite song. (Lucy's was "Wuthering Heights" by Kate Bush; Julia's was Bruce Springsteen's "Thunder Road"; Christy's, rather appropriately, was "A Horse with No Name" by America.)

Robyn's voice softened, and she lifted her chin and smiled.

"I've never won anything before. I need a break. Maybe it'll be fun?"

Lucy and Julia smiled back, but Christy, who was now engrossed in her own private drama, her anger at Vaughn and his inability to be profligate except when it suited him, missed the moment.

"Look, Robyn," said Christy, "you don't have to do it. I don't know how this happened or why Vaughn put it in the raffle." (This was directed at Lucy.) "But it doesn't matter. It's only a few hundred bucks."

Ouch again. Julia looked away. Lucy looked down at Robyn's shoes and saw the black line of the rubber resole around the toe.

"Or maybe you could swap with someone? Is there another prize you'd prefer?"

Christy turned and saw Lizzy Clearmountain, a Reiki practitioner whom she liked, carrying a crate of Spanish wine out of the door.

"Look at Lizzy. She got the Rioja and she's practically teetotal."

A sudden blush in the shape of a hand spread red and furious over Robyn's collarbone and clutched her neck.

"I won this. Fair and square. It doesn't matter whether I like it or you like it. I'm coming."

And she headed off toward the lockers, her rubber soles squeaking with indignation.

"I should have offered her the candle," said Julia.

"She hates us," said Christy.

Neither Julia nor Lucy disagreed.

LIANNE HAD DONE extensive preparations for the horse weekend. She had read *The Horse Whisperer* and watched the film twice and spent the first half hour of the journey discussing with Julia why screenwriters felt they could change books so much.

"I mean, there's no sex in the film. It's stupid. What's the point of Robert Redford being your horse whisperer if you don't get to . . ."

At this point Christy turned up the radio, ostensibly to get the traffic update for the turnpike.

"Well," replied Julia thoughtfully, "with an adaptation you're thinking, *How do I reflect the spirit of the book in a different art form?* It's not necessarily about slavish adherence to the plot. So in the film of *The Horse Whisperer*, the two main characters still have an intense spiritual connection fuelled by the kid and the horse stuff; it's just beyond the physical. Right?"

Lianne did not appear to have listened. Like most people raised by servants, she demanded attention and agreement and was disconcerted by any deviation from that.

"I think it looks like he's in love with the horse and that's why there's no sex."

"*Interesting.* Maybe you should ask our facilitator that?"

suggested Julia. "After all, we're learning about human-equine relations. Right, Lucy?"

Lucy nodded and tried to look enthusiastic. She had loved horses as a child, obsessively reading about them, entering the WHSmith win-a-pony competition every year, and on walks she would canter on her own legs through woodland, making whinnying noises at passers-by to her brother George's embarrassment. In a childhood remarkable mainly for its juxtaposition of high drama and excruciating boredom, it was something that stood out, something that she remembered with happiness. Throughout her twenties and thirties she had often asked herself why she had stopped riding.

Richard knew this. She had been reminded once again how well he did know her. He had never forgotten their honeymoon in Turkey during which he had watched her cantering alone on a white horse along a mountain path, an expression of pure bliss on her face, and so he had insisted she go away with "the girls", as he put it, in some flashback to the vocabulary of his own parents in the seventies. Lucy had resisted. She felt that she had wasted weeks, probably months, of her life in London trapped with "the girls" in one never-ending tedious conversation on the theme of "kids do the funniest things", as they all vied to demonstrate their exemplary motherliness. But as Julia and Christy never mentioned their children unless they absolutely had to (usually in answer to the question "How are your children?"), she felt safe among the like-minded. Now, though, her heart was pounding underneath her seat belt, and she could not mention it. It was only the second time she had been away from her sons since they'd come to New York, and she was overwhelmed with the separation anxiety that had begun the moment she had said yes to Julia. It wasn't healthy, she knew that, and she also knew that many believe co-dependency to be the death of any relationship.

"We have to be open, Lucy," said Lianne. "This is about taking us out of our comfort zones."

Lucy looked out of the window. "I'm already out of my comfort zone. I'm in New Jersey."

Julia roared with laughter and caught Christy's eye in the rearview mirror. Christy knew her well enough to know what she was thinking, which was, *See, she's funny and clever, I insist you like her*. Christy made a non-committal grunt, gripped the steering wheel, and pressed her foot down on the accelerator. Lucy was glad the car was automatic, as Christy was grumpy and would have taken it out on the gearbox. The journey was beginning to remind Lucy of a school trip she had once been on to Stonehenge. Then, as now, the vehicle positively hummed with the undercurrents and strange calibrations of female moods and alliances. Lucy always sensed such things. She did not enjoy that aspect of her personality.

Lianne handed her a sheet of paper, ordering her to read it, and Julia put on her glasses, a pair of jet-black little-old-lady frames that should have made her look like Demi Moore, but in fact made her look like someone had scribbled circles on a photo of her face with a black marker pen. One side of the sheet was background information about horses and the herd mentality and how they always live in the moment, as they have fight-or-flight responses. The other side was quotations, "Aha!" moments, from successful participants in the EAL course. These were in italics, with many exclamation marks. Mike from Millbrook had found it *"Profound!!!!"* Susan from Westport said it *"Changed my life forever!!!!"*

Lucy turned her head to see Julia chewing her lower lip and rocking ever so slightly backwards and forwards.

"What is it?" mouthed Lucy, concerned.

"I'm having withdrawal symptoms," whispered Julia.

"Didn't the doctor give you anything?" said Lianne, who had the hearing of a bat."When I went off cocaine the doctor injected me with some vitamin/antidepressant thing."

Christy was keeping her eyes firmly fixed on the road ahead.

"It's not literally withdrawal," said Julia. "I promised Christy I wouldn't bring my writer's notebook."

"That's good." Lianne had her solemn voice on. "You know what they say about the sessions here? *What is said in the circle stays in the circle.*"

A song came on the radio. An unmistakable melancholy guitar intro.

Lucy and Julia sat up. *"Gordon!"* they exclaimed in unison.

"Who?" said Lianne.

"Ssssh. Turn it up."

Christy obeyed Julia, and they listened in silence to Gordon

Lightfoot singing "If You Could Read My Mind". Julia and Lucy started singing along, and then, harmonizing the bridge.

Lianne could take it no longer.

"I'm sorry. 'He's trying to understand the feelings that she lacks.' What *does* that mean?"

"I know what it means," said Christy sadly, but Lianne just stared at her.

Christy sighed and glanced in the mirror. To her amazement, she thought she could see a tear in Lucy's left eye.

"I love Gordon Lightfoot," Lucy was saying, "I love Jim Croce, too."

"So do I," replied Julia, and they gripped each other's hands.

Christy had another of her out-of-body experiences. She saw herself trapped in a deep dark pit with Lianne and coils of hissing snakes while Julia and Lucy frolicked together in a sunlit garden above. For a moment she wished she was drinking plastic coffee with Robyn Skinner on the train, an extremely unexpected development, but then a positive thought struck her.

She had an emotional dilemma she could bring to the horse.

THEY HAD BEEN LEANING on the wooden fence around the outdoor arena for more than an hour, observing horse behaviour. Or, rather, Christy, Julia, and Lucy were observing the horses and Lianne was observing their facilitator, Darren, who, though no Robert Redford, was a rather manly six foot three, with big hands and no wedding ring, and had demonstrated earlier how to bring a pony to submission using acupressure points and nose massage.

Robyn, who knew all about submission with no nose massage, had left immediately afterwards to "check out the yurt", and, when Lucy went to look for her, was flat on her back on a camp bed, last month's *Vanity Fair* unopened on her stomach, snoring the extreme sleep of the chronically sleep deprived. Lucy put a glass of water beside her and closed the sheep's-wool-and-timber door firmly.

Four horses had been released without halters into the sandy ring. They trotted around, then, one after the other, collapsed onto their knees and rolled over luxuriously on the ground before rising to their hooves and shaking off the dust. There were three geldings, Mitch, Neo, and Captain, and a small white mare, Sahara. They nosed around the ring, munching at the bushes surrounding the fence. The three males relentlessly nipped, niggled, and messed with one another. *So that's what horseplay means*, thought Lucy to herself, in the first of her three revelations of the day. Sahara kept herself to herself and rewarded any male incursions into her space with either a nuzzle and a gentle rebuff or a great big kick. Lucy's second revelation was that this reminded her of most evenings in her apartment.

Julia was wholly absorbed. She found the experience fascinating and oddly relaxing. Christy, to whom detachment came as first nature, was silent and still. And Lucy, caught up in

the rush of her revelations and feelings and childhood memories, felt again a sense of intrinsic Lucyness returning to her,
the thrilling and painful process that had started from the
moment she arrived in New York. More prosaically, all three of
them shared the same momentary insight. *When did I last sit
still for sixty minutes?* Lianne did not. She was pretty much a
daily visitor to the Nails and Tails Beauty Spa in Chelsea.

Suddenly, Darren cleared his throat and asked what obser-
vations they had about the horses' behaviour. Lianne's hand
shot up.

"We can see that horses all have their places within the herd
and they are led by a dominant mare."

"Well done," said Darren. Lianne beamed.

"Really?" said Julia.

Lucy nodded. "I know that from *My Friend Flicka*."

Darren then asked them to consider if they had responded
to any of the horses in the arena on an emotional level. Julia
pointed immediately to the white and bay, Mitch. A handsome
brute with wide eyes, Mitch dominated the others at seventeen
hands.

"I like him. I liked him the first moment I saw him," she
said.

"And is your husband big and good-looking, Julia?" Darren
asked.

"He certainly is," said Christy, curiously.

Darren explained. "We're doing research at the moment
into why humans are attracted to certain kinds of horses.

Early stages, but we're certainly seeing parallels. Mitch is a good-looking, well-bred, charismatic horse, but he's also fragile emotionally and not a leader. He needs someone to look after him."

For the first time in a very long time, Julia had nothing to say so she clutched at a real straw, stuck it in her mouth, and chewed it in what she hoped was a very cool and cowboy-like manner. It tasted disgusting, so she spat it out.

Darren turned to Christy. Before she could speak, Lianne piped up.

"There's no old nag in the field for you, Christy."

She turned to Darren. This was her moment.

"Christy likes old ones. She's married to my dad. He's seventy-two. Right, *Mom?*"

Christy controlled the sudden urge to kick her.

"There isn't a horse that leapt out at me, but if I had to choose, I'd go for that one."

"Neo," said Darren, looking into her eyes.

"*Neo,*" said Christy, looking away.

"Neo *is* older than the others. Twenty-four years old, in fact. He was a champion jumper in his day, but he's still sound and useful in his senior years."

Lianne put her hand over her mouth and sat down on a plastic barrel. The barrel wiggled vigorously beneath her.

"I like the mare. Sahara," said Lucy. "I'm sure it's because I respond to her feminine energy. At home I'm surrounded by males."

Darren turned to Lianne.

"I guess that leaves me with that one. Captain. Though I would have chosen him anyway," she simpered. "Tell me, Darren, what do I like in my horse?"

"I don't believe there's such a thing as a bad horse, but the other riders here find him feckless and headstrong."

Lianne's face fell. The others desperately wished that Darren could have lied, but he was not that sort of person.

"He wants to hang out with the boys, that's all."

Suddenly there was a piercing whinny from a small chestnut horse in the field abutting the outdoor arena. Captain neighed back and trotted towards him, the other horses lifting their heads to watch.

"That's the new horse, Pilot," said Darren, as Captain and Pilot stood nose to nose at the gate. "We're introducing him to the herd."

"Sweet!" said Lianne, but then Pilot, baring his yellow teeth and snorting, spun round and kicked his legs high into the air, crashing his hooves against the wood. Captain cantered back to the safety of the others.

At this point, Robyn appeared from behind the stables, backlit by the glowing afternoon sun, singing a song with a group of small children who trailed after her, adorable in little boots and hats. She was wearing a tight checked shirt over her jeans and had pulled down her ponytail, so her hair fell in long tendrils past her shoulders. Her face was serene and soft and pink, until she saw the other women staring at her, and it turned tense and taut and white.

"Robyn's got good hair," said Lucy.

"And her own tits," said Julia. (Lianne folded her arms grumpily. Her tennis-ball tits had been stitched onto her skeletal chest when she was thirty.)

"Some men would find her very attractive," concluded Christy. (*Despite the wobbly bits beneath that denim*, she thought.)

Such men included Darren, who galloped towards Robyn, asking if she would like to help him tack up the mechanical horse. Robyn smiled, slowly smoothing her hands down over her thighs, and nodded. (Lucy thought she had licked her lips, but Julia disagreed.) Darren picked a schooling whip that was lying on the gravel and the two walked off side by side, as he showed her how to tickle a horse's withers.

"But she's so fat!" said Lianne, outraged by this.

"She's not fat," said Julia. "She's fabulously . . . *fecund*."

Lianne was devastated. Her dreams of a future with Darren on a ranch in Montana where they would wear matching Stetsons and breed horses and children were disappearing.

"Oh, what would I know? I'm never going to meet anyone. I can't even pick a horse that's interested in fucking." Her voice trilled even higher than usual.

"Captain's a gelding," said Lucy, trying to be helpful.

"That's not HELPFUL!" roared Lianne, and Lucy knew she hadn't been.

"They promised me I'd learn something I didn't know. *Fuck and double fuck!!*"

A couple of the adorable children turned and stared.

"*Nice,*" muttered Julia.

"There are children around, Lianne," hissed Christy, unable to control herself any longer.

"Oh, that's right, Christy, remind me that I'm *childless.*"

"*By choice!* You have six embryos on Eighty-third Street."

"I don't want an embryo!"

"*What?*"

"YOU DON'T UNDERSTAND! How could you? When have you EVER not got what you wanted?"

If Lianne had hung around for a moment, she might have got an answer from Christy that surprised her, but she stormed off across the yard towards a wheelbarrow with various metal implements leaning against it.

Julia watched nervously, hoping Lianne was looking where she was going, as all the scene needed now was for someone to have a comedy collision with a pitchfork so it could end.

She turned round and glanced at Lucy. Lucy raised an eyebrow. Christy saw this and felt humiliated. She tried to lighten the tone and nudged Julia theatrically.

"What we need in this herd is a dominant mare. Julia, pin your ears back and bite her for me."

"Don't say that, Christy. Actually, I feel a bit sorry for Lianne." Christy shrivelled a little inside at the reprimand. Julia was right, of course—Lianne was just being Lianne. It was

Christy who was awkward and discombobulated. She always found being near Lianne a trial, but she hated to have such uncomfortable and unattractive feelings put out there for general analysis. And although she felt confident that ever-loyal Julia would soon be making jokes about the events of the day, it was unsettling having Lucy there, who said little, apart from the odd wry aside that had Julia giggling, and watched everything.

"This horse course was a terrible idea. I want to go back."

Julia shook her head.

"It'll be fine. This is all about taking us out of our comfort zones, remember?"

"I'll call Vaughn's driver. I'll leave you my car." (Christy was discovering that being out of her comfort zone made her regress.)

"No, you won't, Christy. We're all here because of you. Stop pouting . . ."

"Why is everyone so mean to me?"

THWHACK!

Christy's tantrum was abruptly halted by a stinging slap to the back of her left calf. She spun round to see Lucy shaking her palm and grinning sheepishly.

"Horsefly. On your leg. Very nasty if you don't get to them in time."

Christy gave a little gasp but said nothing. Julia was pushing the wheelbarrow towards the stables as if to illustrate the point that shovelling shit was preferable to listening to it.

Lucy sighed and stared out at the far hills. She hoped she

could spend a great deal of time with the mechanical horse; otherwise, this was sure to be a very long weekend. She was glad she had brought two bottles of red wine. And delighted she had remembered to choose screw tops.

LIANNE SULKED FOR THE evening in her yurt. This was not just because of her emotional distress, but also because there was no non-dairy option at dinner and she had never spent a night in a bedroom that didn't have en suite facilities. With a quivering lip, she asked Christy to respect her personal space, and so Christy had to forget all about hers and sleep on the floor with Lucy, Julia, and Robyn.

Robyn had spent the day with a broad smile on her face, basking in the attentions of Darren and avoiding any avoidable contact with the others. She curled on her side in the corner, texted her children good night, and looked forward to more sleep. Unfortunately for her, Christy was in no mood to rest.

She was reading *Madame Bovary* with her book group and started a conversation with Julia and Lucy about the travails of nineteenth-century women, dying of corsets and boredom.

"Some chance," muttered Robyn, tucking her knees up against her chest.

Christy looked over at her. After the coldness and friction with Lianne, she was feeling positively warm and fuzzy towards Robyn.

"Are you reading anything at the moment, Robyn?"

Robyn nodded. "*Little Women*, with my daughter, Madison."

Lucy grinned.

"I love *Little Women*. Every girl wants to be Jo March, don't they?"

"Yes," said Julia and Christy.

Robyn shook her head. "Not me. I'd rather be Amy. She knows what she wants, and she gets it."

"*Interesting,*" said Lucy. Christy looked up. She knew Lucy had caught this habit from Julia, who said "interesting" as punctuation. Lucy, meanwhile, had suddenly thought of a game that would while away half an hour and stop the conversation from veering into dangerous territory.

"Okay," she said. "So in *Gone with the Wind*, who would you rather be? Scarlett or Miss Melly."

"Scarlett," said Christy and Julia.

"I love Melly," said Lucy. "She's so brave and good, and she shoots the soldier in her bare feet."

"I like Belle Watling," announced Robyn. "She has sex with Rhett, he pays her for it, and she never has to make a dress out of curtains."

They all laughed. To their surprise, Robyn laughed, too, and she looked ten years younger.

"What do you do, Robyn?" said Lucy.

Robyn looked at them.

"I'm office manager of a budget bed shop on Thirty-ninth and Ninth."

And the laughter was gone. Just like that. Robyn supposed

this was because the others did not know how to bond with someone who had a job like that, a regular, nine-to-five, mostly tedious job that you did for the money because you didn't have a choice.

"Right," said Julia.

"I'm responsible for accounts, personnel, stock control, and special offers. We're doing a top-of-the-range memory foam for eight hundred bucks this month. We deliver free of charge to the whole of greater Manhattan."

"That sounds like bloody hard work to me," said Lucy.

"My husband's a writer. His name's Ryan Anthony James," Robyn said proudly.

It was a non sequitur, but they all relaxed.

"Oh, what has he published?" said Julia.

"*Residua and Fragments.* One hundred and seventy pages. Experimental short stories."

There was a pause as Julia, Christy, and Lucy waited for Robyn to continue.

She didn't.

"I should buy it," said Christy, kindly.

"It's out of print."

(At this point in the same conversation Ryan would always say, "It's what happened to Richard Yates for years. The fate of the serious artist." But Robyn could never quite bring herself to quote him.)

"Ryan works in a gallery downtown, and he writes at night and at the weekends."

"Good for him," said Julia.

Another pause.

"What do you mean?" said Robyn.

"Maybe he needs to be around people some of the time? Being alone with your own head all the time can drive you crazy. Look at me."

Julia had meant this to be an amusing, throwaway line, but Christy and Lucy didn't laugh, and Julia immediately regretted having said it. At least she knew that they would not comment. But she had forgotten about Robyn, whom Christy thought hated them all.

"Is that why you left your husband?" Robyn said.

Lucy glanced at Christy, appalled. The conversation had positively careered into dangerous territory, but as neither of them knew Robyn well enough to admonish her in any way other than *"Mind your own damn business"*, they didn't, and Julia was hung out to dry.

"It's one of the reasons, yes. I went a bit nuts," she said carefully, uncharacteristically choosing understatement of tone and word. "And that was not good for me. Or my family. So I left."

Julia looked very sad, and Lucy reached over and squeezed her arm. But Robyn hadn't finished.

"Didn't you miss your children?"

"Of course I did."

Julia's eyes filled with tears, but not because of the casual cruelty of the comment. She had always known that people assumed she hadn't missed her children. The pain came from the memory of how much she had, and how close exhaustion and overwork had brought her to an appalling decision that might have ruined her life.

"Let's get some sleep," ordered Lucy.

Robyn put her headphones in her ears, selected John Mayer on her iPod, and closed her eyes, aware she had transgressed but unsure exactly how. *Honestly*, she thought, *it was impossible to fathom the rules of these women, who from a distance looked so unbreakable but close up were utterly neurotic.*

"I'm sorry," mouthed Christy to Julia.

"This is ALL YOUR FAULT," mouthed Julia back, shaking her finger in silent, exaggerated fury. She attempted to mime "I am out of my comfort zone" but gave up at "zone" and pulled her blanket over her head.

THE AWKWARDNESS BETWEEN Christy and Lucy had disappeared by now. Christy was grateful that Lucy conformed to her national stereotype and her upper lip was stiff. Lucy had decided to pretend that all the emotional outbursts of the day had never happened. She thought it was the only polite thing to do. So when Christy, on the second bottle, attempted to apologize for her stepdaughter, Lucy stopped the conversation, calling Lianne a "poor dear" and adding, "It must be difficult for you, Christy," while pouring her another plastic cup of red wine. But it was also Lucy, who knew what it was to be desperate and afraid, reliant on prescription medication, and feeling that life had no purpose, who said she was going to the bathroom, but in fact crept over to check on Lianne just before midnight.

Lucy showed Lianne the photo Richard had sent her of Max and Robbie in their Spider-Man pyjamas. She talked about the games they played and what they liked to eat and how they were so similar, and yet so different. And Lianne, who had known so little genuine affection in her life, held Lucy's hand and told her she must be a really good mother. Lucy shook her head. She told Lianne she had spent many months of her sons' childhoods self-obsessed and depressed, but she had realized recently that, as she was the only mother they had, she would have to do better for them. She missed them and would be lost without them. She was hopelessly co-dependent, and it was simply love.

Lianne looked up at her, her wide green eyes staring above the sleeping bag like a baby owl. "It must make your life feel *real*, doesn't it? To have a little person that you made. When you wake up, you hear them breathing. You can reach over and hold their tiny hands. Do you know what I mean?"

Lucy nodded, and this seemed to soothe Lianne, who yawned and wriggled down as Lucy stroked her hair and tucked her in.

Lucy walked out into the night and looked up to see the stars scattered across the black sky exactly as if she were in a planetarium. In the fields beyond, the horses stood, sleeping like statues, the occasional soft snort reverberating. She heard Robyn's distinctive snoring, Julia and Christy chortling together, and knew that peace in the herd had been restored, and she was glad. She shifted her weight onto one foot. She could stand apart from the others and observe from a distance.

For it was Lucy who was the dominant mare. This was her third revelation.

LUCY, JULIA, AND CHRISTY awoke to find Robyn's bed empty and no note. They were relieved, although it occurred to them all individually that Robyn had chosen flight over fight, sneaking off in the middle of the night, because she couldn't stand being around them, and that was not a feeling they were used to. When they told Lianne, she seemed disappointed.

"I quite liked Robyn," she said airily. "It's nice to hang out with a normal person once in a while." And with that she breezed off to corner Darren in the tack room.

"Lianne's wrong about that," said Lucy. "Robyn's many things, but normal isn't one of them."

"That's an awful thing to say about her," said Christy, but Lucy and Julia just laughed at the *pot* and *blackness* of this comment.

"You know what I mean," Lucy replied. "There's a lot lurking beneath that shirtdress and espadrilles."

Julia nodded. "Yeah," she said emphatically, "and I don't want to know what it is."

The women spent the morning with a session each on the mechanical horse, learning stable management and enjoying a sedate hack through the surrounding countryside. These activities passed without incident, but there was a feeling that the Real Work had not yet been done, and they all felt a sense of anticipation.

Darren was not the expert in EAL. That role was taken by Ava, a capable, no-nonsense middle-aged woman with a sharp grey haircut and a military bearing. The combination of this and her therapy-speak was somewhat disconcerting, as if you heard a four-star general order a soldier into a minefield and then ask, *"And what is going on for you right now?"*

Ava announced briskly that the afternoon's exercise was all about teamwork. Julia's heart sank. She was preoccupied. *"Didn't you miss your children?"* was still ringing round her head like church bells at Christmas, and she hated teamwork almost as much as she hated unsolicited insights. (In the first ten minutes Ava had suggested that Lucy seemed like a person "used to doing her own thing". Julia and Christy already knew that. Lucy was the type of English person whose response to any dictatorial behaviour was to nod laconically and continue digging straight down beneath the stove to escape through a tunnel called Tom, Dick, or Harry.)

Julia had done so much analysis on her head that she was nervous about what her body might betray, so if she found herself putting her hands on her hips or slumping in a bored manner she corrected it immediately. It was exhausting and left her no time to consider what they were meant to be doing.

Ava gave them an exercise in the indoor arena. Their task was apparently straightforward. They had to get the mare, Sahara, to walk round the ring with them, but they could not touch her. This would involve *teamwork*. Julia, who considered herself a natural leader and was certainly the most vocal of the group, deliberately stepped back. This did not confound Ava, as she had intended, but it did disorient the others, so Lianne, anxious to impress, took charge. She had a plan. They would all walk round the arena together, and inevitably Sahara, curious, would follow them. This made perfect sense to Lianne. She never liked being on her own and always attached herself to a group whenever possible.

She headed off purposefully, motioning for the others to follow. Christy did. So did Lucy. Julia adopted a neutral lope behind them. Sahara, however, did not move. She simply stood, scratching her rump on a wooden post. Lianne quickened her pace. Then, after the second aimless circuit, she let out a sudden cry, *"SAHARA! Come here!"*

Unlike Nanny Marta, the tennis coach, and the massage therapists, Sahara swished her tail and took no notice.

"SAHARA! I said come here!"

Sahara whinnied tauntingly, then went back to the rump scratching. Lianne stared at her in furious disbelief. Christy, who had seen that expression before, felt very nervous and moved closer to Julia, who was calm. Julia was enjoying the fact that what was going to happen would just happen and she didn't have to make it up. She folded her arms across her chest; then, catching Ava's gaze, she unfolded them again, but in fact Ava was examining Christy. You didn't have to be any sort of expert to read Christy's body language.

After a full five minutes of stalemate, Lucy broke ranks, walked slowly up to Sahara's head, and introduced herself. There was a moment as the two dominant mares eyed each other, but there was never doubt as to who would win. Lucy clicked her tongue against the side of her mouth, and Sahara moved. Lucy told the others to group themselves around the horse, two on each side, and to walk in step. They did so.

Christy relaxed. As long as Lucy was in charge, marching them off over the horizon, she and Julia could frolic together in her imaginary sunlit garden.

It was all going perfectly until Lianne found herself trotting at the back and demanded to know why they had to walk in that direction. Lucy was distracted, Julia stopped, Christy rolled her eyes, and Sahara ambled away.

Ava caught Sahara and led her back to the women. She wanted to know why they thought the exercise had broken down. Julia suggested that they had stopped concentrating.

"Yes, it's all about energy," Ava said, and nodded. "The horse responded to the breakdown in communication between you." She paused. Turned her level gaze on Christy.

"Did I sense some irritation with Lianne on your part, Christy?"

Uh-oh, thought Christy, *here we go.*

"Yes, you did," said Lianne triumphantly.

"Not that I'm conscious of," lied Christy.

Ava looked serious.

"A horse will always discover the truth of the dynamic within a group."

Julia was confused. Was there a right or a wrong answer to that?

Lianne gulped. "The horse ignored me."

No one denied this. The horse had indeed ignored her.

"I can see you're upset," said Ava.

Lianne wiped her face with her sleeve. Ava continued.

"What are you feeling now, Lianne? What has this brought up for you?"

(*Whoosh!* Ava opened the door, and Lianne and her quivering lip stepped in.)

"My parents ignore me," sobbed Lianne. "They always ignored me. My mother only had me because my father decided she had to do something apart from spend his money."

Christy objected. There were things in Vaughn's past, things like his cruelty and his tax avoidance, that she had never acknowledged herself. She could not have them on the record.

"Vaughn was a young man then. He had a terrible childhood himself. He has regrets—"

"*Blah, blah, blah.* You're like everyone else around him, Christy. You do exactly what he wants. Because if anyone says something Dad doesn't like, they get rejected, or pitied, or given money to shut them up. I get all three. Poor Lianne, he says, with her lunatic mother and her sad life and her terrible men. She can't look after herself. So he'll keep writing cheques and I won't rock the boat. He put my mother in a mental hospital, Christy. Twice. Did you know that? And he told the doctors there that I was so useless he didn't even believe he was my father."

Christy stopped arguing. There was nothing she could say to change Lianne's mind, because the fact that Vaughn had been a good husband to her, and that he did treat their two young daughters differently, was the most painful thing of all for his eldest child.

Lianne lowered her head. Christy walked over and touched her shoulder.

"I want the dream, Christy. I want what you all have. I want to meet someone who loves me and make a baby. I don't want to have a child on my own. It's not like having your boobs done. It can't be reversed. I wouldn't be one of those super-capable single mothers. I can't look after my cuticles. You and Dad only organized the sperm donation so you don't have to deal with my abandonment issues."

"Don't say that," said Christy.

"Don't try and shut me up, Christy. I know I'm a problem. But you and Dad want me to be one. What would you talk about if I was happy and well-adjusted? All fucked-up families need a scapegoat."

"I'm so sorry," said Christy softly.

"I'm just telling the truth," Lianne replied, and that, of course, was the most shocking thing of all. The thing that made everyone hate her and call her a madwoman and want to stick her in an attic or burn her at the stake.

And then a strange thing happened. From the corner of the arena, Sahara suddenly trotted over to Lianne and nudged her with her nose. Lianne turned, stroked her flank, and then, remembering the horse massage Darren had shown them the day before, by applying just the right amount of pressure, she encouraged Sahara to bow her head down and chew contentedly. Lianne smiled with delight, the hardness disappeared from her face, and the others glimpsed the fragile, hopeful child within.

Lucy and Julia looked at each other and said *"Profound!"* simultaneously.

And they were not being ironic. They had had an "Aha!" moment, like Mike from Millbrook.

"I think we should do this again," announced Christy.

Lianne became Lianne again. She looked around and wrinkled her nose.

"Nah. I don't think I'd ever get used to the smell."

THAT EVENING, Robyn sat in Two Boots on Avenue A, sharing a large Earth Mother pizza with her two children. She had taken off her shoes and run giddily up the staircase to the apartment in anticipation of Ryan's gratifying delight at her unexpectedly early return and the loud declarations of much missing from her children, Madison and Michael, that had followed. But when Ryan decided to head off to the Writers Room for the afternoon, she was not as disappointed as she should have been. She had wanted to take the kids out for dinner, but she knew that if Ryan came, with his cavalier ordering of extra sides and sodas and sundaes, she could not (unless they ate pasta for the next two weeks).

Michael looked up, grinning in an ecstasy of gloopy tomato. "Did you enjoy your vacation, Mom?"

Madison turned to him contemptuously.

"That wasn't a vacation, that was a mini-break, idiot. Look it up."

Robyn was picking her battles with Madison these days, so she let this go. But Michael had been quite correct. The twenty-four hours on the horse course had been her vacation for this year, and, although it had not encompassed any of the activities usually associated with "getting away from it all", she had got away from her life long enough to remember who she was.

Only time would tell if this was good or bad.

an englishwoman in
new york

PART II

The dream took place in Central Park Zoo but did not feature many animals. One moment Lucy was standing with Max and Robbie, watching the sea lions being fed. The next she was alone, up a tree in the red panda exhibit, peering through the foliage at the throngs of visitors walking past and thinking, *"Who's in the cage?"* She juddered awake at six a.m., curious. Normally her dreams required no interpretation (having sex with Brad, and once with Angelina), but this one must mean something. *Am I in the cage?* she wondered.

It was a perfect early-summer, crisp-cotton New York morning as she walked down West Broadway, although, as she was English, she did have a jacket tied round her waist and a small umbrella in her bag "just in case". She was heading towards TriBeCa and the offices of a film company where Julia had organized a job interview for her. Julia had used the adjective "little" (which seemed to cover both job and interview) and emphasized that what was on offer was the opportunity to read unsolicited scripts and write brief reports on them.

Carmen Ross, a film producer who had been Julia's first employer, and whose curiosity and capacity for reinvention had kept her at the top of her profession for many, many years, had just fired a twenty-three-year-old graduate of the film school at NYU for ambition, and had asked Julia to suggest someone "mature". This mature person must love stories, be content with $75 a day for one day a week paid out of the petty cash, and never seek promotion. What Carmen, who shared her spectacular apartment on Greene Street with two Siamese cats and a lot of tribal art, had actually said was that "it would suit a woman with children", and, when Julia raised one eyebrow, Carmen continued, "You know what I mean", and Julia nodded, because Julia did. Julia had immediately thought of her, and she had immediately said yes. It had seemed like a good idea at the time.

But when she paused outside the SoHo Grand to check out her reflection in the glass doors, the black iron gates reminded her of a cage, and she knew her dream was about anxiety. Her last—in fact, only—serious job interview had been eighteen years ago, when she had followed the traditional route into a publishing house for female graduates by applying to be someone's secretary. Despite the first-class degree in English language and literature, she found herself word-processing in the gardening books department, and spent two years stroking the egos of muddy men with spades and getting drunk at the Chelsea Flower Show. She then moved into editorial and Mind, Body, and Spirit, and quickly knew more about growing medicinal drugs in a window box than anyone ever needs to. After six years of lunches with druids and one-way phone conversations with psychics, she was about to apply for an opening in New Fiction when she got pregnant, and the rest was history. There had been no more interviews apart from the six months a few years ago when she was vetted by elite primary schools in West London. She suspected, correctly, that that would be of no help to her today.

She stood up straight and practised an expression of competence and confidence. She did a mental inventory of the most notable films that Carmen had produced (although Julia had assured her that Carmen never missed an opportunity to mention the awards). She looked at her reflection, she saw herself, and to her own surprise, she smiled, catching the eye of a porter, who winked at her. While she had no interest in the approbation of a twenty-one-year-old wearing a checked shirt and a plastic earpiece, she knew this meant something—specifically, that she looked a lot better in New York than she did in London.

It had started with her hair. Despite her relative youth, her two back-to-back pregnancies had sucked every particle of natural colour from the front section of her dark brown locks. She had not noticed this until dawn broke one day in the guest bathroom in Ladbroke Grove as she cradled croupy Robbie in the steam from the cascading hot shower. She had wiped the condensation from the mirror with her dressing gown only to see her aunt Eva staring back at her. As children, she and George had always referred to Eva as the Badger.

. The moment her nerves and Robbie had recovered, she took herself down to Patrice at the salon in Notting Hill. Patrice spent a significant amount of time staring at her scalp with his thumbs tucked into the pockets of his leather trousers. Patrice examined strands of her hair in different types of light. Patrice told her to trust him. She then sat in the leather chair with a vibrating back-massage feature for *four hours*, while Patrice wove his magic with squares of tinfoil and plastic brushes. The bill was so enormous that she left her watch as security and ran to the nearest cashpoint. Patrice understood. There had been one unfortunate scene over a washbasin when a client's husband appeared, brandishing a credit card bill.

She repeated this every ten weeks for the next five years, often thinking that if he ever bothered to add up the cash withdrawals on the bank statements that lay unopened in a pile next to their coffee machine, he would assume she had a cocaine problem. It would never occur to him that it was the cost of maintaining a series of nondescript brown, blonde, and iron-grey stripes through her chin-length hair with nose-length fringe.

But in New York, she faced a stark hair choice: embrace the grey like a grown-up or get down to the drugstore and buy the $7.99 mahogany dye. She chose the latter, but, after about two weeks, had to buy the "pen thing" Christy recommended and colour in the white regrowth on the top of her forehead so she didn't look like she was going bald. Then she took her dark hair to a barber on First Avenue, and a rotund man called Spiro cut it short, as short as it had been in her twenties, and suddenly people saw her cheekbones.

To match her new hair and her new cheekbones, she decided to change her appearance. For her fortieth birthday, she bought a pair of black leather biker boots and a matching pea coat, which she wore most days with a tailored white shirt and straight-leg jeans. Although it sounds a bit butch, in fact it was all very Inès de la Fressange Parisian chic, and for the first time in her life, when she saw herself in a shop window, or a car mirror, or the glass doors of the SoHo Grand, she smiled. She felt that her outside matched her inside and the rest of her life's dressing had been a series of costume changes that didn't quite work.

"*Hey!*" shouted the porter, and she snapped out of her sartorial self-congratulation. An old woman with grey hair piled vertically on her head in an elaborate series of curls, slippers under pyjamas, and a sleek fur cape thrown over her shoulders despite the sunshine, had shuffled over to one of the outdoor tables and was stuffing the remains of a ten-dollar *pain au chocolat* into her mouth and enjoying it.

"I can't bear the waste," said the old woman, dismissing the porter with an extravagant wave of her hand, and who, with the towering updo and the plastic butterfly perched upon it, had a decadent aristocratic glamour and a look of Lady Somebody in a portrait by Gainsborough hanging in the dining room of the Frick Collection. Lucy decided that if she ever got that confident she would stop dyeing her hair and hurl the pen thing in the bin. But that wasn't today.

She pulled a scrap of paper with an address on it out of her pocket and turned towards Worth Street, and the little interview for the little job.

SITTING ON an uncomfortable chrome stool next to a large bamboo plant, she peered through the foliage at the strategically jumbled framed posters on the walls, and the throngs of young people shouting things like "That's sick!" into their phones. She consoled herself with the thought that they all looked very ambitious. Thanks to her sojourn in Mind, Body, and Spirit, she knew that the offices had once been comprehensively feng shui'd, but all that was left was a small plastic dragon sitting on a windowsill, a broken set of wind chimes lying on top of a pile of dog-eared scripts with felt-tip titles scrawled across their spines, and a solitary crystal hanging over the kitchen door. She was just wondering where the water feature had been placed when Carmen Ross appeared.

Julia had warned her that Carmen wore *outfits*, and

certainly Carmen in ruby-red shoes, belt, bangles, earrings, and beret gave new meaning to the word "accessorized". One of Julia's jobs as Carmen's secretary (although Julia always described her role as "executive assistant") had been arranging the extra luggage allowance for flights to the Cannes Film Festival and ensuring that any hotel room Carmen stayed in had a full-length mirror. Underneath the beret, Carmen's hair was blow-dried and hand-tinted black-brown, and her face a symphony of subtle make-up and full face-lift. That's what somewhere between fifty and seventy looks like, she thought.

She had pulled together a rudimentary résumé that was tossed casually on top of the filing on Carmen's desk. On Julia's instructions, she had creatively constructed a series of non-profit activities to cover the glaring gap in the employment history section ("children's literacy volunteer" to describe reading Percy Jackson books to Max's class, "fund-raiser" to describe begging for prizes for the PTA raffle), but Carmen breezed through this, declaring, "I admire all you stay-at-home mothers so much. After all, it's the hardest work of all."

She was so unprepared for this it reduced her to silence as she decided if it made her feel like a fraud or not. Fortunately, Carmen did not require noise.

"Honestly, the scripts are usually total rubbish. I only do this because I'm polite and old-fashioned and I applaud anyone who sits down and writes one hundred pages of anything." Carmen paused. "Though I do draw the line at the handwritten ones. Those people need psychological help, not a rejection letter."

Carmen stood up, picked up a pile of ten scripts, and handed them across the desk, saying, "I only ever got one good thing off the slush pile", and pointing a bony red-nailed finger at the corner of the room. She, Lucy, looked. And looked again. There was an Oscar, a studded cat's collar around it, on the shelf next to a photo gallery of Siamese and one of Carmen in the eighties in an outfit that would have put the cast of *Dynasty* to shame.

"Do you want to hold him?" said Carmen. She should probably have played it cool, but she didn't want to. She picked Oscar up. He was surprisingly heavy.

"Next time you can take him into the bathroom, look in the mirror and deliver the speech you imagined when you were about thirteen."

"*Read it and weep, Patsy Michaels,*" she said, and Carmen laughed.

"You're English? An Englishwoman in New York. I like that. It's a twist on that song. Who sang that song?"

And Carmen started to trill the opening lines of "Englishman in New York" before forgetting the words and trailing off.

"It's a good title for something," Carmen mused. "Not sure what."

This musical interlude was interrupted by a disembodied voice from the telephone.

"Carmen, it's Bruce on line two."

Carmen groaned and counted to three.

"My new boss. He's thirty-one and says he has the utmost respect for my experience, but one day he's going to call and fire me for age."

Carmen picked up her phone with two fingers.

"Put him through. It's been a pleasure to meet you, Lucy. I have a good feeling. I hope this works out." And Carmen raised her hand and wiggled her fingers good-bye.

Outside on the street, she clutched the scripts to her chest. She knew it had gone well, although she had said only about fifteen words. These words included "hello," "Patsy Michaels" (the first-form bully at Sunnylawn Senior School for Girls), and "Sting".

THAT NIGHT, she attempted to describe Carmen to him, beginning with "She's a force of nature", though somehow that didn't feel right, as it implied that Carmen had sprung fully Carmen-like into the world, and she felt sure that the persona had been more artfully constructed than that.

"Is she married? Does she have kids?" he asked.

"No," she said, walking into the bathroom. "Carmen has an Oscar and a loft on Greene Street."

"I wonder if it was worth it," he said.

As she was fishing a clump of rotting, soggy hairs out of the plug hole, she decided to ignore this because she adored him and she knew that for him, these days, a life without her and his sons was unthinkable.

The buzzer sounded; she cleaned her hands under the cold tap, but when she came into the corridor, he was already in the open doorway, shouting instructions down the stairs. Something was to be "brought up carefully", but what it was she had no idea.

"Into the bathroom!" he said, so forcefully that she turned to see which of the boys had come bleary-eyed out of their bedroom, pyjama trousers round their knees. But he meant her. She obeyed and sat on the toilet, listening to an intriguing soundscape of heavy bootsteps and hammering and Richard-style swearing, "Fuck them all bar Nelson", until he opened the door with a flourish and led her the four paces into the main room, where, in the corner, was a new desk and chair. Her pile of scripts had been lovingly placed on the right-hand side.

"I can't get you a room of your own yet," he said. "But I did get you this."

She rested her head on his shoulder for a moment, and then she walked over and sat down. The desk was reclaimed and had been painted in French country style: a white base, with leaves growing up the legs and meeting in a delicate pattern of foliage and flowers on the top.

"I saw it in the window of the shop round the corner and I thought of you."

Lucy and Richard occasionally experienced love so transcendental that they could communicate their feelings without words. This was useful at this moment, as she could not speak. She looked over at him, and he knew that there would be no gift at a specific moment in her life that she would ever value more.

EVERY MONDAY MORNING from then on, she sat at her desk and read and wrote. The scripts encompassed everything from the high-concept "Tudor zombies take Manhattan and joust in Central Park" to the low-budget "Unhappy couple argue for ninety minutes". Because she had taken to the art of pithy precis like a duck to water, Carmen, who usually listened to script reports over the phone, insisted that they meet, and they enjoyed their weekly chats in cafés downtown about the romantic comedy with minimal comedy or romance, or the Scandi genre script with much snow and sexual violence. And soon she started to understand what made dialogue work, what a "pinch scene" was, or indeed an "inciting incident".

Although Julia said that the only things she had learned off Carmen were that "the time to slow down is when you're most in a hurry" (something Julia wished she had done more often in her life) and that "white, as in white jeans, is a wardrobe basic", she discovered that Carmen was a sort of Yoda of cinema and, as they shared an obsession with the films of the seventies, she was delighted to sit at Carmen's feet and talk about *Star Wars* or *The Godfather* or *Annie Hall* or *Badlands*.

Inevitably, as they were women and they liked each other, they also talked about life.

In Tea and Sympathy, over beans on toast and a stiff Earl Grey, she explained that she had never felt English until she came to New York. When Carmen asked her what she meant, she explained that the broad American definition of "English-ness", as something to do with British bands, or aristocrats, or Windsor Castle, was not something that would ever be applied to her with her nondescript suburban upbringing when she was actually in England.

In Tartine, over milky coffee and a toasted baguette, Carmen explained that Little Carmen had never felt any sense of who or what she was until the 1970s. When Lucy asked her what this meant, Carmen explained that it was not until then that a girl might realize there was a choice about how to be a woman.

"I was a sixteen-year-old in a print dress and pointy shoes, thinking of a future with *The I Hate to Cook Book* (which, by the way, is hilarious), when I read Betty Friedan," Carmen said, "and Betty changed my life. I came to New York and I dared to be different, although, as I'm sure I would have found out eventually, it was the only way I could be."

She remembered his question "Was it worth it?" but said nothing. The next time she met Carmen, however (they were in the spectacular loft on Greene Street, as one of the Siamese had hypoglycaemia), Carmen appeared to have been considering it.

"You know, Lucy, I used to say to Julia that I lived my life so women like her, and you, didn't have to. You can engage with the magnificence of your own potential in the way a man can, see what the options are, and decide for yourselves whether the sacrifices are worth it."

A silence fell. Lucy walked over to the floor-to-ceiling windows and looked down onto the cobblestone street, then across at the cast-iron facades and felt the ghosts of SoHo: the bohemians, the sweatshop workers, the artists. How many of them had come to this city wild with hope? How many had found the magnificence of their potential?

"When did you buy the apartment?" she asked.

"In 1986. Off an actual artist who painted wall-size canvases in drip style and had no heating. Took me ten years to do the renovation. Every time a film got a distribution deal in Korea I thought, *There's another window.*"

The sickly Siamese cleared his throat and crawled listlessly onto Carmen's lap, and they were all conscious of his sour breath.

"I only ever had passionate affairs with married alcoholics so, with hindsight and therapy, I know that I did not want the picket-fence-and-rose-garden fantasy. But I have friends who deeply regret some choices they made for political reasons."

She turned to look at Carmen, whose bony-red fingernails were caressing the cat's head.

"Oh, no. Not me," said Carmen. "I don't think I ever wanted children, really."

On the far wall hung a huge wooden carving of four female

warriors, arms inextricably linked, breasts proudly jutting towards the enemy, brandishing spears and raising their muscular legs in a war dance.

"Sometimes when I think of all the time I've wasted, I feel so sad I don't know what to do with myself," Lucy said suddenly.

Carmen did not agree or disagree, but simply said, "Maybe you're a late developer?"

She looked unconvinced.

"Lucy. I long for the certainty I had when I was twenty, it makes life so much easier if there's only one road to travel, but now I'm older, I think there are as many shades of women as . . ."

Carmen paused, and so she piped up, ". . . drugstore hair colour to cover grey. Everything from ash-blonde warrior to raven-black homemaker."

And the melancholy mood in the loft lifted, although the smell of sick cat did not.

"I'm obsessed with hair colour at the moment," she confessed. "I don't know what to do with mine, what with the regrowth and the frizzing."

"Every woman has a bad-hair decade," said Carmen firmly. "The important thing is, once you find your style, to wear it well."

"Because I'm *worth* it," she said, with a knowing wink to an imaginary camera, and they both laughed. But then Carmen got serious.

"You are, Lucy. Believe me, you are."

· · ·

As Carmen had predicted, one day Bruce, the baby boss, did call and fire her, but it was a confusing experience because he had done a management course on effective dismissal and spent ten minutes out of twelve on "positive focusing". Carmen made three subsequent phone calls: the first was to a lawyer to ensure that the settlement included health insurance for life; the second to a man Carmen had met while shooting a movie in Argentina five years ago, who immediately issued an invitation to stay at his estancia and learn how to play polo; the third to Lucy, to say that from now on the company would be shredding unsolicited scripts, and so she was unemployed, too.

She was sanguine, and Carmen, who was sanguine, too, appreciated this and quoted lines from Tennyson's *Le Morte d'Arthur* about how "the old order changeth, yielding place to new". Then Carmen invited her to come to the opera that Friday night and say farewell or, rather, *"adios"*.

"It's a date," she said, and they agreed to meet by the fountain.

She deliberately came out of the subway onto Columbus Avenue so she could savour every step she took towards the Met. As she approached, the early-evening sunlight hit the sparkling sprays of water and a series of rainbows danced across the magnificent facade, and she laughed at the absurd beauty of it all.

Carmen emerged from behind the fountain, ever youthful in leather jeans, a poncho, and a green felt gaucho hat.

"I left the spurs at home," Carmen said. "I thought they were a bit too *Magnificent Seven*."

They air-kissed with real affection and then headed inside, where she spent her last day's wages on champagne, and they marvelled at the Chagalls and the chandeliers. Then they took Carmen's usual seats in the very front row of the stalls, where they could practically feel the air move as the conductor lifted his arms, the curtain rose, and suddenly they were in a darkened church in Rome as the painter Cavaradossi finishes his portrait of Mary Magdalene and awaits the arrival of his lover, the diva Floria Tosca.

When she was ten, before she had any idea what opera was, she had listened to the twenty most beloved arias as her father drove her to school. He had bought a limited-edition box set of two cassettes, a special offer from the *TV Guide*, and one day, stuck in traffic, through the tinny car speakers, Maria Callas had sung "Vissi d'Arte" from *Tosca*, and her father had started to cry.

"What does it mean?" she had asked, but her father said he didn't have a clue, there was just something about the voice of Callas that had affected him.

In the first interval, Carmen took out an embroidered handkerchief in preparation for this, and when the magnificent soprano began to sing "Vissi d'arte, vissi d'amore", Carmen, too, started to cry.

I have lived for art.

The English surtitles were projected overhead.

I have lived for love.

She smiled at Carmen, and squeezed her hand.

"Thank you. For everything," she said.

Carmen nodded, wiping her cheeks, as one bulging tear sat on her right eyelash like dew on a strand of grass.

"Green shoots are growing, Lucy," she said enigmatically, and Lucy felt a shiver of anticipation.

it might be true,
but it doesn't feel real

When Lucy was living in London she had longed to go to the Hamptons, so when Julia and Christy mentioned they would both be there over the Fourth of July weekend, Christy in the barn in Bridgehampton and Julia in a rental in Amagansett, she thought, *"At last!"* Sitting in her library in Ladbroke Grove, Lucy had spent many happy hours researching houses and reading about the Jitney. She knew in topographical detail which bit of East Hampton was actually in East Hampton and not buried in woodland where you could find deer lactating in your driveway or be bitten by Lyme disease-ridden ticks.

None of this information was of any use in her present

accommodation, however, a budget motel with pink-and-green bedspreads that smelled of cooking oil and a shower that Janet Leigh would have refused to enter, and where they were lulled to sleep at night not by waves rolling along the shore but by trucks rolling along the Montauk Highway.

It didn't matter that Lucy remembered trips to five-star hotels in paradisaical locations round the globe where she and Richard had bickered and complained, and twice he had remembered urgent business in the office and left a week early, chatting to the boys at the infinity pool via Skype as Lucy resentfully sipped the first of her afternoon cocktails. No, she had a nasty little secret. In her hotel bathroom she expected Aveda toiletries at the very least, was pleasantly surprised by Bliss, and once, in Florence, had been delighted by Santa Maria Novella. In the motel on the highway, she had gingerly picked up a yellowing bar of used soap from behind the toilet to examine the thumbprint in its centre.

"OCEAN! Don't be such a girl!"

Lucy looked up from her soggy towel and reverie to see two children, a boy and a girl, arguing on the beach because the boy called Ocean didn't want to go into the water. After glancing over to check that Max and Robbie were still happily splashing with Richard in the shallows nearby, she nudged Julia, who in turn nudged Christy, who reluctantly put her iPad down and listened.

"Leave me alone, Harmony!" the boy shouted, and stuck his nose in the sand and his butt in the air and beat his fists and feet in the distinctive rhythm of tantrum as the girl called Harmony started kicking sand over his Saint Tropez-style shorts.

"Poor Ocean," whispered Christy.

"Poor Harmony," said Julia. "Who'd be a girl in that house?"

"*Houses*, I suspect," said Lucy, as a man and woman marched barefoot toward them past a tower of Boogie Boards. They were clearly the parents of Harmony and Ocean (like the Hapsburgs, father and children had very distinctive chins), and they were arguing.

"He said he wanted to do surf camp," the mother pleaded, her fashion-forward kaftan that had seemed like such a good idea in Bergdorf's wilting around her.

"No. You just wanted to stop me from using the beach pass," retorted the father, taking exaggerated steps through the sand.

"Talk about dis-harmony and ocean," Christy said to Julia, once the unhappy couple was out of earshot. "That's one for the writer's notebook."

"I couldn't use it," replied Julia.

"What? Not even the beach pass?" said Lucy. "That was funny. Getting a beach pass here is a nightmare."

"Nope." Julia shook her head.

Lucy and Christy looked at her.

"If you saw it in a film you wouldn't believe it. You'd dismiss it as unconvincing social satire about the kind of people who summer in the Hamptons and call their kids Harmony and Ocean. It might be true, but it doesn't feel *real*."

And with that, Julia jumped to her feet, brushed the sand off her legs, and expertly zipped up her wetsuit, her right arm angled awkwardly behind her. She pulled a small tube out of Romy's backpack and smeared the zinc cream across her nose, cheeks, and the backs of her hands. It was bright blue and, as she ran to join the surf class on the beach, with her absurdly elegant limbs, her long graceful feet, and her turquoise face, she looked like one of the Na'vi in *Avatar*.

Lucy closed her eyes and took a moment to consider their conversation, but Christy settled herself down again, waved at Sinead and Sorcha, who were happily digging a moat around a palace of sandcastles, and eagerly pulled her iPad back out of her beach bag. She had reached the second part of *The Age of Innocence*, and, as for some reason she had never seen the film, she was engrossed in the twists of the plot. Passionate but too proper Newland Archer had actually married quietly scheming May Welland, but now he was in Newport, staring at the distant figure of his true love, the Countess Olenska, who stood at the end of the pier, watching sailboats go by. Newland, engulfed in the tragic contemplation of his loss, was wondering if she could sense his presence. *"Shouldn't I know if she came up behind me?"* he mused.

Christy stopped reading and looked up across the waves of Ditch Plains. She thought about Newland's self-righteous irritation and wanted to shout at him.

"You got married to someone you didn't love! Of course Olenska doesn't want to see you." She shook her hair back and stared

moodily over the sea, her perfect profile framed beneath her straw panama. She considered a world where the biggest emotions were expressed in the smallest gestures, where a declaration of love was turning to look at someone, where the bitterest betrayal might come on a scented visiting card, where the wave of a white-gloved hand meant good-bye forever. She wondered why, although she wanted to identify with the mesmerizing Countess who trailed her tragedy and the whiff of old Europe behind her, she felt a sneaking admiration for May.

"Christy," said Lucy suddenly, "what Julia just said. That's how I feel when I remember I'm forty years old. It might be true, but it doesn't feel real."

"Oh," said Christy, but she still didn't quite get it.

ANOTHER MORNING, *in the city, Robyn lies in bed and listens to the rumble of the subway train from beneath the foundations of the building. Someone has once told her that it makes them think of a dragon roaring from the subterranean depths, and Robyn always remembers this when summer comes, and she sees the dragon's steamy breath rising through the sidewalks and increasing the stifling heat to unbearable. It's seven in the morning, and already pointless to open a window, so she switches on the fan and throws back her sheet and lets the stale air beat over her as best it can.*

Robyn leaves the apartment early, her bag weighed down with deodorant, foot powder, and a pair of smart shoes as she wears her

Crocs to walk in. The summer is not just a challenge for childcare, but a horror for feet, and, whenever she bothers to look down, Robyn thinks, if I had a dollar for every throbbing bunion, *or, for that matter, every bloodstained Band-Aid hanging off a heel. She moves briskly, but not briskly enough, it seems, for an enormous muscle-bound jogger, sweating through his Duke University sweatshirt, who lumbers toward her with the footfall of a T. rex, and who claps his hairy hands together like a gunshot an inch in front of her nose and bellows, "WAKE UP, LADY!" to get her out of his way. Shocked, she stops for a moment and notices that a small jar of petroleum jelly has fallen out of the pocket of his shorts. She picks it up and glee-fully hurls it into the trash.* I hope you chafe like hell, bully boy, *she mutters.*

In the park by Chrystie Street, she sees a few tiny children running and laughing in the water sprinklers and smiles. Ryan has taken Madison and Michael to their grandparents' house in Anaheim for three weeks. There has been much hemming and hawing about the invitation; Michael has begged her to come with them, even for a week, but in the end common sense has prevailed. What to do with the kids for the long summer months is an annual nightmare, inevit-ably resolved with a patchwork of friends, work leave, any family that can be cajoled into it, and the inevitable couple of weeks at grim, inexpensive sports camps where the children cry as she leaves them because they don't know anyone and are still crying when she returns to pick them up. This year, however, with most of July covered by the trip to California, if Robyn takes two weeks off to sit with them in front of the TV, kick a ball round Battery Park, and chase them through the water sprinklers, they are nearly at the start of the fall term again. Of course the most common-sense arrangement would be for Ryan merely to drop the kids off with his parents and pick them up, but, even as he was protesting that caring for them would be "too much" for his mother, she knew he was looking forward to lying by his parents' pool, eating three cooked meals a day, and writing his blog about the challenges of the artistic life. It is too much, but Robyn has long known that she and her husband have different definitions of the same words. Wake up, lady.

As she approaches Grace Church, she glances at her watch. If she gets on the subway at Union Square, she can take ten minutes, and so she does, entering the church slowly by the back door and slipping into a wooden pew. The stone coldness envelops her as she examines a laminated reference guide to the church, one she has read many times before, and picks out the characters in the Pre-Raphaelite stained-glass windows. At the bottom of the guide is an italicized quote from 1869: "For many years Grace has been the center of fashionable New York."

Robyn kneels down and prays for many things, one of which is a change in the weather.

VAUGHN HAD BUILT the barn in Bridgehampton as his first marriage was collapsing. Although "barn" might imply an Amish-style structure where the most fun you could have would be watching a chicken lay an egg, Vaughn's barn covered five thousand square feet, and had a home cinema as well as wooden beams in the ceiling. It was his pride and joy. He had delayed its completion to try and keep it out of the divorce settlement, but in the end, a sort of time-share agreement had been reached between him and the first Mrs Armitage II over its usage.

When he married Christy, Vaughn had been concerned whether she would feel comfortable about this, but Christy, who did not have a territorial bone in her body, loved the house as much as he did and often remarked on what exquisite taste her predecessor had. Christy was struck by the fact that the flowers in every room complemented the colour scheme and, in the case of the living room, where a huge oil painting of white Madonna lilies hung over the fireplace, an enormous bouquet of matching flowers was always on the table, together with a pair of ornamental scissors to clip out the stamens and the clusters of red-brown pollen atop them. The first Mrs Armitage II, who had a penchant for crisp white French linen, knew how to avoid a stain emergency.

Christy had the scissors in her hand when Vaughn came in and volunteered to take the girls out for a few hours. By the conspiratorial look on their faces, Christy knew that part of this excursion would involve ice cream, but she was delighted. She was planning to surprise Vaughn one day that week by making his favourite dinner, steak and kidney pie, and this was her opportunity. She put the scissors down, kissed them all good-bye, and hurried to the kitchen, where Loretta the Housekeeper had stocked the fridge according to that week's list.

She had just lifted a handful of flour-covered meat into the sizzling casserole dish on the stove when she heard a car turning into the drive. She hid the dish in the oven and, wiping her floury and bloodstained hands on her cream apron, walked into the hall. Now she heard the insistent revving of an engine, which rose to a mechanical squeal. Christy's father had considered it his primary parental duty to teach her and her brother basic automobile skills. She knew this was a car in pain.

Vaughn had remarked only the previous week that the unfenced ditch next to the garage was an accident waiting to happen, and, when Christy came outside, she saw that a small rental car was stuck in it, its front right wheel jutting upwards and spinning as the driver continued desperately to turn the engine on.

"*Stop!* You'll flood it!" she shouted, and at that moment Teddy, the gardener, appeared from the lavender beds and ambled over.

He walked to the driver's door, opened it, and a woman got out. She was wearing a dark suit and black stockings and enormous sunglasses, and when she pulled them off she blinked in the sunlight and looked around nervously, like a goth meerkat. Against the shimmering blues and greens and soft greys of the landscape she looked ridiculous, and she knew it. She took off her jacket and threw it on the back seat. Underneath was a plum-coloured silk blouse that even to Christy's fashion-illiterate eyes looked expensive. (Lucy could have told her it was vintage; Tom Ford for Gucci from around 2001.)

"We'll soon have you out of there," Teddy was saying as Christy approached.

"Just need to give it a good shove."

"I'm so sorry," the woman replied. "I'm an idiot, I didn't realize—"

Her voice was soft and beautiful with a musical inflection, the voice of an American who had studied in Europe—perhaps Italy?—for several years.

"Were you looking for someone?" asked Christy.

"Yes. Mr Armitage. I have a letter for him."

Of course, thought Christy, another upscale begging letter from some foundation or something. Lately she had noticed that such organizations were becoming more creative.

"He's out with the kids. I'm his wife. I'll give it to him. But let's get you out of here first." And Teddy and Christy clambered into the ditch and pushed up, as the woman inexpertly banged the car into first gear.

Once safe on the tarmac, the woman wound down the window. Christy guessed that she was about thirty, although she had the kind of perfect skin that would be ageless if she looked after it (unlike Christy, who had spent her teenage years sunbathing with olive oil), and she had an intelligent face that was also good. In short, there was a look of a younger Julia about her, and so Christy immediately warmed towards her.

"Thank you," the woman said, reaching her hand up to give Christy a thin white envelope. "Tell Mr Armitage I'm sorry. I missed him."

Yes, she had definitely spent significant time outside the States. Her phrasing and the incorrect punctuation gave her away. In another woman it might have come across as affected, but in this one Christy found it charming, despite the nervousness that made her twitch a little and the sweat stains dribbling from the armpits of the vintage silk shirt.

"You look boiling," said Christy. "Come in and have a cold drink."

The woman hesitated.

"I will if it's no trouble, Mrs Armitage."

"Christy. What's your name?"

"Sarah." (Something very funny going on around the *r* here. Perhaps it was France Sarah had lived in?)

"Who do you work for, Sarah?"

"An international foundation. We're restoring some recently discovered Mayan temples in the Guatemalan rain forest."

Christy glanced knowingly at her own reflection in the mirror (she realized she still had the bloodstained apron on, and, as "abattoir assistant" is not a good look, she hastily took it off) and led Sarah into the conservatory to pour her a glass of fresh lemonade. Sarah looked around with a rapt expression on her face, more like a child in sweetie land than a woman entering her fourth decade. She actually gasped when she saw the lawn leading down to the ocean.

"This is the most beautiful house I've even seen."

"That's what I thought, too, when I first saw it," said Christy. "Mr Armitage's first wife decorated it."

"It's *magnifique*. Is she an interior designer?"

"*Non,*" said Christy, at that moment learning that while it was okay for her to be magnanimously nice about Vaughn's ex, it was not acceptable in a stranger. She offered to give Sarah a tour to show that while she might not be *magnifique* as far as choosing upholstery goes, she was certainly *gentille*!

"*The drapes! The carpets! The flowers!*" Sarah exclaimed as they moved up the stairs and along the first-floor hallway, and Christy discovered a talent for real estate brokerage as she opened doors and pointed out arresting features ("The door frames are oversized to give an illusion of space"; "This bathroom is modelled on one in the Villa Cimbrone in Ravello"). Then she led Sarah into a small alcove with a narrow bookcase at the end.

"And this is the one room I did myself."

"The girls' bedroom?" said Sarah, and, smiling, Christy pulled at *War and Peace* and waved her inside the secret door with a flourish.

It was not until they were back downstairs in the living room, and Sarah was staring up close at the brushwork on the lily painting, that Christy realized something. She had not told Sarah that her children were girls and, as the first Mrs Armitage was mentally unstable, she did not allow any pictorial evidence of their existence outside their rooms and strictly instructed them never to leave any of their things lying about. Sarah would not have had a clue *unless she knew before she arrived there.*

Christy flashed back to the cheap rental car in the ditch, probably rented by Sarah that morning after one more lonely night on the sofa bed in the studio apartment in Murray Hill. She saw the letter for Vaughn, probably containing some form of blackmail disguised as a declaration of undying *amour.* Sarah's armpits were guiltily sweaty, indubitably revealing the no-time-for-deodorant, it's-now-or-never haste in which she had left. It was just like the final few minutes of an episode of *Murder, She Wrote.*

Christy had been naive. *"Tell Mr Armitage I'm sorry. I missed him"* wasn't European punctuation, it was Exhibit A for affair.

Vaughn's infidelity was something Christy had not known yet had always known. She loved him, that was for sure, but it was not a madly-in-love, jealous passion that meant the unexpected arrival of the woman in black could ruin her life. It was a "this is my life and I sacrificed things for it, and you, Miss, will never get the third share in the barn" kind of love. Christy knew now that there was one territorial bone in her body.

Meanwhile, Sarah was burying her nose in the Madonna lilies in the vase on the table. She seemed so young and clever and sad, and, if Sarah had been her younger sister, Christy would have said, *if you waste your thirties on married men it will work out only one way and it's bad for you. Don't make stalking your activity of choice on a national holiday. Find a bachelor nearer your own age who will pick a daffodil for you out of someone's plant pot on Fifth Avenue as you walk to Central Park to go boating on the lake.*

But Sarah was not in the family yet, and Christy did not feel any sisterly or sister-wife loyalty to her. And when she saw the beautiful shirt moving dangerously near the lily stamens, and the red-brown pollen that she had not yet cut off quivering, ready to strike, she knew that, were it to hit that silk, there would be no amount of Sellotape could ever lift it off.

"Vaughn's never going to leave me," she said.

And Sarah spun round, brushing against almost every bloom in the fifty-flower bouquet.

"I can see that," Sarah replied, no longer seeming young and clever, merely sad. "I should never have come here. I'm sorry."

"It's all right," said Christy. "But you'd better go. And don't come back."

As Sarah scuttled past her, Christy saw, with only a little remorse, that the hand-dyed plum now had orangey-red patches all over it. And in fashion heaven, the angels wept.

But Christy did not.

She walked into the kitchen and pulled the white envelope from the pocket of her jeans. She sniffed it. It was scented, of course, Miss Dior or something similarly predictable. It did not occur to her to open it; she simply ripped it up, took the casserole out of the oven, and stuffed bits of paper with perfect black-ink-pen handwriting on it and bloody, flour-covered meat into the waste disposal.

Then she went outside to find Teddy and told him to fence round the ditch and not to mention anything about the car or the woman to Mr Armitage.

"Vaughn," she said firmly, "is never to be enlightened."

WHEN HER HUSBAND and the girls returned, all three tired and happy, Christy was lying on the enormous sofa, finishing *The Age of Innocence*. She opened her arms to hug Sorcha and Sinead, and when Vaughn leaned over she tilted her face up and kissed him on the mouth.

"How was your afternoon?" he said, and smiled.

(*A young woman crashed her car into the ditch, I showed her round the house, and she turned out to be your mistress*, thought Christy.)

"I didn't feel like cooking, so I booked a table at the Meeting House," she said.

"Perfect," he replied. "I'll ask Teddy to drive us, so we can have a cocktail."

And he headed out to his office, a distinctly frisky edge to his stride.

Christy leaned back and the girls lay on top of her. She gazed upwards through the golden feathery strands of their hair and looked at the top-of-the-range recessed light fittings imported from Sweden. She breathed in her daughters' smell, felt their flesh born of her flesh, vowed that their life would always be more important than her life, and considered the events of the past three hours.

And finally she understood what Julia had meant that day on the beach. It might be true, she thought, but it doesn't feel *real*.

back to school

September

The kids were all right, of course. It was Robyn, already exhausted by eight-thirty, ashamed of her five-year-old beige skirt and jacket that was the same as wearing a T-shirt reading *I have to work in a badly paid boring job*, who felt trepidation as she approached the school gates.

La rentrée, they call it in France, and for some reason Robyn found herself thinking about chic French women, the kind who take the return to school extremely seriously, using the first few days of term as an opportunity to upgrade their wardrobes and underwear and perform essential maintenance activities on their faces and décolletage. However, Robyn was not living on the Left Bank, but in a former tenement in the Loisaida, which was far too small for the four of them, despite Ryan's protestations that all it needed was more "storage space". The only essential maintenance she would be performing today would be filing her corns in the bath after another day trudging round the bed shop.

Her face darkened, and she frowned. At this moment, a bouncy woman in leisurewear bounced past, grinning *"Everybody happy"* without waiting for a reply. Robyn realized it had not been a question, merely a statement of intent. She glanced around. Yes, everybody did seem happy. All around her, bathed in sunlight, were the shiny people of the West Village.

Maybe it was something in the soya lattes? Or maybe this particular group of adults woke up every morning celebrating the fact that, because of the zoning of their apartments, their children could go to a top public school and they could keep their summer cottages in Quogue? For a moment Robyn missed the old school, the sight of gothically gloomy Lucy Lovett peering in horror over her sunglasses at such things as a poster for *A Happyness Workshop for Siblings*, or the day Julia took over from Christy as Class Mom and reduced half the children to tears by answering the question "What is God?" with "God is something people invented to make themselves feel better about *death*." She smiled, she couldn't help it;

then she pulled herself together. She must stop thinking about Julia.

Ahead of her, something seemed to be happening at the main door and suddenly she was swept into the building. Furious that she had not paid more attention the only other time she had been there (then she had crept furtively into the school secretary's office, guiltily proffered the two utility bills from an apartment they didn't live in to secure the places, and, once she had established where the CCTV cameras were, grinned wildly into them in what she hoped was a carefree, innocent manner but probably made her look like the Joker from *Batman*), Robyn tried to orient herself, but her ten-year-old daughter, Madison, took control as usual and in about a minute had found her own classroom and Michael's and was pointing her face up at Robyn's for a farewell kiss. Robyn held her daughter's chin in her right hand and lowered her face down beside it to feel the extraordinary preciousness of her perfect skin.

"Remember," she whispered in her ear, "if anyone asks you where you live, say 'near Washington Square Park'."

Madison stared silently at her. Robyn was pretty sure her expression was one of contempt, but she decided to ignore it. She hugged her and nudged her gently towards her smiling teacher, who was standing in front of a collage about "restaurants we have visited in our neighborhood", including a photograph of a tall blond child standing outside Babbo.

Robyn took a deep breath; it would all be worth it. This was clearly a superior educational experience for her children.

"*Mom!*" She turned to find Michael beside her, clutching at her handbag. "Why did we have to change schools, anyway?"

"*Because your mother had sex on a yoga mat ten times with Julia Kirkland's husband.*"

What Robyn actually said was, "Because your father and I wanted the best for you."

Both statements were true.

One year earlier

It was all about revenge at first.

Robyn wanted revenge on Ryan for being a schmuck. And, as a pleasant side effect, she wanted revenge on Julia—well, on all of them, actually, all those women, those Mothers at the School who never talked to her, or listened to her, or even looked at her.

She had one theory that it was the cloak of invisibility that settles on middle-aged women, normally used to refer to that fact that men no longer looked at you as an object of sexual desire. Apparently some women find this a relief, but not Robyn. Robyn felt the cloak had wrapped around her at age twenty-eight, with the twenty-eight pounds she had gained after Madison's birth that changed her curvaceous but petite figure into one that might most charitably be described as Rubenesque, if Rubens had ever painted anyone in jeans with a muffin top. Although Julia described her as "fabulously fecund", which Robyn took as an insult until she looked it up in the online dictionary, her two babies seemed to have punched out her waist, and the clip-on, clip-off pregnancies of other women reduced her to fretful rage. When she caught sight of Christy Armitage walking her twins through the playground she had wanted to murder her. Literally. She pondered spiking Christy's solitary miniature cupcake with rat poison at the mothers' annual tea party. She even looked up a few scary sites on the Internet and worked out the exact amount of alpha-chloralose toxin required to cause instantaneous death to someone who was five-foot-ten and weighed about one hundred and thirty pounds. Understandably, this frightened her. That year she made an excuse and didn't go.

Afterwards, she spent a couple of days having an imaginary conversation about it that turned out quite amusing. She tried a little riff on it at Saturday-morning soccer, but it came out wrong and no one laughed and Julia overheard, didn't have the decency to ignore her humiliation, and instead compounded it by putting her concerned face on and asking, "You wanted to kill Christy because she's thin? *Interesting.*"

Worst of all, Julia didn't get out her writer's notebook. Robyn had seen her do it so many times, she had written down something the Hot Dog Stand Guy said, for goodness sake, which could only mean that Robyn was of *no interest whatsoever* to Julia. She was not fit even to be a minor character in some piece-of-shit TV series. In her heart she knew that this was because no one wants to watch a drama about a plump, angry woman who slaves every day to support her family and honour her marriage vows, for better or worse. They can look in the mirror, or on the subway, or at their mother, after all. But this realization did not make her feel better. In fact, if she had written down her interior monologue it would have been italicized with indignation at this point.

Robyn had few choices in her life because of the most important choice she had made. She had married Ryan the year he had been named one of *New York* magazine's most promising writers. That his name, Ryan Anthony James, sounded like that of a successful novelist there was no doubt; in fact, it sounded like the name of someone who writes thick novels with foil titles that sell millions. But Ryan had spent seven years crafting his slim volume of short stories that eight hundred people bought. And one hundred of them were his family and friends. That seemed to be enough for him.

"I'm just an old Romantic," he would say, quickly explaining that this was with a *capital R*, not that he wished to buy her jewellery or take them on a mini-break.

"Art for art's sake," he would say, a lopsided grin lighting up his bad skin but still handsome face. "I love the work. It's not about an audience."

While Robyn had found such idealism thrilling when she

was twenty-three years old, fifteen years on she knew the reality of Ryan was that he might love *the* work, but he didn't like *work* at all. She had lived for years under a false impression about artistic types, which she had drawn entirely from the musical *Rent*, a biography of Zelda Fitzgerald, and her own upbringing. Robyn's mother was "creative"; it was the one thing both her parents agreed on. One Christmas Eve she decided to decorate the tree with miniature goldfish bowls and, as the light from behind her eyes twinkled particularly brilliantly, she and Robyn plopped a tiny orange fish into each one. Unfortunately yuletide itself was one of Mother's bad days, and Robyn, her father, and her beleaguered older brother awoke to find no presents and dead fish in the living room. Another year, the Christmas decorations remained up until summer, the cheap tinsel strung across the hallway a constant reminder that creativity and depression often live side by side, and sometimes when Robyn crawled into her mother's bed and snuggled beside her, looking for love, her mother would tell her how she had so many ideas for poems or stories she just had to write, but that having children had destroyed any chance of her doing it.

Robyn's brother became an accountant and married one. Robyn married Ryan and made a solemn promise to dedicate herself to the cause of his genius and protect him from the responsibilities and messiness of life, giving him the opportunities her late mother had not had, or so she believed. This had been a mistake.

The removal of this illusion was again Julia's fault, as after only the briefest acquaintance with her you would know that she wrote all the time. There was no wandering round waiting for inspiration to strike. She was a workaholic, in fact, and while Ryan might sniff at the "commercial" nature of her output (he had seen an experimental film she had written about Virginia Woolf in 1999 and declared it the only good thing she had ever done), Julia made a very decent living and kept her husband and children in a style that made Robyn want to weep with envy. She was riven with self-recrimination at her youthful gullibility. Didn't she remember reading *Little Women*? Jo March scribbled till her fingers practically bled. This was not a fate ever likely to await Ryan.

At the beginning Robyn had a romantic (with a *small r*) notion that Ryan should stay at home and write while she supported them. In due course this would be rewarded by the kind of life she wanted. This had been vague at first, with fantasies of a bohemian home, interesting friends, a literary soirée or two, but quickly solidified into a life where she didn't have to worry about money. This did not happen. She worried about money all the time, for the very simple reason that they did not ever have enough of it. In fact, after four years and thirty thousand words, although he assured her that his prose was reaching new levels of liquidity, it was Ryan who suggested he take a job. Before she could say "Don't you have a job?" he informed her he had one lined up at a gallery of photography in SoHo. He would be on the front desk from eleven to seven every day, minimum wage, of course, but he could get commission if he sold a photograph. Best of all, he would still be writing, although when and if the companion volume would appear she had given up asking. And so it came to pass that he got to swan over the cobbles of Wooster Street and she trudged back and forth to Hell's Kitchen through months that inexplicably became years, and two uncomfortable pregnancies, and then worked extra hours to pay for the childcare that Ryan did not feel was compatible with his artistic needs (while he supported her desire to experience motherhood, he would have been more than happy with one child, he always said).

Then one January morning, when they emerged from their building, late and arguing, and Michael had forgotten his pencil case and Madison cried when a puddle ruined her new sequinned shoes (and Robyn wanted to cry, too, as she knew they did not have the fifty dollars that month to replace them), and they looked up just as a burst of rain streamed straight down from the sky with the speed and pressure of a series of fire hoses, suddenly she screamed (as she occasionally had done in the bathroom to herself, but this time it came out loud) that they *couldn't live like this any more*. And ignoring the placatory lopsided grin that he rolled out on these occasions, which normally elicited a pseudo-maternal calming response from her, she told him that she had been talking to his parents and that she wanted them all to move to his old home in Orange County. His parents had got planning permission to build a three-bedroom bungalow with study on the vegetable patch at the bottom of their garden. Robyn could work as his dad's office manager, the local public school there was excellent, and the children would have grass to play on, a basketball hoop, and they could all spend time together.

Ryan froze. Robyn tried to pull the kids out of the shower, but he stood, hands juddering, as the rain poured over them. And then theatrically pretended that he had not heard her.

"I'm sorry," he said. "Did you just say you've been plotting with my parents to imprison me in Disneyland?"

Madison and Michael looked at Robyn. They loved Disneyland and were very interested in her idea.

"My children are city kids." He intoned, "They are going to grow up stimulated and excited, not dying of boredom like I did. The best fun I had every summer was hitting a tree with a stick."

"Okay," said Robyn, accepting immediately that she had blundered into the relationship area called bad timing. "Now we have to get out of the rain."

At this moment, three of the young pierced punks who lived on benches in the park scuttled as fast as their bondage trousers would let them and joined them under the flimsy awning. Their Mohicans were wilting, and Michael and Madison stared. Robyn knew the kids were wondering if the spiderweb tattoos on their faces would wilt, too, and wanted to get them away before Michael said something that might result in him being spat at, but Ryan was not done. Robyn knew he secretly enjoyed his biannual explosions, always a response to an inconvenient emotional outburst of her own. He had not fled to New York to skulk away one weekend with a U-Haul back to Anaheim, he thundered. Robyn grabbed each child by a hand and started walking away. So Ryan decided he would lose his temper. The last words she heard as she turned the corner were: "I'm an urban writer. What about my inspiration? *What about my book?*"

She had given him a way out, a way she thought they could stay together, away from a city that took more from them than it ever gave back, and he had blocked it. She would never forgive him. So she raided the account that his parents had set up for Christmas presents for the kids and joined a gym near her office. Then she logged on to goop.com and followed her new friend Gwyneth Paltrow's suggestions on how to coordinate your outfits from Uniqlo.

She was not going to be invisible any more. She was going to have an affair.

SHE HAD ALREADY SLEPT with Vaughn Armitage, so that didn't really count. He was very frisky with all the mothers, which Christy never seemed to mind, to the extent that Robyn wondered if she was relieved. One morning after Robyn politely said good-bye to him at the school gates, his arm tightened so hard around her waist she thought he might be feeling for her kidneys, so she brazenly suggested they have a coffee just to see what happened. Something did. Fifteen minutes of *afternoon delight*, as Vaughn called it, although it was nine o'clock in the morning.

The experience was not one Robyn wished to repeat, although she had a feeling she could. Christy might sleep in Egyptian cotton sheets with a 1,600 thread count, but she still had to feel Vaughn's grey nose hairs rubbing against her thigh. And the scar from his heart surgery ran down his stomach like a red arrow pointing to the fact that he might die on the job, which would be extremely embarrassing and would mean she couldn't do the book sale with Christy, which was the one day in the school calendar that she enjoyed. But Vaughn had been fantastically appreciative of her curves, and it occurred to Robyn that Christy's concave stomach might not be that re-assuring to cuddle up next to, you could give yourself a nasty bruise on her hip bones, so after Robyn had come in late to work, blaming the subway like everyone else did, she looked up "fecund" in the dictionary again.

There it was: *"luxuriant, lush, fructuous* (whatever that meant), *FERTILE"*. She scanned down: *"fruitful in offspring and vegetation"*. Ignoring the vegetation bit, she had an insight into something that might banish the cloak of invisibility to the back of the wardrobe of her life. She was younger, relatively, than most of the other mothers. She had not crossed the Rubi-con of forty, after which the brutal regime of daily exercise and eating nothing but soup and a naughty little crouton stops mak-ing you "fabulous" and instead makes you "stringy", with veins popping out of your arms and shoes that don't fit. Moreover, while other women might consider her fat, men didn't. No, Julia was right, they considered her *fertile*. Her hair, full of nutrients, was thick and long without extensions, and she had her own nails. Once she embraced this, and listened to Gwyneth's advice about updating her wardrobe with some key pieces, she was amazed at the attention she received from the Fathers at the School. She began to scan the locker rooms like an affair-seeking missile.

Within a week one of the chess teachers sidled over, muttering something about showing her his antique pawns, but with his huge bald head he looked like an enormous lollipop and, after the Vaughn experience, she wanted a man she found vaguely attractive. She fixed Richard Lovett in a doe-like gaze from beneath her fringe, but he was so English he didn't even realize she was making a pass at him. He appeared to think she was asking for directions somewhere. So when she bumped into Kristian with a *K* in his Lycra yoga shorts and he suggested she try out his new hip opening workshop on a Saturday morning, as she had a lot of hip to open, she had a feeling she might have struck infidelity gold.

When he rubbed the massage oil into her temples longer than anyone else in shivasana, she knew she was onto something, and that if she took longer than anyone else to disinfect her sweaty mat after class there was a chance their eyes might meet across the incense burner. She did, and they did, and then they did it. "Vengeance is mine," muttered Robyn to arouse herself, thinking of Julia, as her head bumped against the wooden blocks. In fact, it turned out to be rubbish revenge, because Julia never knew. Kristian with a *K* informed her seven sessions into their pathetic fling that Julia was in the middle of an "episode" and had left him, and all Robyn wanted to do was scream, *"Why didn't you tell me? It doesn't mean anything if you aren't cheating on her, if she doesn't get to find out YOU PREFER ME!"*

She still did it with him three more times. She wanted to practise a sexual manoeuvre one of her younger colleagues from accounts had shown her, having recorded it the previous night on her iPhone. (It was the holiday party; there had been free eggnog, and the administrative staff were all huddled in the bathroom, gasping at the sheer athleticism of it.)

So she vented her fury with Kristian that their relationship was not in any way threatening his love for Julia by ordering him around on the mat and telling him to move his leg an inch or so to the right and hold his breath. When she finally got the hang of it she knew it was time to move on, although Kristian protested, saying that he had never met anyone as "free" as her and he would miss her "uncomplicated attitude".

Robyn didn't feel free, but she did feel empowered, until Parents' Evening, when Michael's teacher, Miss Chang, told her that Michael couldn't read and brought back home to her the fact that nothing in her life had really changed.

Ryan went into the idiotically flirtatious manner that incensed Robyn. He assumed at first that Miss Chang was referring to reading *books* and giggled about how uninspiring kids' literature was these days and that he often felt that, if he wanted a break from his short stories, there was a fortune to be made writing for eight-year-olds. Ryan himself had read *Dracula* in third grade. Robyn became distracted thinking about *Dracula* and that among the ways of keeping vampires away, apart from the obvious garlic and crucifixes, was to draw a circle around yourself. She looked longingly at the stub of pink chalk on the desk, wanting to seize it and scribble round her chair, as, after all, marriage to Ryan was sucking the life out of her.

Miss Chang was unmoved. She repeated that Michael couldn't read.

"As in *bat, cat, pat?*" said Robyn slowly.

"As in He. Can't. Read," replied Miss Chang with the weary expression of someone used to ignoring stupid comments shouted out from the back of a classroom. She looked at them across the desk. "How much do you do at home?"

Robyn reached over and put her hand on Ryan's arm. Normally he hated that, but now he found it reassuring. He wanted her to take over, which she did, explaining that they were both incredibly busy and had not been as diligent with Michael's homework as they should have been, and asked what they could do.

Miss Chang sighed. "Practice will remedy it; it's just there are limits to what I can do in a class of thirty-two children, twelve of whom have learning and behavioural difficulties."

"That's just not right," countered Ryan. "How can Michael study with disruptive influences around him?"

Miss Chang looked at her watch. The gesture was as devastating as what came next.

"Michael's no angel."

Ryan fell silent.

"Someone needs to do an hour's reading with him every day."

Robyn looked at Ryan; she didn't get home until seven three nights a week, and Claudia the minder could hardly speak English. Ryan shrugged and folded his arms. Miss Chang looked at Robyn. Robyn knew the look was one of pity.

After this exchange Robyn sent Ryan in the direction of the coffee table, made an excuse, and headed for the disabled bathroom, bumping straight into Julia and Kristian, who had their arms wrapped around each other like young love's dream and were kissing in front of everyone. Robyn was so upset that she didn't even enjoy Kristian's expression of terror when she muttered "hello". She desperately needed to cry and, like a small woodland animal ready to lie down and die, she needed a private burrow to do it in. The bathroom was too obvious, so she made her way to the janitor's storage cupboard, crawled into the corner, pulled a toilet roll from the shelves, and slumped onto the floor.

But she had been followed by a predator.

She looked up through sodden eyes to see Lucy Lovett peering in at her. Of course. Lucy often lurked in unexpected corridors with a faraway expression in her eyes. Sometimes she could be heard talking to herself. Not today. She said nothing, so Robyn felt she had to explain.

"Michael can't read, and I don't know what to do."

"It's because this school is a dump."

Robyn was startled.

"You think so? Miss Chang says it's because I don't read to him."

Lucy, who had felt unsettled about Robyn since the debacle of the horse course, sat down beside her next to the foul-smelling floor disinfectant.

"Fuck off. When the fuck are you meant to do that?"

Robyn winced a little. Despite profanity being delivered in what she imagined was an upper-crust English accent, the good girl from Carolina in her never felt comfortable around it. Lucy and Julia swore all the time. It was very off-putting. But she needed to hear what Lucy was going to say next. This is what it was.

"It's all right for me. I have time. I bring them home and I teach them myself. I don't know how long it'll work, but for the moment it's fine. But you . . ."

Lucy looked at Robyn now, right into her eyes.

"You work harder than any other mother I've ever met. I see you every morning, hurrying, always hurrying. But you never lose your temper with your kids. I admire you. You ought to see me with half the pressure you're under, berating my two for ruining my life in front of Kmart. And passers-by."

Tears were spouting from Robyn's eyes now like a clown's rubber squirty flower. It was all too much.

"I can't do it any more. I'm exhausted all the time. The only recreation I have is the gym." (This was not strictly true, of course. *And sleeping with the occasional husband*, she should have added.) "I stagger through the day and I watch bad TV every night. *How can this be my life?*"

Lucy nodded. She reached for another toilet roll and handed it over.

"Michael can't read," said Robyn again, marvelling that this could possibly be true.

"No, he can't," said Lucy.

Robyn remembered that Lucy volunteered in the classroom twice a week. She knew. Lucy took her hand.

"Thank you," Robyn said, smiling thinly. Lucy smiled back. Broadly.

"You know, if you ever need me to pick them up or you get stuck one evening, let me know. I could drill them with mine."

Robyn stared at her in disbelief, and then the dream-like quality of the scene continued when Julia and Christy appeared in the doorway.

"What are you two doing? Sniffing the fucking cleaning fluids?" said Julia. "The principal's about to tell us the plans for the school summer clear-out. We have to choose a child to put on a bonfire. Or at least I think that's what she said . . . Oh, hi, Robyn."

Julia spotted that Robyn's face looked like a little rabbit's with myxomatosis and decided to ignore it.

"Stop it," laughed Christy.

"I'm coming," replied Lucy, crawling out. "Can I nominate one of my own?"

Then she stopped in the doorway.

"Robyn, I'm always in the park with the kids on Saturday morning, around ten. Why not come? We'll have coffee."

Julia looked up. "I'll come, too."

And they left.

Robyn started crying again. For so long she had wanted nothing more than to sit with the cool girls at the back of the school bus, but she realized now that she could have all along. It was not them stopping her. It was her. She had radiated a mixture of fear and disdain and had created a drama about her own rejection that they were oblivious to. She should never have listened to herself. She should have silenced the long monologues inside her head born out of her exhaustion and desperation.

She was suffused with guilt. Now they had finally looked at her, listened to her, and *seen* her, it was too late. She had fondled the penises of two out of three of their husbands.

Thank God Michael was educationally challenged. She had an excuse to take her kids out of the school.

November

Robyn picked up the message on her phone and felt sick. Sitting in Principal Lorraine's office, she felt sicker. She stared straight ahead at a poster listing the five requirements for the children in the school, focusing on number three: *Always tell the truth*. The letters seemed to dance around before her, like a visual disturbance preceding a migraine and, as the principal had made clear "it's about where you live", Robyn felt an enormous headache coming on.

Michael had been handed a form with his address written on it, had read it and put up his hand to say it was not correct. While Robyn's heart leapt at the fact he could actually read something now, she was furious with herself for not thinking of a good enough reason to make him keep quiet on that subject. She was not creative enough, but that was the story of her life.

At that moment she understood why some criminals actually confess to crimes the moment they are arrested. She was possessed by a powerful urge to tell all. How she had informed Ryan of her plan in a matter-of-fact way, and how he was so terrified of her raising the Orange County issue again that he agreed. At first, that is. Then she told him he would have to persuade his colleague at the gallery, the winsome and utterly infatuated Catalina, who lived in a studio on West Eleventh, that they were going to use her address and that, in fact, Robyn had already told two utility companies to change the name on the bills to his.

"But it's a lie," spluttered Ryan.

She had ignored this, thinking, *Yes and so was you telling me you would win the Pulitzer.*

"Our school is good enough for everyone we know."

"No, it isn't. They're just having fun slumming it at the moment, but there's no way Julia Kirkland and Christy Armitage's kids are going to a middle school that has metal detectors at the gates and where the mothers get arrested for dealing." Robyn actually thought this was an urban myth and *Weeds* had a lot to answer for, but she said it anyway and, if that wasn't enough, there was a killer blow coming. "And Lucy Lovett says she'll *move up the Hudson* if she has to. We need to change and change now. If they get into that school in the West Village they're a shoo-in for a decent middle school; maybe we can even get Madison to be gifted and talented?"

"Huh," Ryan snorted. "That's all about gifted and talented parents."

*Well, then, ours are f***ed,* she had thought to herself, but what did it matter now? All her Machiavellian stratagems had been for nothing in the truest sense that Machiavelli's only criterion for a successful plan was not whether it was right or wrong but whether it worked. She shrank into the chair and waited for the almighty reprimand that she was due (something she herself had avoided her entire school career).

Actually, she had dreaded this moment for so many weeks that part of her was curious to see what was going to happen.

The door opened, and in came Principal Lorraine. She smiled, and Robyn noticed that she had done that weird thing with lipliner outside her mouth, which only heightened the tiny wrinkles around it and made it look like she had no lights in her bathroom.

"We have had experience of this before, Ms Skinner . . ." she began.

Oh, crap, thought Robyn, *she's going to be nice.* She started sobbing immediately. She hated when people felt sorry for her.

"I've been so worried about the kids . . ." she replied, her mind racing. Another plan was forming. She was going to beg. She wondered how abject she could be short of falling onto her knees. But maybe that would do it . . .

Principal Lorraine held up her hand to stop her. She proffered a tissue.

"Separations, divorces, difficult custody arrangements."

Robyn nodded non-committally. She had no clue as to where this was going.

"How long have you and your husband been living apart?"

Eureka! The sudden euphoria made Robyn judder, which enhanced the overall effect of overwrought supplication she was going for. Slowly she lifted her trembling left hand and wiped her eyes. Thank goodness she had left her wedding ring by the sink this morning, something she had been doing with increasing regularity over the last couple of years. Everything was going to be fine.

She told Lorraine that she and Ryan had been in trouble for some time but they had only formally separated in the last few months. It was very confusing for the children, but they were doing their best to make them feel secure and she appreciated the wonderful atmosphere and opportunities offered by the new school.

She sniffed and grinned—oh, yes, why had she been so worried?—and finished by saying that she had not felt so relieved in years.

"It's just facing up to the truth, isn't it?" the older woman said, pointing to bullet point number three.

They even embraced as Robyn left.

So from that day separate letters from the school went to each of them at the two addresses. (Robyn had said that Ryan had moved out of the family home to the Loisaida.) They attended their first Parents' Evening together, but they arrived at different times to school events, went to the holiday musical on different nights, and Ryan decided to leave work early on a Monday and Friday to collect his children and spend "quality time" with them. Robyn wondered if it was her imagination, but she was pretty sure he was enjoying the new arrangement. She had worried he would have some moral objection, but he told her she had been right and he was delighted that the days Madison would come home asking what a blow job was had become a distant, although still unpleasant, memory. Certainly he entered into the subterfuge with great gusto, and what with that, and the fact that Mrs Hernandez downstairs finally died and they colonized all her storage space in the basement and got permission to put shelves and hooks up on the landing out-side their apartment (which the old lady had voted against at ten consecutive co-op board meetings, meaning they had carried buggies, babies, and shopping bags up three flights of stairs every day for seven years), their life suddenly did feel shinier and happier.

Ryan was asked by a couple of fluttering mothers on the PTA to run a creative writing workshop for the fifth-graders after school every week, and he did so, discovering a talent for teaching he had had no idea of. Then Michael chased after an-other child with a baseball bat, and at the ensuing, excruciating "making amends" dinner the victim's understanding parents insisted on, it turned out that the father was one of the seven hundred people not related to Ryan who had read *Residua and Fragments* and loved it. He asked Ryan to contribute to his on-line magazine, and Ryan started writing a humorous column called "Fathergate", which to Robyn's delight meant he did more and more of the childcare, as it *gave him material.*

He was fulfilled, and he actually wrote more and Robyn had another insight that perhaps the reason creativity and de-pression go hand in hand is that if you are born with the desire to express yourself in that way, the grim reality of that life, and the incredible odds against getting your stories published, or your film made or, heaven help you, your poetry read, makes you depressed and the vicious circle goes on and on. Once again maybe she had been so wrapped up in her own private life drama that she had missed the fact that her husband was struggling. She forgave him for the past, she forgave herself for her erotic adventures in the playground, and, when he mentioned that he was beginning to consider moving to Brooklyn, she knew they could have a future. A two-bedroom with study in Brooklyn Heights! This had been Robyn's wildest dream. Her kids could do a gardening class. *Maybe she could have another baby?* No, no . . . She pulled herself together. She had promised herself she would not let her thoughts run away with her any more. Ryan would . . . Absolutely no, and anyway, how would she explain it away to Principal Lorraine without looking like a slut?

In short, at this point in their lives, divorce suited them better than marriage and it seemed they were about to live contentedly ever after, until Principal Lorraine put her cupid hat on, and sat Robyn next to Schuyler Robinson at the antibullying workshop.

THE FACT THAT ROBYN had not even noticed Schuyler was an indication of her newfound peace of mind. He was certainly attractive, despite a distressing fondness for a black leather jacket that should have been retired in 1989, and the fact that he really was newly single meant that, unlike Ryan, he was receptive to the female fluttering that surrounded him whenever he set foot in the school. Principal Lorraine had taken him under her wing and banished his ex-wife to the back row of the school hall. (Schuyler's ex had committed various sins in Principal Lorraine's eyes, including questioning whether global warming was scientifically proven in front of the third-graders on Save the Earth day, but the worst of which was not dyeing her hair, thereby threatening the expensive and time-consuming efforts Lorraine went to in order to turn back time.) She introduced Schuyler to Robyn with the line, "I'm sure you two will have a lot to talk about." Once again, Robyn had no idea where this was going, but, when Schuyler took his cue and started talking about the frustrations of being a weekend parent, she had another "Eureka!" moment. She had been seated in the divorced section of the auditorium.

She knew she would have to gather herself, would have to assume her role for the ensuing conversation, but, thankfully, the lights went down quickly, the whiteboard came on, and Principal Lorraine took to the stage to outline school policy, scribbling up ten bullet points. Schuyler took out his iPad and made notes. Robyn was impressed. At events like this, Ryan inevitably performed, making humorous comments in an audible whisper until he got a reaction from the other parents, but Schuyler took it very seriously. In the break, he told her that he was concerned for the emotional health of his son,

Quinn, who had been traumatized by his clearly not-at-all-amicable separation. He felt that Quinn being an only child was a problem, too, but another child had been out of the question, and he added, ruefully but somewhat unnecessarily, Robyn felt, how difficult it had been to have one. Robyn was sure she knew what that meant. Inadvertently, she flicked her hair, smoothed her hands over her luxuriant belly, and practically felt her ovaries bounce triumphantly inside her.

Schuyler asked Robyn directly how her children had coped, so she blustered and muttered about putting them first and how she and Ryan had done mediation with a fantastic man in Queens, who had a beard that he plaited. She had practised this to herself, the last vestige of her interior monologues, and the two times she had said it people had laughed. But Schuyler looked sad and told her she was an admirable person. Robyn was repulsed by herself. She decided that when she got home, she was putting her wedding ring back on. She would tell Principal Lorraine she and Ryan were reconciled and they would have to deal with the address issue.

And then Schuyler invited her to his farmhouse on the Jersey shore for the weekend. Just like that. He reached over and placed a hand on her thigh and whispered in her ear that he could tell she would look good naked. If it was her turn for the kids, there were permanent staff and a separate children's wing. And he had a top-of-the-range Duxiana bed. Robyn knew better than most people how impressive that was.

When she said nothing, she was in shock, as this put the

covert liaisons in the yoga cupboard to shame, he mistook her silence for some form of bohemian disapproval of wealth (he had heard that Ryan was a published writer and was impressed by it) and made a quip about it not being his fault he had a grandfather who discovered how to plastic-coat paper clips, but he did take his work for a non-profit very seriously. He would send a car for her if that made it easier. Now Robyn felt furious. How could this man, this perfect-affair-material man, suddenly appear just when she had remembered how to be good?

She wanted to reassure him that she was absolutely not the sort of person who found indoor hot tubs or 3-D televisions or six-star vacations in the Maldives vulgar, but she sensed real danger for herself here. So she said it was very kind of him to invite her, but that she and Ryan had agreed they would never expose the children to any new relationship that wasn't . . . *serious.*

Schuyler was a little taken aback, she could tell, he was obviously working his way through the lonely ladies on the lunch nutrition committee, but Robyn was determined not to be a notch on his Shaker-style bedpost. In fact, her only hope was to keep as far away from him as possible, for, if she allowed herself to spend one minute in that Duxiana with him, she would simply have to marry him and that would mean redecorating the farmhouse. And she hadn't a clue about colours.

She buttoned her coat firmly, which had the effect of making him stare at her chest, and picked up her bag.

"I'll send you the notes if you like?" Schuyler called after her. "What's your e-mail?" She shook her head. "No thank you." But at that moment Principal Lorraine appeared in a puff of something and handed them all a leaflet with the names and contact details of all attendees, who she announced could share information and ideas inspired by the workshop.

"I'll send you roses, then," he grinned; in fact, Robyn was pretty sure he winked, and, as she was walking out of the front door of the school, she received what could only be described as an inappropriate text from him about his desire to *harrass* her. Schuyler had spelled "harass" incorrectly, and Robyn was charmed. Ryan crafted everything from texts to e-mails as if they would one day be bequeathed to the New York Public Library.

It was a bad sign that she was becoming irritated with Ryan again. She did not put her wedding ring back on.

January

Quinn's tenth birthday party was to be held at Chelsea Piers. Robyn found the invitation in the trash can by accident—her reading glasses had fallen off as she poured the end of her mug of herb tea into it, and the soggy red paper had stuck to her right lens.

She retrieved the card, smoothing it out by the side of the sink. Ryan had junked it, but that was okay. They had agreed that all party invitations on the West Side were to be destroyed before the children found them. It was just too expensive to go, a hundred dollars by the time you'd got there and back and bought the sort of present, educational *and* fun, that would be expected, and you could always get stuck with paying for drinks and popcorn as you waited for the wall-climbing class to start, or the pottery to warm up, or the clown to dress. But she told Ryan that Madison had found it and demanded to go (her lying had become so much more practised as a result of the few months of the double life of Robyn; she had learned never to embellish and had eliminated any verbal tics that might give her away), and he agreed, adding that Schuyler seemed a good guy. Not the brightest spark in the fuse box but an unusually tolerable member of the lucky sperm club, *ha, ha, ha* (this was how Ryan always referred to the scions of independently wealthy families). Schuyler had made a point of telling Ryan how much he enjoyed "Fathergate", and Ryan was never averse to hanging out with people of excellent taste.

"He has a town house on Charles Street," Ryan added for no apparent reason, and suggested that they all take Madison to the party. This was not what Robyn wanted at all. And she really wished Ryan had not told her about the town house.

"Oh," she said. "It's just that Michael wants you to take him to the movies and I thought we'd split up for the afternoon."

She and Madison were late to the party. Robyn had not known what to wear, and then they had to scan the several events going on, the hellish shrieking reverberating high up into the domed ceiling. The place was full of different children, but characterized by the same adult behaviour, as parents, or mainly mothers, futilely offered celery sticks and raisins to children who were stuffing handfuls of crisps down their throats, and hid empty cola bottles in their bags before other parents arrived to collect their by now hysterical offspring. Finally, Robyn saw Schuyler's leather jacket in the distance hovering by a balance beam, as Quinn crouched in tearstained refusal before it. Madison ran off to join two girls dressed like or by the Olsen twins, and Robyn made her way over to Schuyler, just as his ex, the climate change denier with the grey pixie cut, appeared.

"Quinn, it's a gymnastics party," she said, trying to disguise her exasperation. "It's what you said you wanted."

"*I wanted to tumble!*" the boy shouted. "*It's not my fault there's no tumbling! This is a bullshit party.*"

"Don't speak to me like that." She turned to Schuyler, her own eyes reddening. "You shouldn't let him speak to me like that."

"*Quinn.* Your mother's right—"

Even Robyn, predisposed to view Schuyler through town house-tinted glasses, thought this was pathetic. She had endured many similar scenes in her own home, scenes that never ended well. Fortunately, at that moment Big Dave, who was in charge of activities, appeared and, realizing that his sizable tip was diminishing as Quinn's behaviour disintegrated, stepped into the breach.

"Quinn would like to tumble," sniffed the ex.

Robyn could tell that whatever Quinn wanted, Quinn got, so she was not surprised when Big Dave immediately crouched down and started doing forward rolls across the blue exercise mats. Quinn followed until he twisted his right arm beneath him and started crying loudly for his mother, who dutifully sprang towards him despite the fact that Schuyler tried to stop her by hanging on to her sleeve. Schuyler shook his head, and Robyn looked away to avoid the pain-filled, silent exchange between them that she thought told the whole story of their years of reproductive torture.

When Robyn looked back, Schuyler was watching the other children, Madison in the excitable centre, queuing up to swing on the monkey bars. They then both turned and caught sight of Quinn half punching his mother in the chest as she hugged him. Robyn saw in Schuyler's face his dislike of his own child. *Something would have to be done about that*, she thought. She asked him if he wanted a coffee. He looked at her, nodded, and held out his hand. And as if it were the most natural thing in the world, she took it and led him towards the machine.

He told her that the reason he and his wife had not been able to have more children was not her highly strung, stale-egg infertility but his own less-than-zero sperm count. The doctors had tried to make him feel better by mixing sperm from two donors with the couple of sperm they had surgically retrieved before the in vitro, but when he looked at Quinn he knew there was no part of his DNA anywhere near him, the conclusive proof of this being that Quinn loved anchovies. Schuyler had gone to great lengths to source anchovy-flavoured crisps, and he knew no other children would eat the pizza because it was covered in them.

"Anchovies make me barf," said Schuyler, and they both smiled.

"I'm sorry I came on so strong to you," he continued. "I've been taking my therapist's advice to have some fun. It'd been a long time and, boy, it's amazing how much fun you can have with the ladies if you're . . . up front."

Robyn tried to convey a mixture of understanding and suitably ladylike shock, although she knew as well as he did it's amazing how much fun you can have with the gentlemen if you're up front.

"I liked all the flowers," she said primly. "My office looks like a funeral parlour."

"That doesn't sound very good," he said.

"I didn't mean it how it came out," she replied, not meeting his eyes, though in fact it was exactly what she meant. It was just that something, not someone, had died.

"Well, anyway, I'm sorry. For all of it."

This was a reference to the increasingly suggestive texts he had sent, often late at night, and his one attempt to leave a phone-sex message on her mobile. It had made her laugh so loudly that Ryan had become convinced they were so happy these days they should renew their vows.

"But now I want to get serious." He meant it. Robyn adopted an intense listening pose.

"I want another child, Robyn. I don't care how. I deserve a second chance."

He crushed his plastic cup in his hand and threw it so it landed in a bin twenty feet away. He had excellent ball skills and, unlike Quinn, Robyn suspected he was extremely gymnastic. Then he smiled, looked at his watch, and announced he had to go to find the only cake shaped like a fish in the fridge. It had silver icing shaped into gills and everything, and some pastry chef in the Meatpacking District had slaved over it after his/her shift the previous night.

Robyn knew she was losing him. She recognized from the look on his face that he wasn't looking for an affair any more; he wanted a second marriage and a new baby. If that was what *she* wanted, she reckoned she had about eight weeks to snare him before some gorgeous twenty-eight-year-old, tired of dating and making excuses for the lack of commitment from her male contemporaries ("I feel sorry for him, actually"), would listen to her mother and see Schuyler Robinson not as a tired middle-aged man but a good catch.

Robyn had some serious thinking to do, so she wandered outside and stared over the river. Ryan would be fine, she knew that. He had the ultimate relationship survival skill, self-absorption. It was Madison and Michael who had to be considered. She was not an evil person, after all, but wasn't the fashion of subservience to your children out of vogue?

Weren't things going back to the fifties and Betty Draper-style parenting (a cigarette and a slap) these days?

A bird, a big ugly gull, squawked overhead. She looked up, idly wondering if this might be a sign. The bird released an enormous shit that landed on the side of a yacht called *The Anemone*. The sign was that in New York City, everyone dumps on everyone else eventually.

That night, she had a long bath in Jo Malone nutmeg-and-ginger oil and allowed Ryan to glimpse her moving seductively along the tiny corridor to their tiny bedroom. He followed her, meaningfully throwing his notes onto the floor and removing his T-shirt flirtatiously, a long-standing sign between them that he was available and ready to go. She laughed but escaped from his embraces to run back into the bathroom. "Just a minute," she giggled, and closed and locked the door.

Then she lay down on the yellowing bath mat, gathered herself, opened her legs, and, taking a deep breath, stuck two fingers inside herself, feeling for the wire threads of her Mirena coil. She found the first easily, then wiggled for the other. *Eureka!* She closed her eyes and pulled, hard, until the coil came out in her hand, clear, sticky *fecund* mucus stretching round it like chewed chewing gum. She wrapped the plastic in toilet tissue and threw it into the bin.

May

Christy noticed Robyn immediately on Sixth Avenue, although Julia had said that the effects of Robyn's new life on Charles Street had transformed her to the point of unrecognizability. It was not just the obvious physical changes, her clothes, her skin, her haircut, it was that she smiled.

"Maybe it's love?" Julia had suggested, then begun laughing so hard the muscle she had pulled during Soul Cycle went into spasm.

"You shouldn't be so cynical," said Christy. "Just because Schuyler's rich doesn't mean she didn't fall for him."

Julia recognized that this was a sore spot for Christy and regained her composure. Christy decided there was solidarity between her and Robyn, and determined to be very nice to her if she ever saw her again. She had resolved to ask her to join her book group, until she remembered Schuyler's ex was in it, so instead she asked her if she wanted to go for lunch in Bar Pitti. Robyn was delighted, telling Christy she had all the time in the world these days as she had stopped working *"outside the home"*, they both said quickly, as soon as she had moved in with Schuyler. She had also become a born-again virgin, so there was no embarrassment for her in inquiring solicitously after Vaughn's health.

It was only when they sat down at their table, and Robyn

removed her fun-fur gilet, that Christy noticed she was defin-itely carrying more weight up front. She said nothing. Robyn had always been a little heavy, but Christy wondered if Julia was right and the weight gain was a sign of repenting at leis-ure. (Christy, with her anorexic worldview, could never accept that a woman could be fat and happy.) But Robyn caught her glance and announced proudly that she had not been hitting the dessert trolley but that she was pregnant.

"How?" said Christy, too sharply. When they had read *The Handmaid's Tale*, Schuyler's ex had told everyone about his lack of sperm motility.

Robyn, sagely accepting that in the circles in which she now mixed there was no such thing as too much information, an-swered calmly that the baby was in fact Ryan's, the result of a moment of passion inspired by the realization that their life together had ended (Christy blinked a little at this) but that Schuyler had been overjoyed at a second chance at fatherhood.

She shrugged happily and ordered a primi pasta and the kidneys in a cream sauce.

"Everything's great. Ryan's living with his colleague from the gallery on West Eleventh, so the kids see us both all the time. Nothing's really changed for them. Except they've got two happy parents."

Christy was disoriented by the matter-of-factness of it all. She ordered two primi salads, one beet, one artichoke, and wanted to ask how life could be so straightforward, but felt she could not without revealing her own private torments, so instead she said, "So you met Schuyler and you knew he was the one and you just went for it?"

"I'd been unhappy for a long time. And there was just one moment when I was standing by the water, and I saw a beautiful white bird and it skimmed up into the clouds, flying free, and I knew what I felt and I thought, *Robyn, you need to fly free, too.*"

Christy had no idea Robyn was such a poet.

"I bumped into Lucy Lovett the other day and told her, and she said it was another wonderful/terrible New York story. *So Lucy.*"

Robyn paused as she was overtaken by heartburn. "Then she said something else. She said I had taken on the city and I'd won. I didn't have a clue what she meant." Robyn's heartburn eased, but her confusion did not. "What do you think?"

Christy rolled her eyes dismissively.

"Robyn, I don't know what Lucy's going on about half the time," she said. "Julia says it's like Mornington Crescent, whatever that means, and it's a cultural thing, but she seems to understand her."

But Christy did understand. Lucy had meant that Robyn had exactly the right combination of bravery and ruthlessness required for success in New York, and when the opportunity for a new life had presented itself, she had taken it. Christy knew this because when her opportunity had come, she had not.

"Julia *adores* her," said Robyn meaningfully.

Christy smiled weakly and stabbed an artichoke.

"I think I really love Schuyler," Robyn continued, "but I'm not going to lie. I really love my new life, too. It's a better fit for me. I've been on a long, tough journey, and this is the right ending. I don't feel guilty about *anything*. I'm riding into the sunset. Ooh. The baby's moving."

She said this blithely, her unabashed reincarnation as a Real Housewife complete, and then stood up to go to the bathroom, explaining that the baby had kicked her in the bladder. Christy felt like someone had kicked her in the heart.

When Robyn returned, Christy was examining the dessert menu. To Robyn's surprise, Christy said she would share the chocolate mousse, and they started talking about private schools.

cabin fever

Julia's trick was to cook the turkey upside down. This guaranteed moist juicy breast meat and not the white sawdust-tasting astronaut-chew food people were used to. She had learned this from a cookery demonstration she went to the year she had lived in London, during which she had embraced the full Victorian ideal of Christmas, the holly wreaths, traditional English carols, even brussels sprouts, with the zeal of a convert. Ever since, she strove annually to have at least fifteen family members sitting round her dining table pretending they liked one another, for, as she always said, "Christmas won't be Christmas without any alcohol-fuelled arguments."

Last year her teenage nephew had obliged by setting fire to his hair gel with the end of a joint and, although Kristian had saved the day and possibly the youth's chances of future successful sexual congress by hurling a jug of pomegranate bellini over him, when Julia's unmarried brother Andy, in whose bag the illegal substance had been found, explained that he was taking it for medical reasons only (he lived in Vermont), he and Julia had had a violent dispute, ending in a headlock straight out of WrestleMania, about how Andy had ruined everyone's life with his burgeoning addictive behaviours the year before Julia had left for Barnard.

So Julia had promised Kristian that they would experience the magic of the next holiday season alone, just the four of them, in the cottage upstate, and her parents clearly felt the same way, as they booked themselves onto a three-week cruise in the Caribbean in order to avoid the four days towards the end of December when all hell broke loose. But as November drew to a close, Julia started feeling like a failure, and, under the pretext that it was good for the children to experience the communal table, she invited Lucy and Christy and their families, and for different reasons they both said yes.

Kristian was sanguine about it. He wanted Julia to be happy, because over Thanksgiving, which Julia considered merely a warm-up in the turkey stakes, they had made a Big Life Decision, one he was sure was the right thing for their family. But he worried Julia had not fully reconciled herself to it. He knew this because she had not told Christy, and this was hanging over her like the scent of the eucalyptus candles she began lighting as soon as she woke up on Christmas Eve.

Outside, the elements had bent to her will. It was picture-perfect. A fresh dusting of snow had glazed the garden, the bare trees stuck into the white like twiglets in icing, and Romy's snow*woman*, accessorized with yellow straw hair, a conical bra made out of plastic cups, and false matchstick eye-lashes, stood proud in the middle of it, like a snow Madonna on the Blond Ambition Tour.

It gladdened Julia's heart to see Romy and Lee running out-side in their fleeces, hurling themselves onto the ground and making snow angels. Kristian was happily hauling logs on the sled. All she needed was Judy Garland singing, *"Have Yourself a Merry Little Christmas . . ."* on the soundtrack, and that was easily remedied by pressing the remote play on her iPod, as a selection of holiday classics was already ready to go. She peeled squash and sang along, thinking of Judy and her heartbreaking voice that could bring tears to your eyes with the tiny sob at the end of a line. *"From now on our troubles will be out of sight."* Julia fervently hoped so. She had colour-coordinated her two Christmas trees in the hope that she would find the perfect moment with Christy, the two of them alone in front of the glowing fire, or outside, ruddy-cheeked in the snowscape, where she would make her announcement and they would hug and be happy. That was how she planned it, anyway, and no one knew better than Julia the power of setting up a scene correctly.

In fact, it had been easy to avoid telling Christy anything over the last few months because she had been increasingly preoccupied and distracted. If Julia hadn't known her so well, known that Christy kept no secrets whatsoever from her, she would have sworn she was up to something furtive herself. Christy did not answer her mobile phone, even though she had put a special *boinging* ring on it to tell her it was Julia calling, and didn't ever seem to have the time to chat. This had happened before in their relationship, and Julia assumed it was for the same reason. For while Christy was resolute about not letting her girls become spoiled and extravagant and talk about their full money boxes or bringing child-size cuddly toys home from far-off places by buying an extra seat in first class on the plane, Vaughn was a very rich person, and Julia had long known that the lives of the very rich are not the same as those of the medium or fairly rich. Occasionally, Christy had to get involved in very-rich-person activities such as renovating ski lodges or flying to Barbados to play in charity golf tournaments, which made her distracted and distant, as she never liked to admit to them.

So Julia had begun ringing Lucy when something chatworthy happened; and that was how she had ended up telling her the news first, and realizing that Lucy had somehow usurped Christy in her affections. Julia also realized that this feeling would never be entirely mutual, as Lucy's best friend was Richard and, despite Lucy's occasional intimations about the "ups and downs" they had endured in the past, now they were the happiest couple Julia knew, herself and Kristian included.

Romy was shouting something outside, and Julia looked out of the window and witnessed Lucy and Richard's arrival, the rumbling of the tiny rental car muffled by the duvet of snow. It was like watching a silent film as their boys tumbled out of the back seat, scrapping, and Richard leapt out after them, lifting the smallest up and spinning him round, taking in the 360 degrees of expansive views around them. Lucy appeared now, a guitar case in her right hand, and when she handed it to Richard he threw his other arm around her, gesticulating and talking and thinking and talking again.

Kristian came over, embraced them, and led them to the former Oat Store where they were going to camp out together. Julia had been embarrassed offering them this accommodation (Christy had pre-empted it by saying she would check her family into a suite at the Luxury Olde Inn down the road, as Vaughn always made clear that he liked nature as long as it wasn't natural), but Richard had enthusiastically announced that he had been awarded thirty Cub Scout badges (including air activities) in the three years his father had been posted in Hong Kong, and it would be good for Lucy to learn how to tie a reef knot and melt snow in an empty baked-beans can. Julia had then felt embarrassed to tell him the building actually had a bathroom, electric heating, and wiring for cable TV, so she had whispered it to Lucy, who visibly relaxed and surprised Richard by her enthusiasm for the survivalist experience.

Lucy bounded up the path, marvelling at the size of the enormous footprints she made in her wader boots.

"It's like yeti tracks," she said, kissing Julia firmly on the cheek in the doorway.

"What's a yeti?" asked Max, pausing only briefly to drop greying chunks of wet snow on the tiles before hurling himself towards Lee, who had two-player Guitar Hero ready to go in the den.

"A great hairy beast," Julia called after him. "Nothing at all like your mother."

"You haven't seen my legs," said Lucy. "I don't shave them after the clocks change for winter."

"Really? Does Richard go for that?"

"Yes, he's got some posh-boy thing for the peasantry. It makes him feel very *droit de seigneur* pillaging a filthy local maiden. ROBBIE! What the *hell* do you think you're doing?"

On the path behind her, Robbie had pulled down his track-pants and was sending a yellow arc of urine rippling into a flower bed.

"I am mortified," declared Lucy for good form's sake, though it wasn't actually true, but Julia just smiled and went out to peer at the evidence as one day at her very worst, exhausted, white-as-a-sheet former self on the Crime Show, the Asshole had told her that her eyes looked like piss-holes in the snow, and she had often wondered what that really looked like. (Boreholes with a greenish-yellow tinge at the top. *Interesting.*)

She returned to the kitchen to see that Lucy had pulled open the oven door to peer at the enormous brisket roasting inside, the smells enveloping the room with the promise of satisfaction and happiness and all good things.

"I'm glad I didn't offer to bring any food. I mean, you are so domestic goddess."

"I know," Julia said, and grinned. "And you wait till tomorrow. I'm only getting started. It'll be the full monty . . . isn't that what you lot say? *All the trimmings round the bird.*"

Lucy flinched involuntarily. Not only had Julia's approximation of an English accent (a cross between Joan Collins and Rupert Everett) sounded exactly like a sadistic art teacher she had loathed, but the very use of the word "bird" for turkey brought back all her unfortunate memories of Christmases in her childhood which mainly involved overcooked or undercooked "birds" and, one year, a sherry-soaked argument between her parents so ferocious that it ended with her mother throwing a sherry-soaked trifle, in its glass dish, at a group of carollers from the local Church of England and breaking the vicar's baby toe.

Julia didn't laugh when Lucy explained this. Whenever she got such throwaway glimpses of Lucy's childhood, she marvelled at how her friend had ever survived to become halfway sane.

"Oh, well." Lucy wanted to move on to the happier present. "Now. Have you told Christy yet?"

Julia shook her head and started to make gravy. Lucy's eyes widened as she pondered the implications of this. Julia had promised a stress-free holiday among friends, and, while she could not imagine a trifle-throwing competition breaking out between them, she had witnessed enough of the intense nature of their friendship to be concerned about how Christy might take Julia's news. She glanced up at the clock.

"When are she and Vaughn due?"

"The middle of April," boomed a male voice behind them. "How did you know?"

Lucy and Julia turned to see Vaughn, charismatic and handsome with the new, carefully trimmed white beard he had grown, in an Italian duffel coat, carrying four bottles of whiskey with a huge designer poinsettia balanced precariously on top.

"Know what?" said Julia, rather more aggressively, thought Lucy, than one would normally expect when welcoming guests for a holiday lunch.

"Know that Christy's pregnant," replied Vaughn, refusing to falter, in the voice that had launched a thousand hostile takeovers.

At this moment Christy appeared, ravishing in a white ankle-length coat, the two girls beside her in matching red capes, all their hoods and eyelids flecked with fresh snow. As she stood next to Vaughn, it was as if Merlin had married a benevolent Snow Queen and they had given birth to two Little Red Riding Hoods. Christy was carrying three Bloomingdale's big bags full of presents wrapped by the service. Mindful of her condition, Lucy hastily took these.

"It's really starting to come down out there," Christy said. "Thank goodness it's so warm in here." But as she said this her voice trailed off as she felt the temperature around her dropping once again.

"What's up?" And she looked at Vaughn.

"The ladies were talking about due-*ness*, and . . . I misheard . . . so I let our . . . *news* slip."

"So many congratulations to both of you," said Lucy warmly, kissing Vaughn on both cheeks and embracing Christy while leaving space around her stomach with appropriate sensitivity. It was as if such news were a completely normal occurrence, and Christy blinked in surprise. There was such a depressing lack of drama about Lucy sometimes.

At least over by the oven it was not only the gravy that was simmering.

"Why didn't you tell me?" said Julia, and then, "*How could you?*"

And so Christy, caught off guard, disoriented, who had had a speech ready for when she and Julia were alone later that day, possibly by the glowing fire, possibly ruddy cheeked in the snowscape, felt robbed of her moment delivering the news of her Big Life Decision. Now disappointed, she decided to deliberately misunderstand what Julia had said.

"How dare you? What do you mean *How could I*? I'm not that old. And neither is Vaughn."

"I have to disagree with you about that, my dear," said Vaughn, who was working out how quickly they could make a dignified exit, "but as I told her, Julia, at least I won't have to deal with the appalling teenage years, because I intend to be dead."

He reached for Julia's hand and gripped it. They had always got on well. She looked at the liver spots on his paper-thin skin and the veins knotted beneath it.

"I'm sorry, Vaughn. You know I didn't mean—"

"I know, sweetheart. But even this won't keep me alive forever, and other people will think and say it, and we would be well advised to prepare ourselves."

Christy knew this remark was directed at her, just as she knew her continuing obsessive secrecy was all about avoiding tut-tutting and raised eyebrows and too-long pauses before half-hearted congratulations, so she adopted a mama-grizzly tone and directed it back to Vaughn.

"I don't give a damn what anyone else thinks. This is only about my family."

"I rather think, Christy, that this is all about *you*," he replied.

"I'm not feeling very well," she said. "I'm afraid I'll have to go back to the inn."

"No one's going anywhere at the moment, baby." Vaughn

pointed to the window, where at least four inches of snow were piled up on the outside mantel; picture-perfect had become *The Shining*.

Julia glanced at Christy, whose face had blanched and whose eyes were like piss-holes in the snow. Then she glanced over at Vaughn. He was shifting uncomfortably from foot to foot, reacting physically to the unusual feeling of being stuck somewhere he didn't want to be, in this case a wood-framed cottage inside a snow globe, complete with two colour-coordinated Christmas trees, small shouting children, and the ever-present threat of someone trying to start a board game. He was staring at the bottles of whiskey on the table with the meditative intensity of a Buddhist monk. It was obvious that his attitude to his impending new fatherhood could best be de-scribed as ambivalent and, even as Julia was furious with Christy for keeping it all secret, not to mention her weird jealousy as she was reminded of how much she would have liked a third child herself if she had not been so terrified of post-partum psychosis, she wanted to protect Christy from the way Vaughn could be when he decided to, and so she decided to get a grip.

"I'm *delighted* for you both," she said, chivvying Lucy and the girls to round up the others for lunch and absentmindedly handing Vaughn cutlery to set the table with, forgetting that he had not done such a thing for at least thirty-five years.

(He obeyed, of course; the situation had all the elements of the first act of a play. Not a tragedy, perhaps, but certainly a drawing-room farce.)

"Yes. It's wonderful," replied Christy. "The best news ever."

(Who else, Vaughn wondered, was going to come bouncing in through the door, overhear the end of a conversation, misconstrue it, and utter an ill-timed revelation?)

"I'm so glad you feel that way." It was Kristian, who had entered carrying the coal bucket and ran over to embrace Christy by vigorously rubbing his chest against hers to avoid putting his blackened hands on her.

"You know I've thought for a long time we needed to get out of the city and so I'm just thrilled that you support us. It'll mean so much to Julia. Right, darling?"

Christy looked at him, confused. Kristian looked at Julia, confused.

"You have told them, haven't you?"

"*Told us what?*" said the Snow Queen snowily.

"We're moving to LA in the New Year."

There was a pause. Then Christy burst out laughing.

"Good one." She looked at Julia. "*You? LA?* You loathe all that sunshine and positivity. What you gonna do? Grow organic vegetables and build a henhouse?"

"Well, yes," said Kristian, his lower lip starting to tremble.

"You can't leave the city, Julia. You only look right next to concrete and glass. And you're not safe driving a car. I've never heard such a ridiculous idea."

But to Christy's amazement, Julia walked over to her husband and put her arm around his waist.

"No, Christy. We are going. Next month. The kids are

starting school there. I'm sorry, I tried to say something, but you've been in a strange mood for weeks and . . . now I know why . . ."

Kristian felt nervous. He was concerned that he was in trouble for doing something, but he had no clue what it might be.

"Christy's *pregnant*," Julia explained, and although this was part elucidation, it was not all.

"I need a drink," said Vaughn.

"Absolutely," said Kristian, suddenly feeling on safer ground. "Let's celebrate. I'll get the champagne."

"No, no," said Vaughn. "I'll have whiskey."

Christy hadn't been listening to any of this. A sudden hopeful thought had struck her.

"Are you feeling . . . *okay*, Julia?" she began, with a meaningful look at Kristian. "Isn't this sort of thing, a mad irrational decision that could have catastrophic consequences for your life, exactly what the doctors told you could precede a manic episode?"

"I don't know, Christy," Julia replied frostily. "What's your excuse?"

"We want food! We want food!"

Vaughn shuddered. Max and Robbie were marching in at the head of a line of children, Lucy and Richard laughing indulgently behind them. Julia, who had now totally lost interest in her perfect hostess thing, plonked the lunch onto unwarmed plates with the gracelessness of an underpaid school dinner lady and poured herself a four-unit glass of red wine while

Christy stared accusingly at her. They both sank into their chairs and sulky silence, leaving it to Lucy to hurl herself once more unto the breach by regaling the table with stories on a tangential holiday theme.

The first was about a job in Yorkshire she had once had with her friend Camilla. Lucy and Camilla, wearing green tights and red sweaters to give a sense of elfishness, had been employed by a farmer to take five live reindeer, dressed up with bells on their horns and red coats with a white furry trim, round to local fairs in nearby country towns. Then they would charge the parents of small children for the delight of a ride in a sleigh, a small cart on wheels that had been covered in festive wrapping paper, to visit Santa, who would inevitably be an unemployed actor of wide girth who would equally inevitably encourage Lucy and Camilla to sit on his knee. Kristian smiled encouragingly at Lucy, hoping that this monologue might continue with an amusing anecdote not involving bottom pinching, a moral, or perhaps an unexpected insight into Lucy's personality, but no, Lucy had finished at the point where it was simply a humiliating but successful business opportunity.

"What happened to the reindeer in the spring?" he asked.

"Oh, two of them caught TB off a badger and died, and I think the other three . . . you know . . ."

Kristian did not know, so Lucy was forced to make a small throat-slitting gesture with the forefinger of her right hand.

"When you cure reindeer meat, it tastes like prosciutto,"

said Richard cheerfully, kissing the side of Lucy's face. Then he looked over at Vaughn. "We're going to hear the patter of tiny feet ourselves soon."

Before Vaughn had time to begin to make sense of this, Lucy elbowed Richard in the chest and explained.

"We bought a puppy—it's coming in a week. Right, boys?" Max and Robbie elbowed each other in the head, fell off their chairs, and rolled on the rug.

"It's my lovely little girl at last," giggled Lucy.

Christy looked up, triumphant. She had been waiting for a wry joke or a wistful comment to indicate that Lucy had secretly always wanted another baby. She had been looking forward to this on the journey.

"Would you like to have another baby?" she asked.

Lucy did not bat an eyelid. By now she was used to the inappropriately personal question as small talk. It was, she knew, simply a fact of life in New York.

"God, no," she replied. "I'm far too old."

"You could adopt," Christy retorted, feeling quite desperate now. (She knew Lucy was several years younger than she was.)

"No, I'm temperamentally unsuited to the process. I wanted to get a puppy from the dog rescue, couldn't see why we couldn't give a home to some runt thrown out of a lorry on the Interstate (Julia had told Christy that this was how some English people dealt with unwanted pets—Christy had found it very disturbing), but honestly, after five minutes of them telling me about all the questionnaires I'd have to fill in, and making a date for the accommodation inspection, and practically having to swear on the Bible I'd never go away on holiday, I told them, no, that's okay, I'll just buy one."

"Darling Lucy," said Richard affectionately. "Please don't equate the adoption process with dog rescue."

"All I'm saying is, unless I could be handed a child from somewhere, and preferably one of at least five years old, I wouldn't want another one. Does that sound terrible?"

"No," intoned Vaughn. "It sounds eminently sensible."

And he downed another triple whiskey with a ruthless, manly efficiency that made the other two men feel soft and inadequate. (Kristian, in particular, made a mental note never to use moisturizer again.)

So that was that. Christy fell silent. There would be no validation for her reproductive superiority. Lucy changed the subject.

"Now, who wants to hear about the summer I waitressed in the Aloha Motel in Atlantic City, where I had to wear a grass hula skirt and balance a live parrot on my shoulder?"

Christy struggled to conceal a yawn. She had no wish to hear the end of this story, which, if Lucy continued true to form, would be that the parrot was now deceased. Fortunately, Lucy's boys intervened by making loud groaning noises and demanding to watch television.

"Nonsense," barked Lucy briskly. "We'll play charades. Come on, children. Follow me." And to the other adults' amazement, they did.

Vaughn stood up and repaired to a bedroom with another bottle, where he sat on a yoga ball and thought about his life. Richard and Kristian fled the melancholy silence of the kitchen to act out *Harry Potter and the Deathly Hallows* using Julia's incense sticks as magic wands.

Now alone, Christy spoke first.

"I'm sorry, Julia. This isn't how I wanted to tell you."

"Ditto," replied Julia, but she said nothing more, and neither did Christy. They both knew this was not the right moment for their conversation, but whether there would ever be a right moment they did not know. Something big had happened between them, Christy was sure of it, and, although she should have said that she was delighted for Julia, too, she was gripped by a terrible panic that it was the beginning of the end of their friendship, which would dissolve into three illegible scribbled lines on a holiday card every year. Worst of all, she realized that in the past she would have known, but today she found it impossible to tell what Julia was thinking.

In fact, what Julia was thinking was that at least with family when they were annoying or deceitful you could shout at them or make incredibly nasty comments in front of or behind their backs or give your siblings Chinese burns and everyone would shrug and accept it. But such behaviour was not possible with friends, even when they did not behave like friends. So she turned up "O Holy Night" to squeeze out the silence between them, and Christy walked out into the hallway, where Lucy and Richard were now standing hand in hand, peering into the swirling whiteness and talking about arctic exploration and one Captain Oates from Scott's tragic expedition who had walked out into a blizzard, announcing, "I'm going out—I may be some time." Christy hoped no one was getting any ideas from this.

Lucy demanded they hush and listen to the wind as it whistled and howled around them. Now she started talking about traditional Irish music, in particular a tune that a group of sailors said they had been given by the wind. Richard listened with a kind of awe. To him, Lucy was the most fascinating person he had ever met. As Christy watched them, an overwhelming sadness came upon her.

She peeped round the door of the den to see all the children rapt in front of *The Sound of Music*, so she climbed the wooden staircase to find Vaughn. Vaughn was always able to parachute in and out of situations at will, and if anyone could haul himself out of a snowdrift, it was him. In the distance she heard his voice muttering and discovered him in the master bedroom, watching Fox News and shouting at the television.

When he saw her he calmed his tone, and told her that they were going to have to stay the night, as travel was impossible. She was amazed at his equanimity.

"I'm tired," he said, though whether this was a general statement or specific to today she could not tell. Then he turned back to Sean Hannity.

Christy lay down beside him and absorbed the events of the day so far. *Julia. Leaving. New York.* Unthinkable. Of all the possible dramatic twists to the plot of Julia's life, this one had honestly never occurred to her. For the fact was that Christy needed Julia to get through the next stage of her pregnancy. She had planned on them going to the scans together like a glamorous lesbian couple and watching the baby wave at them in black and white. Julia might even be present at the birth this time, and would certainly visit Christy on a daily basis as she lay blissful but broken apart in the few weeks after delivery. Such acts were things she would never expect of Vaughn. After all, wasn't that how most women got through the vicissitudes of new motherhood? It was the daily snatched conversations over neighbourhood coffees with other warriors on the front line of maternity that saw you through the battles of sleep deprivation, hormonal fluctuations, and the annihilation of your former self.

Julia's presence was vital to Christy's picture of herself and the new child. Christy had made her decision knowing that her life would change but assuming that everyone else's would stay the same.

"You'll miss Julia when she leaves," said Vaughn matter-of-factly, switching off the TV, his eyes beginning to close.

"Yes." Then she whispered to herself, "I didn't think I'd be doing it on my own."

But Vaughn had heard her.

"You won't be on your own."

And she smiled and snuggled up beside him.

"You'll have to get a nanny now. I suggest two," and he curled onto his side and fell asleep immediately.

She stared up at the ceiling, which was plaster, and beamed, very cosy, very un-Julia, in fact, and rested her hand on her swelling belly, waiting for the fluttering and gurgling that told her all was well, new life was coming. Perhaps unsurprisingly, she thought about the first Christmas and Mary, nine months pregnant on a donkey, jigging over hills into Bethlehem. *What a nightmare!* she thought.

She was awoken about an hour later by the sound of a guitar playing, a soft, plangent series of chords, and then a young boy, his voice high and pure like the angels that appeared to the shepherds that night, began to sing.

In the bleak midwinter
Frosty wind made moan.

She stood up carefully—the nausea of early pregnancy had left her, but sudden movements made her dizzy—and crept out into the hallway.

Earth stood hard as iron,
Water like a stone.

Outside, halfway up the stairs, Julia was waiting for her. "It's our favourite carol," she said.

Christy nodded.

"You've got to hand it to Christianity, really," Julia continued. "The nativity, it's such a powerful, beautiful story of hope." She paused. "Of course, the whole God-is-a-child thing is a bit weird."

Then she looked at Christy.

"But the birth of every baby is a miracle."

Christy smiled and walked down towards her, and they went into the kitchen and sat in front of the glowing embers of the fire in there, and they delivered their speeches softly to each other.

Christy was brief and pithy. She described how she had been overcome once again by feelings of entrapment, but this time it was about the years and the girls slipping away from her, the circumstances of her marriage to Vaughn (or rather the state of affairs between them), and the nurse she would inevitably become, dictating her choices. She had decided that there had to be one thing in her life just for her, so she had given Vaughn an ultimatum. The thing she wanted more than anything else was a baby and, knowing that when a woman wants a baby only a baby will do, Vaughn, determined not to lose her, had reluctantly agreed to the defrosting of two of their previous embryos, taking comfort in the extraordinary unlikelihood of the odds and their compromise, which had been they would try only once. Yet Christy had become pregnant and, although she had miscarried one of the twins early on, she had clung to the other with all her might. It was a boy. Unto them a son would be born.

This, finally, had banished Christy's cabin fever.

Now it was Julia's turn, and by contrast she was long-winded and meandering. She started by describing her life as a Venn diagram, with circles and oblongs representing children, work, marriage, and friends, and how increasingly it seemed impossible to make everything coexist in a harmonious pattern and she feared she was slipping back into the kind of behaviours that had sent her out of her mind and into the Wellness Center before. It was just harder to stay up all night glugging Red Bull laced with vodka in Malibu, where eighty-year-olds jogged past you on the beach at six o'clock in the morning and drinking two delicious lychee Martinis was viewed with the same horror as shooting up heroin, apart from by the people who were shooting up heroin, of course. But she had already lost Christy by this point, so she started again with herself, Kristian, and the kids stuck in the car park that the Holland Tunnel often became at weekends and holidays.

The children, tied into the back seat, were moaning loudly about the fact that neither she nor Kristian would allow them to play with what were always contemptuously referred to as "electronic devices", and Lee almost decapitated himself by craning his neck out of a window to try to watch *Up* on a screen in the land cruiser in the lane next to them. That day, the Wednesday before Thanksgiving, after they had finally given in and handed over their mobile phones switched to game apps, they emerged from the tunnel into horizontal rain lashing against the windscreen like a carwash, Kristian had good-humouredly turned to Julia and, laughing, said, "How d'you feel about Southern California?" and she had said, "You're right. It's time." Kristian had then stalled the car in shock, causing a trumpet of car horns from behind them, which underlined the solemnity of Julia's statement.

Romy was already showing distressing signs of creativity and the accompanying emotional fragility, so while Julia continued to encourage her ten-year-old towards a sensible occupation (when Christy asked her what such an occupation might be, Julia replied "cardiac surgeon"), she feared it was too late. Romy was already on the first chapter of a novel called *The Fear in Me*, was the lead singer in her band, and it was increasingly apparent to Julia that a new stage of family life was upon her—a stage where her daughter needed her not to expend vast amounts of energy obsessing about who was the lead in the school play but just to sit on the end of her bed every night and talk about how it felt to be, well . . . like her.

Julia had held out hopes that Lee, who was extremely good-looking, sensibly intelligent without being flashy, and brilliant at sports would not require the same level of maternal time investment. This made him her favourite, though she would never admit it to anyone, even Christy, mainly because he was far less exhausting, although she knew that it was also because she, who had been the tall, skinny, brainy girl humiliated by the cheerleaders and whose best friend was her hamster, was delighted to have given birth to one golden child. But even he had started writing acrostic poems about the different seasons, and Kristian reported that in the one called

W

I

N

T

E

R

he had written *Wishing for fields and mountains* at the beginning.

One thing was for sure. Julia knew when to hold them and when to fold them. She would never lose her passion for New York, but she could love it from a distance. Within a fortnight she had found a house just off Broad Beach to rent, a good school with huge windows and a soccer pitch nearby, and a tenant for the loft on Rivington Street. Lucy and Richard were making noises about buying the cottage upstate because Lucy had come into some money after her mother died. Julia was not even annoyed when Kristian declared this was all synchronicity; she was finding his New Agey-ness endearing these days, and anyway, he was right. The kids would be surfing, and he would be running breath workshops in Montecito within days of their arrival, and, while she would never be a person described as "laid-back", she might no longer be one who hovered on the edge of a nervous breakdown at least once a month. No, everything had clicked into place with a devastating momentum.

"And it's not like I'll never see you again," she finished. "I'll have to stay at your place when I come back for work."

Christy reached over and took her hand.

OUTSIDE, THE SNOW had settled, and, from the bustle in the hallway, they realized that Lucy and Richard were bundling the children into their outdoor clothes and snow shoes.

"Where are Christy and Julia?" called Richard, as he headed out.

"In the den, probably," replied Lucy. "Leave them, they need a little chat."

"Even I, insensitive male that I am, could tell there was a bit of aggro."

"Oh, they'll be fine," whispered Lucy, and they could hear the grin in her voice. "It was just a storm in a PMT cup."

They could hear Richard laughing behind the closed front door.

Julia looked at Christy apologetically.

"I like her," said Christy, and they hugged and wished each other happy holidays, though inside they didn't know whether to laugh or cry.

one thousand
words a day

It was dark outside, although the bars on the tiny windows in the dingy classroom wouldn't have let much light in, anyway. Lucy sat at the desk, arranging her pens and blank pad in a neat pattern in front of her. She looked up and smiled nervously once at the other people in the room: four other women aged between eighteen and eighty, and two grey-haired men who looked more scared than she was. She picked up her pen and wrote the date, January 21, underlined it using the spine of the *People* magazine that she had in her handbag, and quickly stuffed it back in. It wasn't quite the image of herself she wanted to portray in a creative writing class where the serious-looking woman next to her was reading *Freedom* and nodding earnestly every couple of paragraphs.

Julia had given Lucy the course as a present before she left for LA. They were sitting in Café Mogador having a farewell breakfast when Julia handed her an envelope which contained details of the place and time of the course (every Wednesday night for the next eight weeks, seven until ten o'clock) and a receipt indicating she had booked Lucy in and paid for it.

"Don't worry, it wasn't expensive," she said reassuringly. "It's taught by Ryan James—you know, Robyn Skinner's ex. Don't know if he's any good, but it doesn't matter. I just really feel you should do it. You need to *do* something, Lucy."

Lucy nodded. In Julia she had found a friend with whom such directness could be given and taken without rancour, in the spirit of the generosity Julia always showed. The question of whether writing could indeed be a suitable occupation for Lucy had been vexing them for many months now, and she and Julia had discussed different possibilities at length. For although her life was full and busy and exhausting these days (with young children and housework and volunteering at the school and being happily married), Lucy still found herself considering *Is that all there is?* and wanted something more, something that was not just about financial independence, though that was certainly a desire that had been reawakened in her, but would give her the confidence to sashay through middle age like Tina Turner, with her skirts hiked above her fantastic legs. Julia encouraged her in this determination.

"What are we all meant to do, Lucy?" she would say. "Lie down and die? *I don't think so.*"

Lucy didn't think so, either, which is why she thanked Julia from the bottom of her heart and promised faithfully she would attend.

At that moment, Julia's attention had been diverted by a text coming through called *News About You!* Julia explained that some underpaid minion in her agent Clarice's office had the job of scanning all media for references to clients.

"It's very interesting," she said. "Sometimes I learn things about myself I never even knew."

Today however, the minion had made the colossal error of telling Julia that a Julia Kirkland had died yesterday of complications of emphysema at the age of 103. This threatened to ruin Julia's morning, as she couldn't help but wonder if it was some strange portent, but after another cup of coffee she brightened—103 was a damn good age, after all—and suggested to Lucy that she make it the first line of a story. *That morning, Julia learned she had died*, or something like that.

"I wouldn't want to write about you," replied Lucy.

"It wouldn't be about me, necessarily. Or if it were, you could just change my name."

Lucy suddenly remembered Richard telling her what Kristian with a *K* had said about Julia before she had ever met her.

"Is that why all artists need the 'splinter of ice'?"

"Oh, please," Julia snorted dismissively. "Kristian's always banging on about that, but I think it's just silly. All artists use things that have happened to them, whether they paint, or act, or write. It helps to make sense of everything. Anyway, my dear, in case you hadn't noticed, you have the splinter of ice, too. With you it's the ability to distance yourself from people and observe them."

"That doesn't sound like a great thing when you say it out loud. You know, for a person to be like that. *Distant.*"

"Why? I think it could give you a voice. A way of writing about life the way you see it. You have a distinctive view of the world. That's why you should use it. Mark my words, Lucy. You have something to say."

Lucy smiled. "I'm going to miss you."

"Ditto," said Julia. "You'll have to come visit me in Lotus Land. Make sure Kristian doesn't force me into buying a juicer and doing family yoga."

"That'll never happen."

"You're right." She glanced at her watch. "Gotta go. The new tenant wants me to change the blinds to match the sofas. He's German," she added, as if this were an explanation.

Lucy was dragged back to the moment by the appalling noise of chalk and nail scratching on a blackboard and saw Ryan, central-casting creative writing teacher in glasses and a brown corduroy jacket, his body language indicating his enjoyment of this intoxicating combination of pedagogy and tight jeans, scrawling words with a flamboyant flick of his right wrist. *Stop it!* she thought, as she caught herself doing this, *holding herself back and observing* as, despite Julia's words ringing in her ears, she had resolved to stop the *distant* thing. Surreptitiously she slid her plastic magic magnifier out of her wallet and peered through it at the blackboard, on which was now written ONE THOUSAND WORDS A DAY. She glanced around to see her fellow participants dutifully copying this into their notebooks. Lemming-like, she followed suit.

Ryan spun round, ran his chalky hand through his boyish crop of hair, and grinned. "That's all you need to know," he said.

Lucy re-evaluated. When Ryan was with Robyn she had never thought him the remotest bit attractive.

"One thousand words a day," he continued. "That's the thing about writing. You sit down and you do it. I hope this course will give you some tools, but if you can't commit to the thousand-words-a-day rule"—he paused, catching the eye of the most obviously attractive female in the room, a twenty-five-year-old social studies student called Dianne—"stand up, take your stuff, and leave!"

Lucy wondered if anyone had ever actually gone at this moment and what would happen if she did, but Ryan was now circling the room, soliciting introductions and expressions of intent. There was the lovely Dianne, who wanted to express herself. Roger and Stu, who wanted to do that, too (Stu on the instruction of his therapist). Marian, a stick-thin eighteen-year-old, who planned a career in songwriting, and her mother, serious-looking Jennifer, who wanted to do "something for herself". Betty, an unfriendly, wizened septuagenarian who really did have the face she deserved, tut-tutted at this (although Lucy knew exactly what Jennifer meant) before ranting on about why all contemporary fiction sucked for about five minutes, *"It's psychotherapy masquerading as plot"*, and finally announcing that she had been working on her memoir for the last ten years.

Finally, Ryan turned to Lucy and actually saw her. By the way he double-took, she knew he was trying to remember how he knew her, failing, and then worrying about the increasing number of senior moments he had experienced recently, so she put him out of his misery by declaring that their kids used to go to the same school. She told the room that she had studied literature, worked in publishing (when Ryan flinched, she assured him she had been a lowly editorial assistant in nonfiction), taken time out to be with her children and support her husband's career (when Betty flinched she wanted to say that Richard's career was brilliant no longer and they were all the better for it, but it felt too convoluted and disloyal), but somehow a few years' break had turned into ten as if by magic. Then she told them that she had turned forty this year and, although everyone said to her it shouldn't be a crossroads, it sure as hell felt like one, so she had decided to get off her arse and try something she had always felt she could do. For, after all, what was the point of reading a book and thinking *"I could do that"* when the only valid response would be, *"Maybe, but you didn't, did you?"*

Jennifer smiled and clapped her hands together, reflecting the waft of approval emanating from round the room; even Betty could not think of a sneering riposte, and Ryan nodded in a sincere manner. Lucy stared down at her empty pad with the date neatly written across it, considering how pathetic it was that she could experience an intoxicating sense of achievement simply by speaking in front of strangers.

To begin, Ryan asked them to think of a headline in a newspaper or on the Internet that they felt could inspire a story. Who were the characters? What were the events? How would they tell it? Lucy immediately thought of an article she had seen in the *New York Post* and laughed out loud, startling herself as much as everyone else. Ryan looked at her curiously, so she had to explain. The article was about a pensioner who had poisoned forty-seven police officers with dodgy tuna melts over a two-year period.

"Great," said Ryan, hoisting himself onto Dianne's desk, his manly thighs spreading slightly so she had to pull her pencil case away. "Let's run with that. Betty, who is this woman?"

Betty was not amused. "Why would you ask me? And why do you assume it's a woman?"

"Fair point," said Ryan, thinking *What big ears you have, Granny*, and asked Roger for his thoughts. Roger tactfully suggested it was a man called Stu, because he couldn't think of another name on the spot, who harboured a secret resentment towards the police because—

"His wife left him for a station sergeant," piped up Marian. And Jennifer added, "With a big nose," and they both laughed ruefully in tones redolent of private meaning.

"Yes," said Stu in the deep, husky tones of a presenter of late-night jazz, which startled everyone, as he had not spoken up to this point, "and my, I mean Stu's, restaurant was closed down after I fled to Paris to train as a pastry chef because of malicious claims by my ex and her husband."

"This should be set somewhere else," said Dianne. "How about Corleone. It's in Sicily."

"Do they have tuna melts in Italy?" remarked Betty sourly.

"If it were an American restaurant they would," said Ryan, both chivalrous and grammatically correct.

And Lucy, though silent, was happy. And while she hoped fervently that Ryan would not end the class with any profound statements along the lines of the longest journey beginning with the first step, or some such version relating to a large book and a single letter, as she looked around her she knew it was true.

Anyway, he didn't. Ryan was much less annoying as a teacher at night school than as an unhappily married parent you had to make small talk about the school nits epidemic with at the Halloween barbecue.

Lucy tried to get into a groove. After the boys went to school she would spend half an hour cleaning and tidying the apartment, take the puppy to relieve itself in Tompkins Square Park, walk along First Avenue to Abraço to buy the best cup of coffee in the neighbourhood, and then return ready to sit down in front of the laptop. Ceremonially, she placed the coffee on her right, a pad for notes on her left, the puppy by her feet, and then she removed a Post-it from under the desk, the days when they were used to give orders to the staff long gone, and stuck it on the wall in front of her.

One thousand words a day was written on it.

That was the easy part.

She enjoyed the challenge of the writing exercises Ryan set them. She described a memorable incident from her school-days (this was pure fiction, as she did not want to share the truly memorable ones), she dramatized a historical event from her own perspective (the morning of August 31, 1997, when she had awoken to Camilla shrieking down the hall of their flat in Bayswater that Diana, Princess of Wales, had died), and she wrote a surprising monologue for a fictional character (she imagined that Melanie Wilkes in *Gone with the Wind* hated Scarlett O'Hara, which was how Lucy herself felt). But once her homework was done, the lure of displacement over-whelmed her. She would stand up, gather the latest of the never-ending piles of washing, and walk to the launderette thinking about the evening's dinner. Often she took a short detour to see if *Hello!* had come into the International News-agents on Fifth Street. One day she rang Julia in desperation, looking for inspiration, but Julia was lost in Beverly Hills, late for a breakfast meeting with someone so famous she couldn't say who it was, and had just spilled a double macchiato down her James Perse lounging T-shirt while doing a U-turn, so a garbled "Write something you'd like to read yourself" was the best she could do. It did not help. Lucy struggled to type a single word a day.

Her fellow classmates did not seem to have such difficulty. She had had a long chat with Roger the previous week about how he had written not one but three unpublished books. He would come home after a day working in the archives of the New York Public Library, cook himself dinner, and then write for a couple of hours. This in itself seemed to give him great pleasure, and he described how seeing letters form his words on the screen in front of him made him feel alive. Lucy found this inspirational. She found the sight of Marian, Dianne, and Jennifer reading their paragraphs out loud to one another before class moving. She came to admire Betty's dogged refusal to accept that her own life was less valuable or interesting than anyone else's. Even withdrawn Stu opened up, telling her he loved books because he was fascinated by typefaces and the effect they might or might not have on the reader. Because she had worked in publishing she was able to discuss with him the different meanings of regal Times New Roman or perky **Arial** or reassuring **Rockwell**.

There was no doubt about it, Lucy loved books and words and using phrases like *a concatenation of circumstances*, but, although comfortable with the life, as she had always relished a certain amount of aloneness, she quickly came to feel that she was not cut out to be a writer. Take adjectives, for example. How could you ever describe something in a new way, a way that wasn't a cliché? When Lucy thought about the snow at Julia's over Christmas, the only adjective that came to mind was "white". It was frustrating and she was useless, and Julia had been quite wrong to give her false hope. She would have to train to be a teacher, the only other profession she could think of to do, despite the fact she disliked all children except her own. She lamented her hubris at length to the puppy inside and outside the apartment, and because the little dog woofed adoringly whenever Lucy paused for breath, passers-by thought she was training her and not crazy.

She was full of fear and self-loathing as, halfway through the course, she trudged into the classroom fifteen minutes late, the sound of the boys' hysterical refusal to eat their spaghetti ringing in her ears. Ryan introduced her to his partner, Catalina, who had arrived in leather leggings, bearing cup-cakes for the break, and at whom Dianne was staring viciously. Perhaps because of the presence of the leather leggings, Ryan was on top form this particular evening, announcing that the session tonight was inspired by William Carlos Williams, doctor and poet, and his philosophy that poetry could be about the everyday circumstances of life. Ryan scribbled *NO IDEAS, BUT IN THINGS* on the blackboard and allotted the group fifteen minutes to write a free-form poem about a specific incident in their life with no embellishment or allusion other than what *actually happened*, before disappearing out of the door with Catalina.

Oh, God, thought Lucy. *Now it's like an exam I haven't prepared for*, which was a nightmare she still occasionally endured, sitting bolt upright in the early hours of the morning, trying to remember how to use a slide rule to calculate average speed using distance travelled/time taken. But then she reminded herself that she had always been very good at exams and the trick with an exam was to answer the questions. So she focused on thinking about something that had actually happened that afternoon and, to her amazement, she started to write.

She had just dotted the full stop at the end when Ryan reappeared, ever so slightly dishevelled with what looked like photocopier ink on his neck, and told them to read their poems. Lucy was anxious to get her turn over with so she could concentrate on the others, so she hurried through her effort, which she called "Homework with My Nine-Year-Old". Dianne point-blank refused. (Lucy guessed she had written about a romantic incident designed to inflame Ryan's jealousy, then thought better of it.) Marian, in monotone, described hiding in a wardrobe the day her father walked out to live with the woman with the big nose, which left Jennifer in tears as she read her poem about growing a beautiful sunflower from a seed. Roger told of the day he touched a first edition of *Leaves of Grass*, Betty of her hip replacement, and Stu recalled being on vacation in Jamaica and his taxi driver being shot in front of him, brains spattering all over the windscreen (*No wonder he needs a therapist*, they all thought).

Ryan did not congratulate or criticize, he listened and made constructive comments, and all felt proud and energized and excited, apart from Dianne. But now that she had witnessed the reality of Catalina, and was liberated from the burden of flirting with Ryan, she, too, started to concentrate.

Meanwhile, Lucy's block had disappeared, risen like a portcullis, allowing invading ideas to storm in, and, as she looked round the room, sentences were forming, images appearing, *no ideas, but in things*. And wasn't that what Julia had been trying to say to her all along? Begin with what you see and go from there.

That evening she came through the door and found Richard half asleep on the sofa, the *Times* crossword half finished across his chest.

She leant over and kissed his forehead. His eyes flickered open, and he looked at her and told her she looked beautiful, and he asked her what she had done at her class. She replied that she had written a poem in fifteen minutes and he asked her to read it, which she then did. He told her it was good and he was proud of her and she should really give writing a go and, if she did, she'd have to give it at least a year or two to see.

She lay on top of him, her head pressed into his neck, and whispered, "Thank you" and said she would and what she wanted to thank him for was not only his generosity and support, financial and emotional, but also the gift of taking her seriously, despite all the years and all the reasons not to.

All she had to do now was take herself seriously.

HOMEWORK WITH MY NINE-YEAR-OLD
by LUCY LOVETT

(with apologies to William Carlos Williams)

You should walk away
I tell my son at the kitchen table.
He looks at me
Blue-eyed, curious, pencil in hand.

When the feeling starts,
I say, the red mist.
Like Taz the Looney Tune, he says,
Yes, but Taz never walks away

so it isn't the best example.
When Patrick laughed at me
it felt like wasps were buzzing
in my brain. Let them out

I reply. Now, long division. (A long groan.)
And, look! You have four bonus words
for spelling. Paragraph,
Business, Communication, Literary.

Oh, sweet Jesus, he mutters,
glancing up to see if anything explodes.
But it's only the sweet corn boiling
for I have walked away.

Lucy was touched when Johanna Riordan, great with child, at the end of a wonderful, gossipy lunch in the penthouse, handed her a beautiful leather-bound notebook and a packet of pens. She needed it. She no longer measured out her life with school plays or sports days or soccer tournaments. Ideas and stories were flooding her, images like the woman with a live snake around her neck, the horizontal rain that coursed through the avenues, Robbie peeing in the snow upstate. As she walked through the lobby and saw the handsome doorman playing with a couple of toddlers who lived in the building, Lucy reflected on Johanna's life, immured in luxury, and what would happen if she fell in love with someone else. She jotted down this idea, which she called "The Doorman", felt a little guilty, as Johanna had given her the notebook, then remembered what her friend Rosanna had said about changing names. She thought about Rosanna, the first proper writer she had ever been close to, and her heroic struggle to be true to herself as well as those who depended on her. Rosanna had once told her that she loved the movie *Julia*. Lucy decided that was what she would call her.

The epic historical novel, the sci-fi spectacular, or the big thriller would have to wait. Lucy had no clue how to write one of those. But if she wrote some stories about events in her life or the lives of women like and unlike her, it might turn into something. A book that she would buy at an airport, or waiting for a train, or read exhausted in bed, in the twenty minutes her body gave her before she sank into comatose sleep. And if she would read it, maybe someone else would too? But soon she stopped thinking about that. And then she understood what Ryan meant by *If you want to write, you just have to write*. One thousand words a day. Whatever the ending of your writing, if you have the willpower to do it and it keeps you sane, why not?

She noted down words to describe her feelings about New York, and soon the city became a character, as real to her as any other. She cut out pictures from magazines and took photographs and stuck them in her notebook. She thought about her life back in London and her life now. What she had wanted to be and what she had become. She thought about sentences and how they might work together, and she wrote incredibly long ones (which sometimes she broke up by using brackets) just for the fun of it. Some days, many days, she wrote nothing; she clawed at a couple of ideas, she stared at the keyboard, she composed a humiliating critique of her ideas by one such as a Miranda Bassett that made her cry.

Then came the horse course, the Hamptons, the opera with Carmen, and Ryan (Evan), and the Mother from the School she would call Robyn who ran off with the fantastically handled Schuyler Robinson, whose name she would have to keep, at least until copy-editing. And finally, she realized that she'd have to be a character herself, or rather a version of herself with some of the tedious and unpleasant bits edited out. Or maybe left in. Maybe that was the point.

After three months, she gathered all her notes into one document, but before she could start she needed a title. She looked out of the window at the last sleet of spring and typed the first thing that came into her head.

AN ENGLISHWOMAN IN NEW YORK

She paused. It looked okay.

She rocked back and forward on her chair and took a big swig of coffee.

She cracked her knuckles and stretched out her fingers.

They arrived in early September. No one could have guessed the weather.

She had begun.

acknowledgements

Thank you to my beloved husband, Joseph O'Connor, for everything.

Thank you to our sons, James and Marcus, and our families, especially my mother, Monica Casey, Sean and Viola O'Connor, Fidelma Casey, and Eimear O'Connor.

Thank you to Amy Einhorn, my editor, and all at Amy Einhorn Books/Putnam, and thank you to Kate Parkin and all at John Murray (Publishers).

Thank you to my agents and friends, Nicky Lund and Lizzy Kremer at David Higham Associates in London, and Allison Hunter at Inkwell Management in New York.

Thank you to all those colleagues and friends who encouraged my writing through the years and the different careers, especially Georgina Abrahams, Jane Wellesley, Lavinia Warner, Dorothy Viljoen, Maggie Pope, Martha O'Neill, Mary Callery, Andrew Meehan, Charlotte Cunningham, much-missed Maeve Binchy, Sarah Barton, Emma Broughton, Gavin Kostick, Michael Barker Caven, Michael Colgan, and all at the Gate Theatre in Dublin.

Thank you to all my friends, old and new, in England, Ireland, and America, for their enthusiasm, support, and inspiration, especially Amy Jackson, Katey Driscoll, Angela O'Donnell, Dianne Festa, Cathy Kelly, Rosamund Lupton, and Rebecca Miller.

And remembering always, my father, John Casey, and my friend Dominic Montserrat.

about the author

Anne-Marie Casey was a script editor and producer of prime-time television drama for ten years before becoming a writer full time. Her film and TV scripts have been produced in the UK and Ireland, and her theatrical adaptation of *Little Women* enjoyed a sell-out run at the Gate Theatre in Dublin in 2011. *An Englishwoman in New York*, her first book, was inspired by her time living in Manhattan and her love-love relationship with the city. She is married to the novelist Joseph O'Connor. They now live in Dublin with their two sons.